S/YA

AUG 0 9 2010

By Royal Command

A JAMES BOND ADVENTURE

CHARLIE HIGSON

Disney • HYPERION BOOKS

New York

S

For information address
Disney • Hyperion Books
114 Fifth Avenue
New York, New York 10011-5690.

First American edition, 2010.
1 3 5 7 9 10 8 6 4 2
V567-9638-5-10060
Printed in the United States of America
This book is set in 11.5-pt. Caslon.
Reinforced binding
ISBN 978-1-4231-2526-6

Library of Congress Cataloging-in-Publication Data on file.
Visit www.youngbond.com
www.hyperionbooksforchildren.com

SUSTAINABLE FORESTRY INITIATIVE
Certified Fiber Sourcing
www.sfiprogram.org

THIS LABEL APPLIES TO TEXT STOCK

For Vicky

* * *

In memory of Kate Jones

* * *

*My thanks to Franz Hink of the Kitzbühel ski school
for teaching me how to ski and showing me the mountains.*

PART 1—KITZBÜHEL

CHAPTER 1—WHAT WILL BE WILL BE

Colonel Irina Sedova of the OGPU hated tractors. She would be happy if she never saw a tractor again as long as she lived. She had built tractors, she had driven tractors, she had unveiled statues of tractors, she had made countless speeches in foreign towns singing the praises of tractors . . . Russian tractors, Communist tractors, the greatest tractors in the world!

She had endured the Great War, the revolution, and the civil war that followed it. She had lived through the terrible famine of 1921, where, in the frozen, impoverished countryside, people had been reduced to eating anything they could—weeds, grass, rats, leather shoes, even each other. She had survived the purges of the last ten years, and three assassination attempts, but she would gladly have lived through it all again rather than spend another minute with one of these infernal, godforsaken machines.

But here she was, on a cold March morning, watching a parade of them drive around a square in an ugly industrial quarter of Lisbon for the benefit of a group of bored Portuguese businessmen and local officials.

The twenty tractors, from the Chelyabinsk Tractor Plant, were of varying designs, but they shared several things in common. They were noisy, they were dirty, and they were ugly.

Colonel Sedova had grown up on a farm in the Ukraine.

Back then, at the end of the last century, there had been no tractors. Farm work was done by horse and ox and peasant. It was only after the revolution that they had started to appear in Russia, or the Soviet Union, as it was now called. They were the symbol of the new Russia, of a fabulous modern world. They would revolutionize agriculture just as Lenin had revolutionized everything else. When the new tractor arrived in a village, there would be celebrations. It would drive slowly into town at the head of a long procession, followed by men and women and children waving flags and singing patriotic songs.

Having fought bravely and fiercely in both the war and the revolution, Colonel Sedova had joined the Ministry of Propaganda, and one of her first jobs had been to make a series of films in which the hero was a Russian tractor. Later on she had joined the Obedinennoe Gosudarstvennoe Politicheskoe Upravlenie, the Russian secret police. Her job then was to run spies and secret agents throughout Europe, with the aim of undermining foreign governments and eliminating anyone who might be working to harm the new Communist regime.

At last, she had thought, I can get away from tractors.

It wasn't to be, however. A group of Russian secret agents would attract a great deal of attention in a foreign country unless they pretended to be something else. All spies needed a cover. So Colonel Sedova and her team traveled the world pretending to be part of a Soviet trade delegation selling Russian tractors.

She sighed. The life of a spy was not as romantic as it was presented in popular novels. Most of her time was spent being bored to death.

But this morning she had a mission.

She looked around. Nobody would notice if she left now. The Portuguese would want to talk to the engineers about tedious things like engine sizes and power output and haulage capabilities. She would not be missed.

She muttered something to her secretary, Alexa, stepped backward into the shadow of a warehouse, then slipped away down an alley to where her car was waiting. It was a brand-new black unmarked Citroën Traction Avant. She loved this car. The French might have been enemies of the mother country, but they certainly knew how to build automobiles. Her driver, Anatoly, opened the door for her, and she climbed in and settled back in her seat, breathing in the scents of wood and leather. The scents of luxury.

"To the Alfama district," she grunted, and Anatoly set off, driving quickly and efficiently through the streets of Lisbon. He took a few random turns and switchbacks to make sure that they were not being followed, and once he was sure they were clean, he pressed on toward the old part of town.

Sedova, known by most as Babushka, the Grandmother, didn't pay any attention to the passing scenery. She was lost in her thoughts. Concentrating on the mission ahead.

What exactly was Ferreira up to?

A small group of spies working together was called a cell. The members of a cell would only know the identities of their fellow members. This meant that if one was caught and interrogated, he would not be able to give away any information about the rest of the spy network. Only the leader of the cell would know the identity of the next person up the chain, and sometimes the identities of other cell leaders, but, once again, if they were ever found out they would be able to betray only a handful of other spies. A cell structure was a secure structure, but if a cell leader turned bad it could cause problems.

Martinho Ferreira ran the most important Communist spy cell in Lisbon from a bookshop that specialized in works on art, music, and architecture. Ferreira reported directly to Franco Fortuna, the Soviet officer for southern Europe, who was based in Rome and reported to Moscow.

There was a problem, though, and Colonel Sedova had been forced to break cover and come down personally to deal with this business. A cipher expert at the OGPU headquarters in Moscow had noticed a change in Ferreira's reports, subtle differences that would perhaps not have been noticeable to most people, but to the trained and deeply suspicious eyes of the expert, they stood out glaringly. A careful search in the files revealed that the changes went back several months. What had happened? Why was there this change? Had Ferreira's cell been infiltrated? Had he been turned by some foreign power? The Germans, perhaps, or the British?

Babushka would find out. She would find out and she would deal with it.

They came to the walls of the Castelo, swerved around a rattling wooden tram, and started to wind their way down through the labyrinth of narrow cobbled streets and small squares of the medieval Alfama quarter toward the wide gray expanse of the Rio Tejo.

The bookshop was on the northern edge of the district, near the flea market in the Campo de Santa Clara. Anatoly stopped the car by a row of dirty orange houses, then applied the hand brake but left the engine running.

"Leave the car here and go to the rear of the building," said Babushka, climbing out of the Citroën. "Watch for anyone going in or out. Follow them if necessary. I will go in the front."

Anatoly nodded and cut the engine.

Olivia Alves looked up as the bell above the door rattled and chimed. She peered with some curiosity at the woman who came in. She didn't look like the usual customers they got in the shop. In the three months Olivia had been working here, the trickle of customers had for the most part been professors and students from the university, or bearded bohemian types. Neither did the woman look like any tourist she had ever seen, though she was certainly not Portuguese. She was from a northern country, Germany perhaps. She was short and stocky and dressed all in gray. Gray woolen stockings. Gray lace-up boots. A skirt and jacket that were too tight for her and strained at the seams. Her hair was gray, too, and her skin. She had a flat peasant's face and small watchful eyes. She made a brief show of looking at the books on the shelves, and then marched over to the desk where Olivia sat reading a book on Tintoretto.

"Is Senhor Ferreira in?" the woman asked in clumsy Portuguese.

Olivia nodded toward the rear of the shop. The woman grunted and walked off. Her back was wide and solid as a lump of rock.

Babushka had to duck her head to get under the low arch

that led into a warren of book-lined corridors and tiny rooms that lay behind the main shop. She plodded steadily between the shelves until she eventually spotted a bearded man sitting in an alcove, studying some papers under a desk lamp and eating a sandwich that smelled of garlic.

He looked up as she approached, and slipped a pair of glasses down from his forehead onto his nose. He had a long droopy face that had a melancholy look about it.

Sedova studied him for a moment, then spoke in her stumbling Portuguese. "Are you Martinho Ferreira?"

"But of course," the man replied.

Sedova now slipped into her native Russian. "Tell the girl to go for her lunch," she said. "And close the shop."

The man smiled vaguely, pretending not to understand.

"I am Sedova."

The man paled, dropped his sandwich, and jumped up from his ancient, rickety chair. He hurried off and Sedova heard low voices, then the opening and closing of the street door.

Sedova walked over to the desk and cast a quick, professional glance over it.

Something caught her eye: a scrap of paper with a name on it. A name from her past. She frowned and quickly slipped it into her jacket pocket as she heard the man returning.

He came through, smiling and wiping his palms on his jacket.

"Babushka," he said, extending a hand, and went on in fluent Russian, "I am honored to meet you. I have heard so much about you."

Sedova did not shake his hand.

"We need to talk," she said.

The man fussed about, clearing a space for the colonel to sit. They were in a cave of books, and every surface, including the floor, was piled high with dusty volumes.

Sedova remained standing, and the man returned to his chair.

"Is there a problem?" he said.

Sedova did not reply. She was quietly studying the man. She had never met him before, but she had seen his records and the photographs kept on file at OGPU headquarters.

This man looked similar, but he was clearly not Ferreira. He was a good two inches too short and his nose was the wrong shape.

"You are not Martinho Ferreira," she said.

The man shrugged. "I am not," he said. "Martinho is not here at present."

"Then why did you say you were him?"

"You cannot be too careful." The man laughed and fished a bottle of vodka from his desk.

"Would you care for a drink?" he said.

"I do not drink," said Sedova.

"If you will allow me." The man poured himself a hefty measure, the bottle rattling against the rim of the glass.

"You know who I am?" said Sedova.

"But of course. You are Colonel Sedova. Everyone in the network knows who you are. You are famous."

"What is your name?"

"My name? Cristo Oracabessa. I work with Martinho." He returned the bottle to his desk drawer.

"When will Martinho return?" said Sedova. "I would dearly like to speak with him."

"Alas. He will not be returning," said Cristo, raising a pistol above the edge of the desk as he did so. "You are too late."

Sedova recognized the gun—it was a Soviet design, a Tokarev TT-33 semiautomatic. A very efficient weapon.

She remained calm. She had no doubt that the man would use the gun. He knew her reputation. He would have heard all the stories. They called her "the Grandmother," but there was irony in it. She was a hardened killer. She would do anything to survive. Along with many others, she had eaten human flesh during the great famine. It was good to keep the story alive. A fearsome reputation was a necessary thing, but it all seemed so long ago now. She couldn't remember what the flesh had tasted like. As far as she was concerned it was the same as all the other boiled gray meat she'd had to endure over the years.

Yes. This man would know the stories.

He would know that there would be no second chances.

There was a film of sweat along his upper lip.

"It seems you thought I might be coming," said Sedova. "Me or someone like me."

"I hope you are not expecting me to explain myself before I kill you," said the man.

"I do not expect anything," said Sedova. "The Portuguese have a saying: *O que será*."

"What will be will be," said the man, and he pulled the trigger three times, aiming at the largest part of his target, Sedova's torso. Each bullet found its mark, and the combined force of the three of them was enough to knock the woman off her feet. She fell into the bookshelves behind her and collapsed to the floor beneath a cascade of books.

So Cristo, if that was his name, was not stupid. One bullet might not have been enough, three was plenty, and any more would have been a waste.

The man let out a deep sigh, his lips fluttering, and started to walk cautiously toward the colonel.

You did not live to be fifty in the OGPU without learning a trick or two. Sedova had learned to be cunning and wary and distrustful. She had been shot once before, during the civil war, and still had a nasty scar in her side where a comrade had clumsily removed the bullet. It had been enough to teach her that she never wanted to be shot again. Which was why she had taken to wearing a steel-enforced corset with a leather backing. With thick layers of fat and solid muscle underneath, it would take more than a bullet from a TT-33 to reach any of her vital organs.

When she landed she made sure that she kept her arms bent and her hands drawn back, ready to strike. Now she lay perfectly still, holding her breath in and her eyes open. She was careful not to allow them even a tiny flicker but followed the man's movements with her peripheral vision. She would wait. She was used to waiting.

At last the man came near. She could smell garlic and alcohol on his breath, never a pleasant combination. Closer and closer he came, the gun pointing at her head. She would have to act quickly and decisively. He would not make the same mistake twice, and a head shot would be fatal.

The man's head blocked out the light. She could hear his breathing.

Now it was time.

She punched both hands forward. One knocked the man's gun to the side, the other powered into his face like a steam hammer, shattering his lower jaw. The force jerked his head back and to one side, snapping his neck. He was dead before he realized his mistake.

Sedova grunted. She had not meant to kill him. The man was weaker than she had calculated, but when your life is at stake you do not take risks.

She stood up and dusted herself down. Her stomach felt bruised and painful; one of the slugs had penetrated the corset and was pressing into her ribs. She plucked it out with her immensely strong fingers and slipped it into her pocket. She soon found the other two bullets, then picked up the gun and wrapped it in a handkerchief.

It was a shame. The cell had been compromised and would need to be wound up. She would have liked to interrogate the man. Find out who he really was and what had happened to Ferreira. And what he had meant when he'd said that she was too late.

Too late for what?

She took the slip of paper from her pocket and looked at it again, making sure she hadn't misread the name written on it.

She hadn't. The two words were perfectly clear.

James Bond.

What did it mean?

She would find out, but it would mean a lot of hard work. She would have to search the place from top to bottom, tediously trawl through the man's papers and try to find out what was going on.

She prodded the man with her foot and cursed him.

The life of a spy consisted of long periods of boredom punctuated by brief intense moments of fear and death.

The rest was all just tractors and paperwork.

Graf von Schlick pressed his foot down and felt the Bugatti Type 55 Super Sport surge hungrily forward. These winding Alpine roads really tested her to the limit. Tested him as well—a moment's loss of concentration and they would go spinning out of control and down the side of the mountain. Liesl at his side gave a little shriek as the wheels hit an icy patch and the car slalomed drunkenly across the road surface.

Von Schlick laughed.

"Don't you trust me, my darling?" he yelled as she clasped his arm.

"You are trying to scare me, Otto."

"On the contrary! I am trying to wake you up. It is only when we are close to death that we feel fully alive."

Liesl wasn't sure about this. She felt most fully alive eating chocolate in a nice hot bath while her gramophone played something smooth by the latest American jazz crooner.

The car slithered around a hairpin bend, and they continued their descent between high banks of clean white snow.

"So what did you make of my little cottage?" von Schlick asked. By cottage he meant his ancestral home—Schloss Donnerspitze—a monstrous medieval castle built high into the side of the Schwarzkogel above Jochberg. To describe it as a cottage was ridiculous. It was a huge pile of massive gray-black stones, ugly and domineering, like a great bully squatting on the mountainside, sneering at the puny houses below.

Growing up, von Schlick had found the castle cold and dark and oppressive. It was built on a giant's scale, and he had never been happy there. He envied the farmers' children in their pretty and cozy-looking wooden chalets, with flowers around the doors in summer and peaked hats of snow in the winter.

He had left the castle at the earliest opportunity and gone to university in Vienna, where he had bought himself an attractive modern house near the Karlsplatz. It was everything the family castle wasn't—light and airy and clean and warm. His mother had stayed on at the *Schloss*, all alone with a dwindling staff, until she had died four years ago, at which point Otto had had the place closed down and packed in mothballs. He had vowed never to return and had been considering selling the hated pile.

Otto's life was in Vienna now, not here in the backward and boring countryside. He had married Frieda, a minor aristocrat, and they had lived a city life of parties, opera, theater, nightclubs, eating, drinking, and dancing. It was only when he stopped and took a breath after five years of marriage that he realized he had nothing in common with his wife. He was certain he didn't love her, and in fact he wasn't sure he even liked her.

He began spending time with a string of younger, more exciting women who had meant little more to him than the contents of a packet of cigarettes. To be smoked and thrown away, forgotten. Things had changed, though, when he had set eyes on the charming Liesl at the theater. She was an actress and a dancer, and Otto was utterly captivated by her.

It was soon after they had met that Otto announced to his wife that he was tired of city life and had a yearning to return to his roots in the Tyrol.

"From now on," he told her, "I will be spending my summers at the *Schloss* and I will winter here in Vienna. Apart from the odd weekend's skiing."

"Then you will be spending your summers alone," said his wife. "I have no desire to set foot inside that gloomy carbuncle."

"So be it," said Otto.

What his wife didn't need to know was that he had no intention of spending his summers alone. His plan was to install Liesl in the *Schloss*. She could still act if she wanted, during the winter season in Vienna, but her summers would be spent at Schloss Donnerspitze, where she could play at being a *Gräfin* and mistress of all she surveyed.

They had driven over this morning, taking the road from Vienna at breakneck speeds, their helmets and goggles protecting them from the worst of the icy winds. But when they arrived at the *Schloss*, Liesl had felt more dead than alive and had needed a large brandy to restore her senses.

Her first sight of the castle had not been encouraging, and now, on the way back down the mountain, she told Otto that she had grave doubts about moving here.

"But, *Liebste*," Otto pleaded, slowing down slightly so that he wouldn't have to shout, "you did not see the dear old place in its best light. When the sun comes out and the grass is green and the shaggy-haired dairy cows are gamboling in the flower-filled meadows, their bells tinkling so sweetly, then it will seem like a fairy-tale castle. You *are* my princess, after all," he added.

"We shall see," Liesl said, wrinkling her pretty nose.

"Trust me!" said Otto, and he slammed his foot down on the accelerator once more as they hit a straight.

"Please, darling, you have made your point," Liesl shouted. "You must be more careful. Slow down."

Otto was just about to say something clever when they screamed around a blind curve and came upon a car stalled in the road. He applied the brakes with ferocious force and wrestled with the wheel until he had subdued the Bugatti and brought her to a halt less than three feet from the other vehicle.

Liesl was on the verge of tears, but Otto was laughing with relief. The girl was right—he would need to be a little more careful in the future—but today he was filled with a wild, careless spirit. He had almost believed the rosy picture he had painted of life at the *Schloss*. Ah, it wouldn't be so bad. He would drum up some friends, bring them down for parties—all manner of smart types had summer villas in the Alps.

There were two men standing by the car, peering at the engine under the open bonnet. They seemed unperturbed by the near accident.

"Are you in trouble?" Otto called out. The road was narrow here, and the other car was stopped right in the middle so that there was no way he could go around them.

One of the men lifted his head and looked at Otto. He

had the smallest eyes Otto had ever seen on a person; they were almost completely hidden behind thick, fleshy eyelids.

"Do you know about motorcars?" he said in German, with the hint of a foreign accent. Otto surmised that he was probably Russian.

Did he know about cars? What a question! Otto had driven in the 1932 German Grand Prix, in the racing version of the car he was sitting in now, the Type 51. *Did he know about cars, indeed.* He loved cars—why, he sometimes thought he loved them more than he loved women.

"I know a thing or two," he said, climbing out. "What seems to be the problem?"

He strode over, placed his hands on the car, and leaned in to take a look. He could see no immediate and obvious problem, though there was a strong smell of petrol.

"It is possible you have a leak in your fuel pipe," he said, and glanced inside the car. A third man was at the wheel, his face completely wrapped in bandages, his eyes hidden behind dark glasses.

He was sitting very still.

Otto looked away quickly, not wanting to stare, but the sight had unnerved him. He felt a chill of fear. He wanted to be away from here.

He studied the engine once more and at last spotted something: a wire to the alternator had come unattached.

"There," he said. "I think I see your problem."

Liesl was checking her lipstick in the side mirror. She looked over at the other car just as the two men stepped away from it. Otto had his head buried inside the engine. Liesl frowned as one of the men stooped down and picked up something that was lying hidden in the snow. It appeared to be a small box attached to a wire that snaked under the car. She was about to say something when the man pressed a switch on the box and a great gout of flame billowed from the engine, engulfing Otto's head and shoulders. He gave a hideous high-pitched shriek and fell away, clutching his face.

Liesl knew she was in danger; her first thought was to get out of the car and run. It would take too long to slide over the seat, take the wheel, start the car, and put it into reverse gear. But even as she reached for the door handle, the man with puffy eyes stepped up to the car and swung a knuckle-duster at her chin.

She heard a loud pop and was overcome with a terrible sick feeling. Her brain seemed to be fizzing. Then she was walking through snow, surrounded by a hazy whiteness.

No.

It was snowing inside her head.

So cold.

Whiteout . . .

CHAPTER 3—HITLERJUGEND

"**Y**ou are a cheat."

"I am not a cheat."

"I say you are. How else do you keep on beating us?"

"I keep on beating you because I am a better cardplayer."

James Bond was in a faintly ridiculous situation. He was on a train in the Austrian Tyrol somewhere between Innsbruck and Kitzbühel, surrounded by a knot of angry blond-haired German boys. He had thought at first that they were boy scouts; they wore a uniform of khaki military-style shirts with black ties and shorts, which were draped with fussy leather belts and straps. But he had soon discovered that they were *Hitlerjugend*, Hitler Youth, on their way to a camp in the Alps. He had heard about the organization, how every boy in Germany from fourteen to eighteen was encouraged to join and go to training camps, rallies, and field exercises.

The journey overnight from Boulogne on the transcontinental Arlberg Express had been uneventful, but when James changed to a local train in Innsbruck he had found it swarming with the boys. The carriages were full of them, like miniature German soldiers, their uniforms decorated with swastikas and the stylized S, the Sig Rune, that they shared with the SS.

A group of them had been sitting on the floor playing

cards in the corridor, and to pass the time, James had joined them. He had won a great deal of money from them, but the more he won, the more they kept trying to win their money back and the more they kept losing. In the end, James had felt so guilty about what was happening that he had thrown down his cards and told them he had had enough. They had insisted, however, that he carry on and give them another chance. When James refused, a bulky, thick-lipped lad called Gerhardt had grabbed him by the shirtfront and threatened to thump him if he wouldn't play anymore. James had pushed him away, but the boy wouldn't back down. His face was red and he was trembling with anger.

"I say that you are a *cheat*," he repeated, jabbing James in the chest with a finger.

"I don't need to cheat," said James, who had spent much of his early life in Switzerland and spoke fluent German.

Gerhardt swayed from side to side in the cramped space as the train rattled around a bend. "I am used to winning," he said angrily.

"That's because you are used to playing with this lot," said James. "And quite frankly they're pretty hopeless. So maybe you've learned a valuable lesson today."

James was a good cardplayer. He had picked up most of his skills from his foul-mouthed Chinese messmate at school, Tommy Chong. Tommy was an excellent player and a good teacher. Winning at cards takes skill, nerve, experience, and luck. And James had plenty of each. These boys, though, were enthusiastic and inexperienced, which is not a good combination for gambling.

"You have taken all my spending money for the trip," said

a small, bony lad called Artur, who seemed close to tears.

"You should have stopped gambling before you lost it all, then, shouldn't you?" said James, trying to disguise the growing note of impatience in his voice. "What do you want me to do? Just hand it all back?"

"Give us the chance to win it back," said a third youth.

"Yes. Double or quits," said Artur.

"No," said James. "I've given you enough chances. Face facts. I'm a better player than any of you, and if you carry on, you'll all end up with nothing."

"Well, if you will not give us the chance to win the money fairly, we will have to take it," said Gerhardt, jutting his big chin out aggressively.

"Don't be stupid," said James. "You may be dressed up like toy soldiers, but I'll bet you know nothing about fighting. Believe me. If you take me on, you will lose again. My advice to you is to spend a little less time learning to march about waving flags and a little more time learning to play cards. Until then, you should steer clear of any game more complicated than snap."

It was perhaps not wise of James to taunt the boys like this, because the next thing he knew Gerhardt had grabbed his arms from behind.

"Search his pockets," he barked at his companions.

The others looked unsure and hesitated, which gave James just enough time to stamp down heavily on Gerhardt's instep. The boy yelled and let James go. James drove his elbow into Gerhardt's gut just as Artur threw a clumsy punch. James neatly stepped around it, turned, grabbed the boy's arm, and jerked it up into a half nelson behind his back.

"Agh," Artur grunted. "Let me go—you are hurting."

"That's the idea," said James. "I'll let you go when you lot promise to stop this stupid fighting."

"All right, all right," said the boy, and James pushed him away. Gerhardt had other ideas, though, and he lunged at James.

James was ready for him this time. He easily ducked Gerhardt's blundering attempt at a right hook and brought the heel of his own right hand up hard under the boy's chin. Gerhardt's head jerked back, his teeth clacked together, and he must have bitten his tongue, because blood started to pour from his mouth. He clamped both hands over his lips and moaned.

Two more of the youths squared up to James, but he gave them such a brutal look of cold fury that they backed off and put up their open palms in surrender.

James took a handful of change from his pocket and flung it to the floor of the train in disgust. "There you are," he said, "you can have that. Sort it out among yourselves. But if you are not prepared to lose with good grace, don't play cards for money."

James turned and walked away down the corridor while the youths scrabbled on the floor and bickered over the coins.

James didn't feel very pleased with himself. He could have handled the situation better and avoided a fight, but he had to admit that he was tired and grumpy. He'd been traveling for two days now—by train to Dover, by ferry to Boulogne, then through the night across northern France and Switzerland into Austria. He had slept very little in that time and had

had nothing more to eat than some sandwiches that his Aunt Charmian had packed for him.

Also, he had been dogged by the nagging feeling that someone was watching him, following him. He couldn't put his finger on it, but a sort of sixth sense had set his nerves jangling. It had started in Dover when he had spotted a man in a coat and trilby hat who seemed to be staring down at him from a walkway. The man was standing in front of a bright window that turned him into a featureless, black silhouette, so James had no idea if he really had been looking at him, or even what he looked like.

After that he noticed other things, small things: a glimpse of a man's watchful face out of the corner of his eye; a face that disappeared as he turned to look; a figure in a crowd that stepped into the shadows when he glanced toward it; footsteps behind him that seemed to have no owner.

He told himself that he was imagining it. After all that had happened to him in the last few months, he was bound to have developed a persecution complex. He was wound as tight as a watch spring. He needed to calm down and relax. He was greatly looking forward to arriving in Kitzbühel and meeting up with the school party from Eton that was spending their Easter break in the mountains.

To try and clear his head, he fetched his coat and walked all the way to the back of the train, where there was a little open-air observation deck. He tugged the door open, stepped out into the cool breeze, and stood leaning on the rail, looking at the passing scenery.

They were clattering along a narrow track that ran through a valley just beginning to emerge from its winter cloak of snow. Above, the great purple-blue Alps poked out above low clouds, their flanks gleaming with swathes of white. They passed a cluster of wide-roofed chalets that reminded James of his childhood in Switzerland. It had been the middle of the night when they had passed through Basel, where he had grown up, so he had seen nothing of it, but now he felt a slight pang of nostalgia. Soon, though, the chalets were obscured from view as they entered a small forest, and his thoughts turned away from those times before they had a chance to become painful.

The steam from the engine caught in the pine trees, and for a few minutes it was like traveling through thick fog; then the trees thinned and they were out in the open again and the bright mountain light.

The door behind him opened, and he turned to see one of the Hitler Youth come out. James tensed for a fight, but the boy gave him a friendly smile and held out his hand.

"Don't worry," he said in English. "I am not looking for trouble. I wanted to apologize for the behavior of the others."

"Apology accepted," James said, and shook the boy's hand.

"My name is Eugen," said the boy, leaning on the rail next to James. "We are not all like Gerhardt."

"I hope not," said James.

"If you do not join the Hitler Youth they make life very difficult for you," said Eugen. "I hate it. Oh, there are some fun parts. We go to the countryside and walk and ride our bicycles. There is comradeship. But the training is hard. Do you know what Hitler said?"

James shook his head.

"We had to learn his speech by heart," said Eugen, and

he laughed. He then reverted to his native language and did a fair imitation of the German chancellor, his voice clipped and harsh.

"'My program for educating youth is hard,'" he ranted. "'Weakness must be hammered away. In my castles of the Teutonic Order a youth will grow up before which the world will tremble. I want a brutal, domineering, fearless, cruel youth. Youth must be all that. It must bear pain. There must be nothing weak and gentle about it. The free, splendid beast of prey must once again flash from its eyes!'"

It was James's turn to laugh now. "I think Gerhardt took it all to heart somewhat," he said. "But I'm afraid there's more to being tough than having the 'free, splendid beast of prey' flashing from your eyes."

"Oh, there is more," said Eugen, and resumed his impression of Hitler. "'That is how I will eradicate thousands of years of human domestication! That is how I will create the New Order!'"

He stopped and looked around guiltily. "I hope nobody can hear me. I would never dare do this among other Germans. They would have me hung." He turned to James. "The worst thing is they teach us to hate. To hate anyone who is not one of us. Gerhardt and the others will be confused. We have been told many times that the English are weak and ineffective."

A blast of wind whistled along the valley, and James shivered, thrusting his hands deep into his coat pockets to keep warm. "In the end we're all just people," he said. "It doesn't matter where we come from. You are who you are."

"I had a friend," said Eugen, looking away down the track

as it spooled out behind the train. "My best friend. A Jewish boy called Siggy Canter. We had grown up together. I never really thought about his religion. But I am not allowed to see him anymore. I am scared for the future."

James could say nothing to reassure Eugen. He had seen enough of the world to know that bad things happened all the time and that human beings had a tendency to be cruel and destructive. He hated gangs. Where weak people joined together to become one strong entity and bully anyone they didn't approve of. The Hitler Youth was just another gang. The Nazi party in Germany was a gang. The Bolsheviks in Russia . . .

He once more made an effort to put aside any depressing thoughts, and the two of them chatted together until it got too cold. As they went back inside, Eugen put a hand on James's arm. "I hope there will not be another war," he said. "I hope I will never have to face you on a battlefield with a gun in my hand."

It was late afternoon by the time the train did an almost complete circuit of the town and pulled into Kitzbühel station. There had been a recent heavy snowfall, and many excited skiers from the towns and cities along the route bundled off the train, carrying their skis and poles.

James stepped down from his carriage and took in his surroundings. Kitzbühel was 2,500 feet up in the eastern Alps, sitting in a lush valley ringed by mountains. Behind the station was the Kitzbühler Horn, and opposite was the huge flattened peak of the Hahnenkamm, linked to the town by a cable car. Away to the north, standing out against the sky like a line of broken gray teeth, was the range known as the Wilder Kaiser.

James found a porter and discovered that his hotel was in easy walking distance. He felt the need to stretch his legs after the long journey and set off after the man into town. They crossed a river and a main road and then took a curving street that ran below the twin fairy-tale churches that dominated Kitzbühel—the tall, narrow Liebfrauenkirche and the baroque Andreaskirche, whose tower, like so many in the Tyrol, was topped off by what looked like a sultan's turban. It started to snow as they came into the main street, the Vordere Stadgasse, and light powdery flakes drifted aimlessly in the air. The porter cheerfully pushed his laden trolley along the well-made pavement, pointing out the sights to James. There was a picture-book feel about the old medieval town, and it was hard to believe that people lived and worked in these outsized, brightly painted doll's houses with their red, green, and blue shutters and overhanging eaves.

The shops were closing for the day and the locals were thronging the streets. They were mostly stout Alpine types, the women as sturdy-looking as the men. Some were dressed in traditional Tyrolean outfits, the men with feathers in their caps, the women in heavy embroidered dresses, which only added to the feeling that James was on a vast stage set.

As they passed a pastry shop, James felt the hairs on the back of his neck tingle, and he glanced back. For a moment he caught sight of a man standing out from the crowd, in an English coat and hat. But as James blinked a snowflake out of his eyes, the man seemed to melt away.

James told himself he had imagined it. Hopefully, he

would see fewer phantoms after a hot meal and a good night's sleep.

They entered an archway that ran right through a building at the end of the street, and James followed the porter down the road on the other side to where a wrought-iron sign announced their arrival at the Hotel Franz Joseph. The porter took James's luggage into the reception area, James tipped him, and the man scuttled off out into the darkening evening.

The reception was dominated by a large painting of the emperor Franz Joseph, after whom the hotel was named. James was just admiring his great handlebar mustache and huge bushy sideburns when there was a shout, and he turned to see his friend Andrew Carlton coming toward him, a broad smile on his face.

Andrew was a couple of years older than James, but they had made friends when James first arrived at Eton and had shared many adventures together in the secret club they both belonged to—the Danger Society.

"You're bang on time," said Andrew, clapping him on the shoulders. "I'll say something for the locals: they know how to make their trains stick to their timetables, whatever the weather. Don't bother with the paperwork; it's all taken care of. Everyone else is having supper. Eat early, sleep well, up with the sparrows. Come on through. Someone will take your bags up."

Before James could say anything, he found himself being marched off by Andrew through the hotel. All the wood-work was elaborately painted or carved, and there was barely a square inch of wall that wasn't covered by an Alpine painting, or a mirror, or a stuffed deer's head.

A cheer went up as James entered the restaurant, even though, when he looked at the twenty-five or so boys and masters assembled around the long wooden table, he recognized only a few faces: Mr. Merriot, his classical tutor, sitting with the other masters at the far end; Freddie Meyer, a German pupil James had somewhat lost touch with since his first half; two boys from his House, Tom Llewellyn and Teddy Makereth; and a couple of others. They all smiled and waved and called out to him. There was a jolly, festive atmosphere. The boys were evidently enjoying their trip.

Andrew had saved a place for him, and he sat down next to another friend, Gordon Latimer. He quickly caught up with all the Eton gossip, and Andrew and Gordon told him what had happened in the run-up to his best friend, Perry Mandeville, being sent down for putting several sheep in the Head Master's bedroom. Perry was the founder and captain of the Danger Society, and since he had left Eton, the club had shut down.

It was a shame that Perry wasn't there. James would have liked to see him, but he was glad of the other familiar faces. He had missed the last half at Eton and had only just got back from Mexico, which was why he was two days late in joining the others.

Now, though, he was safely among friends.

He told them a little about his recent adventures but left out most of what had happened. It was buried deep inside, along with many other secrets. All James wanted was to return to being an ordinary schoolboy. He was looking forward to three weeks of walking and climbing and, with any luck, learning how to ski.

"You're sharing a room with me and two others," Gordon explained. "One of them's a decent enough sort, Grenville Warner; he's about your age, I think. I'm afraid the other one, Miles Langton-Herring, is a bit of a bore, with a deep love of facts and figures. You know the sort, reckons he's an expert on everything and won't let you forget it. He could blither for England at the next Olympics. That's him down there, talking with his mouth full."

James looked along the table to where Gordon was pointing. He saw a large boy with wavy brown hair and a ruddy complexion. He had big, horselike teeth, but was good-looking in a somewhat burly, rugby-playing sort of way. He was talking loudly and quickly and laughing a lot—presumably at his own jokes, as nobody else around him could get a word in.

James smiled. He had never expected to feel this way, but it was good to get back to his normal school life. The problems were all small and easily solved. Nothing could scare him. He understood now that school was a simple time when you could be yourself, enjoy yourself, and not have to worry too much about the big world that was waiting for you outside like a hungry wolf.

He went up to bed that night with his belly full and his heart light. The hearty Austrian food—soup with noodles, *Wiener Schnitzel* and *Apfelstrudel*—had been just the ticket. He even felt strong enough to face the dreaded Miles Langton-Herring, who was sporting a pair of pajamas monogrammed with his initials. Miles barely paused to take breath after introducing himself before launching into a long and dull history of skiing.

James fell asleep to the sound of his pompous, fruity voice droning on. . . .

"Of course skiing is by no means a new invention. There are cave paintings from thousands of years ago showing men with skis strapped to their feet. But for a long time skiing was simply a way of getting about on the snow. Nobody ever thought of climbing to the tops of mountains just to ski down them. The Norwegians developed the art of cross-country skiing, but when they brought their sport to the Alps, they were faced with bigger mountains and steeper slopes and so new techniques had to be learnt. An Austrian called Zdarsky developed the Lilienfield technique at the end of the last century, but it was Hannes Schneider who developed most of the modern techniques of skiing. . . ."

Outside, a man in an overcoat and trilby stood in the dark space between two big square houses, smoking a cigarette, shielding its glowing tip between cupped hands. Apart from the small adjustments as he smoked, he barely moved at all and seemed unaffected by the cold.

One by one the lights in the hotel went out.

It was quiet now. Nobody moved in the streets. Nobody approached the entrance to the Franz Joseph.

At last the man dropped his cigarette to the ground, where it joined a small pile of butts, and he ground it out carefully before slipping away into the shadows.

CHAPTER 4—AUSTRIAN WALTZING BLOOD

James was first up. Before the alarm had even gone off, he climbed out of bed, went over to the window, and threw back the curtains. The valley was still in shadow—the sun had not yet cleared the top of the Hahnenkamm—but the sky was thrillingly clear and blue. He pushed the window open and drew in a breath of the deliciously cold air. It tasted different from any other air he had ever breathed, sharp and clean and somehow empty.

James's room was at the front of the hotel, facing the Hahnenkamm. There were small patches of brown, dead-looking grass spotting its lower slopes, but higher up it was blanketed with snow. He could see the Hahnenkamm-Bahn, the cable car that ran to the top, parting the pine trees in its path in a long straight line. At the summit the cable-car station was sitting in a halo of light.

The scene promised so much. He was impatient to get out there.

Miles Langton-Herring stirred as the cold air filled the room. He sat up and swore at James. James merely laughed.

"What time is it?" Miles grumbled.

"About a quarter to seven," said James.

"We've another fifteen minutes before we need to be up."

33

"Stay in bed, then," said James. "It's all the same to me."

"At least shut that blasted window, can't you?"

James closed the window and went down the corridor to the bathroom, where he washed quickly and combed his hair. He then dressed in silk long johns and a long-sleeved vest. Over this he wore a flannel shirt and woolen jumper, heavy cotton twill trousers, and thick socks. Finally he put on his boots and picked up his leather gauntlets. They were joined by a string so that they wouldn't get lost if they fell off in the snow, and he had to thread them through the sleeves of his waterproof red wind-cheater.

He was first down to breakfast, and filled up on bread and pastries, eggs and ham and cheese, which he washed down with pure mountain spring water and a strong coffee. He couldn't remember when he had last felt this carefree.

As he worked his way through his breakfast, the other boys slowly trickled in to join him. For the most part they looked tired and bleary-eyed. They shuffled about, speaking quietly, and obviously wished they were back in their warm and cozy beds.

Mr. Merriot came over to sit at James's table. He looked brighter and more alert than his fellow masters. In fact, James had never seen him look anything other than comfortably at peace with the world.

"I didn't have the chance to welcome you back properly last night," he said, sitting down and taking out his pipe. "How have you been? Actually you need not answer that question. Us English, eh? Always asking each other how we are, and never expecting an honest reply. In your case, I know perfectly well how you've been. Your aunt filled me in on everything."

He glanced around the room, leaned in closer, and went on in a lower voice. "It seems we can't keep you away from trouble, can we, James?"

"It seems not," said James with a wry smile.

"But somehow or other you keep bouncing back!" said Merriot, a little louder. And he stuck his pipe between his lips. He made no attempt to light it, however, and merely sucked the stem thoughtfully as he busied himself with buttering a slice of toast.

"I predict an interesting future for you, young Bond," he said, once he was satisfied with his work. "I think you will be either a great hero or a great villain."

"I don't really want to be either," said James. "If it's all the same to you, sir, I've had my fill of adventures. I sometimes feel I've been missing out on some of the ordinary things that other boys get up to in their lives."

"I think you'd be hard-pressed to find any red-blooded boy in England who wouldn't want to swap lives with you, James."

"Maybe," said James, "but I've come to the conclusion that it's really rather better to hear about adventures than be part of them."

"I believe you may be right," said Mr. Merriot quietly, looking off out the windows at the glorious morning. "I suppose I had my fill of adventure in the Great War, and, *yes*, the reality was very different to what one reads about in books. You'd think war was just a big noisy game if you hadn't actually been in one."

"Wasn't it also something of an adventure running for England in the 1924 Olympics?" said James.

"It was certainly exciting," said Merriot. "But that is

behind me now. All I do these days is teach others. Though, in its way, teaching can be equally as thrilling."

James tried to suppress a smile.

"Ah," said Merriot, who didn't miss a thing. "He thinks I'm an old fool. Rambling on about the glories of teaching. But teaching another person to do something really well and seeing them succeed is as rewarding as doing it oneself. When you won the cross-country event in the Hellebore Cup, my heart was beating like a drum. I had never felt such excitement and such pride."

"Well, sir," said James, "despite what I might have said just now, I don't think I could swap winning a race for merely teaching someone to win one."

"Aha," said Merriot. "But the glory soon passes. Standing on top of a mountain, the only way is down. There's no getting around the fact that the moment when you are at your very best is the moment you begin to become worse and worse. Others will come along who can run faster, jump higher, hit harder, and you will be forgotten. Your winning moment will only be a memory. Your fame is already fated to die. It is much more satisfactory to be a good teacher and give your knowledge to others instead of thrilling the crowd for one brief moment. For you, James, I think the moment of glory is all. For men like me it is different. We are playing the long game. I am happy to be a teacher, though I shan't be out there on the slopes teaching you to ski, you'll be glad to hear. That honor goes to a local chap called Hannes Oberhauser, who is really first-rate. Austrian instructors, especially those from the Arlberg school, where he learnt his skills, are the best in the world. You should see him in action, a picture of grace and elegance. It's those few drops of Austrian waltzing blood in his veins, I think."

After breakfast James was taken to a large wooden hut opposite the hotel, where he selected a fine pair of hickory skis edged with steel. They were taller than he was and curved up steeply at the end. His parents had taken him skiing for a couple of weekends when he was younger, but he remembered little about it. He had to be shown how to fasten his boots into the bindings that held the skis on, first strapping his toes into fixed metal plates and then pulling what looked like long springs around his heels to grip them in place. It was awkward and uncomfortable, but once done he felt secure on the skis. He then picked out some lightweight bamboo sticks that had small hoops at the ends loosely attached by a latticework of leather straps. He was looking forward to getting out onto the snow.

An hour later he was standing on the lower slopes of the Hahnenkamm with the other novices, feeling considerably less confident. It was hard enough just standing up on the long skis, let alone trying to move forward. The instructor from the Kitzbühel ski school, Hannes Oberhauser, was very patient and encouraging, but James felt as if he would never get the hang of it.

Hannes was a small tanned man in his thirties, with a cheerful open face and short fair hair. James had noticed that he walked with a distinct limp, but once he put his skis on he moved freely over the snow as if they were a part of him.

"We have a new boy with us today," he said when everyone was ready. "So I will need to spend a little time alone with him to get him started. The rest of you, practice your stems."

The other boys moved off clumsily down the gentle slope, their knees bent and knocking into each other, their skis turned in at the tips.

"I don't think any of them will ever be world-class skiers," said Hannes with a smile. "But that is not the point. The point is to enjoy yourself, yes? And to do that you must learn the basics." His English was good, with only a light accent. He explained to James that he had taken classes, as most of his pupils were from England.

"I will teach you to ski with safety and with style," he went on. "I have seen young people like you take to skiing quickly and shoot off down the slopes with very little practice, but they are only pretending to ski. I call them *ski-savages*. They do not have control and go wherever their skis take them—people like that will never become really good skiers. You must learn to be master of your own skis, and ultimately master of the mountain. It may seem boring and slow at first, but, like anything, if you do not do the groundwork, you will only ever progress so far.

"The first thing you must master is the snowplow, the horror of every beginner. It is not only for slowing yourself down and gaining control, it is also the basis of every turn except for those at high speed. You have watched the other boys, now you try it. Make a V shape with your skis, the tips almost touching, the back ends as wide apart as possible. Press the knees forward and keep your heels flat and the skis very slightly on their inner edges. Don't dig them in too much, though; merely caress the snow with them."

James did as he was told and gingerly moved off down the

slope. He felt ridiculous and clumsy, trying to keep his legs in the right position to control the skis, which had a mind of their own, but he slowly got the hang of it. The trick was to use just the right amount of edging. Too much and each ski pulled in the direction they were pointing until they crossed over one another; too little and the skis tended to drift apart until he was doing painful splits.

"Very good!" Hannes shouted, whizzing down to where James had stopped at the bottom. The other boys were waiting there, chatting, and Hannes ordered them back to the top. James watched as they side stepped up the hill with little chopping movements. He soon found that getting back up the slope was almost harder than coming down it.

"Skiing is not so difficult a sport, really," Hannes said to James as they struggled up. "For sure there are special techniques to learn, but mainly you will need courage, a sense of balance, a desire to practice, and a great deal of patience. A sense of humor will come in useful as well, because to start with, you will find yourself spending more time on the ground than on your skis."

He was right. In the first ten minutes James fell over sixteen times. But he kept at it, and in the next ten minutes he fell over only half that number of times. After an hour he felt fairly confident, and the gaps between falls were getting longer and longer.

Along the way he learned that the most important law of skiing was that you must lean forward so that your body was at least at a right angle to the slope. This was known as *Vorlage*. There were many German terms to learn. Like *abstemmen*, to brake; or its opposite, *schuss*, to go straight down the slope.

Something he was warned against trying just yet by Hannes.

"Look at the slope," he explained. "It is not man-made; it is a natural thing, full of curves and bumps and holes and hazards. You must learn to choose the right line. The most direct route down a slope, the steepest line, is known as the *fall line*. Nine times out of ten you will not take the fall line, but you will curve gracefully from side to side and come down in a long series of sweeping S shapes."

Another thing James learned about was the *Hocke*. "The famous Arlberg crouch," as Hannes described it. "A most misunderstood term. You will need to bend the knees, but not so far that you are sitting on your skis as some people seem to think. The crouch must be combined with a forward leaning, the *Vorlage*. Now you try. Cross the slope from one side to the other with your skis parallel. When you wish to stop, simply pull them into the snowplow. . . ."

James dug his sticks in and pushed off. This felt much more satisfying than the awkward snowplow. He cut through the powdery snow in a clean, straight line, angling slightly downhill. Oberhauser stayed at his side, shouting out instructions.

"Keep your weight on the lower ski and the upper ski advanced. Lean away from the slope with your upper shoulder forward. If you find yourself falling, don't fight it, go with it, relax, and fall smoothly."

This was easier said than done, thought James, as he felt his skis slip out from under him and he was sent tumbling into an untidy heap, arms and legs going in all directions.

Hannes laughed and helped him up.

"You will get there with practice. You must develop a

feeling for the snow. But you are learning fast. After lunch you will join in with the others."

Lunch was soup followed by spicy German sausage with bread and cheese, taken on benches outside a chalet restaurant that sat to one side of the slope. James realized just how tiring the morning had been. There were aches and strains all over his body, and his knees and ankles felt as if they had been kicked by a mule. His boots were caked with snow and sat like heavy blocks of ice around his feet. He had to stamp some feeling back into his toes. But the food restored his energy, and by the time they returned to the slope, he was raring to go again.

His progress was slower in the afternoon, though, as he had lost his one-to-one tuition and was now simply part of the group. There was so much to take in, and most of it went straight out of James's head once he started skiing. What with the tension and the concentration and the noise of the skis sliding over the snow, he was deaf to Oberhauser's shouts. His muscles seemed to find the right shape, though. His upper body settled into a comfortably upright position, leaning forward with his back slightly bowed, his arms relaxed and held in front.

"You must turn off your brain and let your body guide you," Hannes said to them at the end of the day as they were taking off their skis. "Skiing, when it is done well, is ballet dancing to imaginary music."

Over the next few days, James worked hard. The trickiest skill to master was turning, which was much more difficult than he had imagined. Instead of leaning into the curve, you had to lean away from it or the skis would not behave. The problem was that they were long and straight and rigid, and weren't designed for turning corners. Oberhauser explained that in order to change the direction of the skis you had to lift them from the snow or they would simply run straight ahead as if on rails.

"When you need to make a turn, you use an up-and-down movement." He illustrated this by bobbing up and down quickly. "You will be surprised, but if you stand on a set of weighing scales and crouch down suddenly, you will become lighter for a moment. It is that fraction of a moment of weightlessness you must use to lift your skis from the snow and turn them."

James practiced, combining the up-and-down movement with a body swing, and one afternoon he suddenly cracked it and found himself carving an elegant S in the snow with his skis as he sped down the slope. This gave him immense satisfaction, as most of the other boys were still clumsily shuffling about in nervous snowplows.

As he was taking off his skis at the end of the day, the sun passed behind the Kitzbühler Horn and an icy wind came whistling up from nowhere. He shivered and looked up toward the peak of the Hahnenkamm. They had had a jolly day playing on its flank, but he understood only too well how quickly the mood of a mountain could change. There had been a bleak memory lurking at the back of his mind since he had arrived here, and now it fought its way into his thoughts.

His parents had died in the Alps, west of here, near Chamonix in France. It was true they had not been skiing at the time, but climbing. All the same, they had clearly underestimated the power of the mountains and had paid with their lives. James knew he would have to be careful here. Only last year, four masters from Eton had died climbing on Piz Roseg in the Swiss Alps. And they were not the first.

As James watched a group of boys throwing snowballs at each other and laughing, he wondered if everyone else was as aware of the dangers as he was.

CHAPTER 5—YOU'RE GOING THE WRONG WAY!

The weather held for the next few days, with fresh snowfalls during the nights and bright sun during the days. The conditions remained perfect for skiing, and James progressed fast. He loved to learn new things, and he loved to keep active. There was no better feeling at the end of the day than to have tired, sore muscles and an inner glow of warmth. And by throwing himself into the skiing and keeping busy, he managed to banish all dark thoughts about his parents. He grew to love the mountain and he missed it when he was back at the hotel.

So his days were spent swishing down the lower slopes, and in the evenings, after a huge stodgy meal, he would go up to bed early and almost instantly fall into a deep, untroubled sleep. The only sour note was sounded by Miles Langton-Herring, who would often wake James by noisily blundering around their room when he came up later, presumably to take his revenge for being woken early that first morning. Once he was sure James was awake, he would start to talk. This was the most annoying part. Miles was a show-off. He would boast about both his prowess on the ski slopes and his seemingly bottomless well of knowledge. The worst thing about him was that while he appeared to know more facts than could be contained in the world's largest encyclopedia, he seemed not to know the most important fact of all—that nobody was remotely interested in a word he had to say. He was a bore, and like all bores, he didn't realize it. Long after everyone else had finished a conversation, Miles would still be barking away, like a dog locked out in a yard by its owners. James soon learned to tune him out, as if he were an unwanted radio station, but it made it very difficult to have a conversation with anyone else while he was around.

Miles was in a more advanced skiing group, so at least during the days James didn't have to listen to his loud, fruity, donkey bray of a voice. By the end of the week, though, Hannes reckoned James was good enough to join the experienced skiers on the upper slopes of the Hahnenkamm.

"We are going to ski all the way down from the top of the mountain," he explained. "There is a fairly easy run, which will be perfect to test the abilities of a skier like yourself."

So it was that on Saturday morning James found himself climbing aboard a gondola on the Hahnenkamm-Bahn for the 1,500-meter ascent to the summit. He was with Hannes, a master called Mr. Eastfield, and a group of ten boys. They stood in the narrow gondola clutching their skis and chatting excitedly.

The car latched itself onto the moving cable and they jolted out of the lower station and lurched up the slope. They passed through the outskirts of town and up over the tops of the houses, their roofs covered with thick white snow. There was no sound apart from a low bass hum punctuated by the occasional rattle as they went over one of the supporting towers. Soon they were climbing much more steeply between impossibly tall pine trees that shot straight up toward the sky.

"Every year there is a famous race down the mountain," Hannes told James. "The Hahnenkammrennen. Perhaps the most important skiing race in the world. It is a very tough course, and very dangerous, but don't worry: it is not the course we will be taking today. It will be great fun."

"I can't wait," said James.

"You know," said Hannes, "you have it in you to be a really first-class skier, James. I have never known anyone take to it as quickly as you. Most beginners would have needed six weeks at least to become as good as you. You have natural balance, you listen well, and you seem to have no fear at all."

"I'm enjoying it," said James. "I should love to be as good as you one day."

Hannes smiled. "If you are really serious about it," he said, "you should go to Hannes Schneider's school at St. Anton in the Arlberg. It is where I learned to ski, and where I was taught to become an instructor. St. Anton has become the university of skiing, the mecca for all those who love to ski. There is a man there called Fuchs who could make you a world-beater. I only usually teach novices and tourists. My real passion is for climbing."

James looked out to see that they were now so high they were above the tops of the pine trees, which clung to the almost sheer side of the mountain, sprouting from between the jagged rocks. Looking out through the rear windows, it was easy to imagine that they were thousands of feet in the air, as if the gondola were airborne and flying up the slope like a glider. Below them, Kitzbühel had become a toy town. Unfortunately, the weather had changed this morning, and the sky was gray. It had the effect of turning the view into a black-and-white photograph. All color seemed to have been drained from the scenery. The pretty doll's houses of Kitzbühel looked gray, the snow was white, and the pine trees a dense black.

A gust of wind whined through the windows, and the steel cable zinged as they passed an empty gondola coming down the other way.

A few minutes later they cleared the top of the slope and left the trees behind. The land flattened out into rolling pillows of snow crisscrossed by animal tracks, probably left by chamois, the mountain goat native to the Alps. They arrived at the top station, and there was a flurry of activity as they clambered off and carried their skis out into the daylight. It was noticeably colder at this altitude. James felt the wind bite into him. He arranged his black cotton scarf in such a way that it partially covered his face, and tucked it carefully around his collar so that no icy fingers of draft could snake down his neck.

It was another world up here. The top of the Hahnenkamm was flattened so that there was a panoramic view of mountains all around: the Kitzbühler Horn, Resterhohe, Pengelstein, Gaisberg. It was breathtaking. James stood for a moment just taking it all in. The scenery was perfect, and perfectly untouched. He felt like God on the first day of creation looking out over his handiwork.

"We will spend the morning skiing up here," Hannes announced. "There will be a lot of walking involved, I am afraid, but there are some good fast runs to test you. Now let us put on our skis and go!"

As they were strapping on their bindings, James noticed

Miles Langton-Herring in an excited huddle with three older boys. They were sniggering and keeping well away from the adults.

"What are they up to?" he asked Andrew Carlton, who was next to him.

"Drinking," Andrew said flatly.

"Alcohol?" said James.

"They have a flask of schnapps that someone at the hotel got for them," said Andrew. "They think they're being terribly grown-up."

James laughed. "I know in Switzerland they send those big Saint Bernard dogs to rescue people in the mountains with barrels of brandy around their necks, but I didn't know you were supposed to get drunk before you set off."

"They're idiots," said Andrew. "If they *do* get drunk, then they probably *will* need rescuing."

Hannes came over to give James a pair of snow goggles.

"This will be very different from the nursery slopes," he said as James put the goggles on. "You will have to make quick decisions. Up to a certain point you can use your brain, but at speed you have to rely on muscles and human instinct. Pay attention to the ground in front of you. Slopes change from convex to concave, from steep to gentle, all the time. There are waves and bumps and holes to look out for; they will all affect your speed. Keep ahead of your skis like I have taught you. And most important of all—enjoy yourself!"

When they were all ready, they set off. This was indeed very different from anything James had experienced before. They were moving fast down a track with a wall of snow on one side and a frightening drop on the other. If he lost control, he would find himself going down the mountain rather more quickly than he was hoping. They followed each other in a long snaking line. Some boys cried out with the thrill of it; others had their teeth gritted as they went down in grim silence.

James's heart was hammering against his ribs, but he soon managed to relax, and after a few minutes had forgotten the danger and was simply enjoying himself, a wide grin hidden behind his scarf.

The run ended in an exhilarating sprint down a wide steep slope into a small valley. The boys swished to a halt at the bottom and compared notes.

Then it was skis off and a long tramp up a snowy track to the top of the next run.

This was the pattern for the rest of the morning. A few brief minutes of wild excitement and then a good hour's climb back up again.

James was surprised to find that there were one or two buildings up here, including a restaurant that served good hot food, which had to be delivered by cable car.

The weather lifted as they ate lunch; the sun came out and the glorious scenery was lit up, shining and crisp.

It didn't last, though—when they were ready to ski again the sun had disappeared and the sky was heavy with clouds.

It seemed to take ages for everyone to get ready. James was in his skis and leaning on his sticks a long time before most of the other boys, and he was getting impatient as they fussed about and chatted and pushed each other over in the snow. He noticed that Miles and his gang were among the last to be ready, and their faces were flushed.

Mr. Eastfield addressed the unruly rabble.

"We've had a good morning," he shouted, banging his gloved hands together for warmth. "But I've been talking to Herr Oberhauser and he fears that the weather is closing in. We should be all right if we set off soon, but please be extra careful this afternoon."

James looked over at the Wilder Kaiser. A thick, flat, gray streak of clouds had obliterated the tops of the peaks, as if a frustrated painter had smeared a dirty brush across the top of a painting.

They had to ski some way to get to the top of the run down into Kitzbühel, and there was a deal more walking involved. By the time they arrived, thin wisps of clouds were scudding by, and the peak of the Kitzbühler Horn on the far side of the valley was hidden in a murky haze that was creeping down its flanks toward the town.

The Hahnenkamm looked incredibly steep here, and James felt a flutter of fear. Was he really good enough to cope with this run?

"The weather can change very quickly," said Hannes once they were all lined up. "So we stay together and observe all the safety rules. The more dangerous parts are marked off with rope, so stay on the right track. I will lead and Mr. Eastfield will follow behind."

Hannes zipped over the snow to James, smiling broadly.

"If you can make it down here in one piece," he said, "then you can call yourself a skier. Some of the run is very steep indeed. Just remember: the steeper the slope, the faster you go, the more you must lean. You must constantly adjust your angle, like the needle of a compass, as the slope changes.

Air resistance is nothing at slow speeds, but when you are traveling fast it is a very strong force, so you must lean well into it, until finally with great speed you will feel as if you are lying against the air."

He winked at James, shouted some encouragement to the others, then dug his sticks into the snow and pushed off down the slope. James was relieved to see that he didn't *schuss* straight down, but cut across, then swished around in a long elegant curve and went back the other way. The more confident skiers were right behind him, and the rest followed in ones and twos, keeping to the same path the instructor had taken.

Now it was James's turn—he could hold it off no longer. He pulled his goggles down over his eyes, leaned forward, and shunted himself onto the slope.

He grinned as his skis rattled over the newly compacted snow. Gravity would take hold now and convey him all the way to the foot of the mountain. All he had to do was try not to fall over.

For several minutes their progress was steady and straightforward, then they hit a narrow section of the run where turning was harder, and they were forced to take a steeper path. They sped up and James felt his heart race faster with his skis. He passed a couple of boys who had taken tumbles and was feeling like he was king of the mountain before his brief moment of elation came to an abrupt halt. Five boys had collided and fallen in a tangle of bodies and skis amidst much laughter.

The whole party had to stop. The bindings had come away from one of the boy's skis, and Hannes set about trying to fix it. Everyone else sat around, and gradually their high spirits turned to moans and grumbles. Muttered complaints started to be leveled at the boys who had crashed.

"You've held us all up now."

"Just when it was getting exciting."

"You're really wasting our time."

"Back to the nursery slopes for you saps."

While Hannes was busy, and before anyone knew what was happening, thick clouds descended on them. Almost instantly the view was wiped out, and all anyone could see was a milky whiteness. The clouds were cold and damp, and they muffled all sound. With white snow carpeting the ground, there was a ghostly, dreamlike quality to the scene.

Hannes found Mr. Eastfield.

"We will have to sit it out," Hannes explained. "It is too dangerous to ski in this fog."

"Should we not make our way back up to the cable car?" Eastfield asked.

"It could take an hour, perhaps two. It may stop running before we get there, and even walking back up might be dangerous. It is best to stay here and wait for a gap in the clouds. We will be all right."

Far from lifting, however, the clouds seemed to grow heavier as they waited, and then it started to snow. Thick flakes drifted lazily between the pine trees.

Some chocolate was handed around to lift their spirits, but the boys mostly ate in gloomy silence. James noticed Miles and his friends sitting apart and taking sneaky gulps from a silver drinking flask.

They had given up hope of ever moving on when the

clouds suddenly lifted, and they were surprised to see the view appear out of nowhere. It had been easy to forget that they were thousands of feet up on the side of a mountain, and this sudden reminder was startling.

Hannes and Mr. Eastfield ran around shouting encouragement and getting everyone to hurry. They snapped their boots into their bindings, pulled on gloves and goggles, and slung their backpacks over their shoulders, and the conditions were still fine as they at last set off again in a great unruly mass.

They had not been going for five minutes, however, when they came to another pocket of clouds. James watched everyone ahead of him disappear into a white wall, and he could do nothing but follow them. In the confusion, the group became scattered. There was shouting from all sides, but it was impossible to tell who anyone was or which direction to go in. Then James spotted Miles scooting purposefully off to the right, and went after him, assuming he knew where he was going. He soon realized that Miles was lost, however, as the sounds of the skiing party faded behind them. James called after him and sped up.

"Hey, Miles, you're going the wrong way!"

He saw Miles turn and fall, and he swooshed up to him, stopping in a flurry of snow.

"Oi, watch out!" said Miles. "You've covered me. And what do you mean by shouting at me like that? You made me fall."

James apologized. It was simpler than protesting.

"I think my damned ski's come loose," said Miles, and he started tugging at his bindings.

"Don't," said James. "You're making it worse. Let me."

"I can manage, thank you," said Miles, and he pushed James out of the way.

James could do nothing but stand there watching as Miles fumbled and cursed at the straps and refitted his ski agonizingly slowly. The sound of the others had been swallowed up in the fog, and James was becoming increasingly worried that they wouldn't be able to find them again. He peered into the murk and strained his ears, but he had lost all sense of where they were. When he turned back, Miles was taking a drink from his flask.

"That won't help," said James.

"Warms you up," slurred Miles.

"It also gets you drunk," said James. "I don't think it'll be very safe to be drunk up here in these conditions."

"What do you know about it?" said Miles. "I don't expect you've ever taken a proper drink in your life."

James didn't respond to this gibe and merely said that they should hurry up. At last Miles got shakily to his feet and slipped the flask into the pocket of his wind-cheater.

"This way," said James, turning around.

"No, it's this way," said Miles.

"No," said James, "you were heading in the wrong direction."

"Don't tell me what I was doing," said Miles. "I'm a much more experienced skier than you."

Before James could stop him, Miles stubbornly set off almost straight down the slope, so fast that he was quickly out of sight. James had no choice but to follow him. He was getting very scared, but left to himself, Miles might get into serious trouble.

CHAPTER 6—THERE IS MORE THAN ONE WAY TO COME DOWN A MOUNTAIN

James skied furiously after Miles until he had caught up with him. The snow here was deep and unbroken, so he knew that they couldn't be going the right way. He tried to get this through to Miles, who shouted him down and then veered off at a sharp angle—taking them even farther away from where James reckoned the rest of the party should be. Almost immediately Miles cried out, and when James caught up with him, he saw he had got in among some trees and become snarled on a root.

James skied over to him and dragged him to his feet.

"This is madness," he said. "You're coming back with me, back to the others." He physically twisted Miles around and shoved him in the other direction. Miles grumbled under his breath, but carried on.

They were traversing the mountain here and could walk on their skis between the trees. It was slow going and tiring as well.

For several minutes they picked their way along. The trees thinned, and gradually James's hopes rose that they would soon come across the others.

But then Miles stopped again.

"What is it now?" said James.

"A rope."

Miles picked up a frayed end of rope. James saw the other end tied to a tree.

"It marks the edge of the run," said James. "We must have crossed it somewhere up above. We're back on track. We should start to head down again."

"We didn't cross any ropes," Miles scoffed. "I knew you were taking me the wrong way. We must have gone right over to the far side of the run; we need to turn back around again."

James could see fear in Miles's eyes. He could smell it coming off his damp skin. A mixture of sweat and alcohol and something animal. It was making him irrational. If he got too desperate there was no telling what he might do.

"Look about the place," James pleaded. "This is the run. The snow here is clearer, there are no trees. That's where we should be."

"If this is the run then where are the tracks?" said Miles angrily. "The others would have left tracks. They are obviously back that way."

"Don't talk rot," James snapped.

"I am not talking rot," said Miles. "I know about these things. You should listen to me. I've been skiing many times before. I know about mountains and suchlike."

"You don't know about anything," said James. "You're a pompous, overblown windbag. And, what's more, you're drunk. I'm not taking orders from a drunk."

At this Miles lashed out at James and clipped him around the head with a clumsy punch. Taken unawares, James slipped over on his skis and struggled to get up again. By the time he had gotten to his feet he could just see Miles's back as he sped off in completely the wrong direction.

James spat blood from his mouth and saw it lying black on the snow.

For a moment he considered letting Miles go. It was clear that this idiot was going to get them both killed. But James knew that he couldn't leave him alone on the mountain. If anything *did* happen to him, he would never forgive himself.

He called vainly for help a few times, his voice getting swallowed up in the fog. There was no answer but silence. He shouted one last time, then shook his head, pulled up his scarf, tucked into a crouch, and set off after Miles, oblivious to the cold and the ache in his legs. He felt a fool for letting his temper flare up like that. It was important not to lose one's head in these conditions.

He had to stop Miles, calm him down, and somehow get him back onto the right path, but that was easier said than done. There were a lot of rocks here, most of them hidden below the surface of the snow, and tree trunks would suddenly loom up out of the whiteness. Thin branches whipped at his face as he sped past. He leaned well forward, his knees slightly bent, trying not to tense up, keeping his body loose and elastic, reacting to every bump and dip in the ground. Twice he fell over, landing face-first in the snow, and each time he merely picked himself up, wiped his goggles clean, and carried on.

At least the only way Miles could go was down, so in one sense they were headed in the right direction, but they could have no idea of what lay ahead of them, and Miles was taking a course closer and closer to the fall line. Soon he would be heading straight down the mountain, and not angling across the slopes at all.

James's only hope was that Miles would fall, but he

seemed to have the luck of the devil. Or maybe he really *was* the world's greatest skier, as he had often boasted.

James sped on; his eyes focused on the twin tramlines Miles had carved into the snow. He laughed—was it possible that the boy had found an easy way down the Hahnenkamm after all, and James's fears had been unfounded?

Suddenly he burst out of the clouds into an impossibly steep, wide-open patch of virgin snow. There were no trees here, and James at last saw Miles up ahead. He was careering along, completely out of control, his arms waving, standing first on one ski and then the other, wobbling drunkenly from left to right. It was like a long, long fall. Miraculously, though, he stayed upright.

James saw his chance to catch up with him. He would risk taking the fall line. He gripped his sticks tightly and leaned so far forward that his nose was almost touching his skis, and then shot straight down the slope in a wild *Schuss*.

This was like weightless sailing. He was almost flying over the snow crystals. He had mastered gravity. The pressure of the wind in his face was immense, however, and if he didn't lean far enough into it, he knew that it would flatten him.

James was so intent on watching Miles, so keen to overtake him, so lost in the joy of speed, that he wasn't paying close enough attention to what lay ahead. He was brought brutally back to reality, however, when he heard Miles cry out in terror, and the next moment the ground beneath his feet rose sharply and then disappeared altogether.

They had skied right off a cliff.

Now he really *was* flying. He was high in the air above the clouds, with a view right out across the valley, and the only way was down. He knew that he was dead. The mountain had claimed him after all. For a second or two it was as if he were just hanging there, and then he dropped into the white fog with terrifying suddenness.

He yelled, and then could make no sound at all as the air was sucked out of him. Tattered clouds tore past and he watched in horror as the ground rushed up to meet him. He held his nerve, though, keeping his balance, his skis parallel, the tips raised. In a flash he saw that he might have a chance. The slope was still very steep here; he would be landing at an angle. There was a slim possibility that he might just be able to land on his skis. He braced himself for the impact, and when he did land, it was surprisingly gentle; his skis kissed the snow and he was thundering down unharmed. He gave a whoop of triumph and the next thing he knew he was tumbling head over heels down the slope.

He had no idea how far he rolled, but when he finally came to a halt, he lay there, alternately laughing like a madman and sobbing. Nobody would ever believe what he had just done, because nobody had seen it . . . except, perhaps, Miles.

Miles? Where was he? James sat up and looked around. He had dropped right out of the bottom of the clouds. Visibility was good, though the sky was darkening. His blood froze as he saw, not ten feet away from where he had stopped, a second drop that would have spelled certain death. He approached the edge. Below were just jagged gray rocks. Had Miles gone over?

He peered down. There was no sign of him. He called out. And then again. Louder this time. He waited. Had he heard something? A feeble response? He screamed Miles's name, until his voice was hoarse. Yes. There it was. From farther up the slope, a faint quavering response.

James chopped his way up sideways with little six-inch steps, keeping his skis straight and using his sticks for balance.

"Keep calling!" he shouted. "Let me know where you are, Miles."

"I'm here," came the weedy response. "I'm up here."

"Where?" said James, trying to look into the ceiling of clouds above him. "I can't see a thing."

Then a cold wind raced across the mountain and the clouds were ripped away. There was Miles, lying awkwardly in the snow among his sticks and skis, like a squashed black bug. It took James five more minutes to get to him, and he slumped down, exhausted, fighting for breath.

"I thought you were dead for sure," he said.

"So did I," said Miles. "I'm not really sure what happened. I think I must have knocked myself out for a moment."

"You skied off a cliff," said James. "Now will you believe that we've gone the wrong way?"

"Sorry," said Miles. His skin was as white as the snow, and his eyes a livid red.

"Are you hurt?" James asked.

Miles looked at him, swallowed hard, then slowly nodded his head, fighting back tears.

"Where?" said James.

"All over," said Miles. "But I'm worried about my leg. I'm scared to look, but it hurts like hell and I can't move it. I think it might be broken."

James steeled himself, fearing the worst, then glanced down. Miles was right: his lower right shin was bent forward at an impossible angle. There didn't appear to be any blood or bone sticking out through his trousers, but there was no possibility that he would be able to ski any farther. Particularly as one of his skis was missing altogether, and the other, though still attached to his left foot, was snapped completely in half.

"It's bad, I'm afraid," said James, and now Miles burst into tears.

"What are we going to do?" he wailed.

"We're going to get you down," said James. "And we're going to get you to a hospital."

"Get down?" Miles snapped angrily. "How? I can't bloody move."

"Yes you can," said James hotly. "You're going to bloody well have to. Unless you want to die up here."

"I'm not going to die, am I?" said Miles fearfully, gripping on to James's arm.

"Not if I can help it," said James.

"What can *you* do?"

"Listen," said James. "If we work together, you'll be fine. But if you annoy me any more, I'll leave you here. Is that clear?"

"Yes. Sorry. I'm just a little scared."

"We're both scared," said James. "And we have a right to be. We're both still alive, though, and I aim to keep it that way." So saying, he took off his scarf and tore it into three long strips.

"What are you doing?" said Miles.

"We need to make a splint for your leg."

"Don't! You mustn't touch it. I won't let you . . ."

"Be quiet and help me get this ski off," said James.

Together they undid the binding, and James put the

length of broken ski against Miles's shin.

"I'm going to have to try and straighten your leg," he said. "And it's going to hurt. Maybe you should have a slug of that schnapps you've been swigging."

Miles nodded, his face turning from white to green. He took out his flask, unscrewed the cap, and put it to his lips. Quickly, while Miles was distracted, James grabbed him by the knee and ankle and tugged. There was a crunching sound. Miles screamed and fainted but his leg was more or less back at a normal angle. James checked. There was still no blood, which was a good sign. As James was using the strips of scarf to bind the ski tightly to Miles's shin, Miles woke up. When he saw what James was doing, he writhed and groaned and bit the end of his leather gauntlet hard between his teeth, but he was brave enough to let James finish, and once it was over he seemed relieved and much calmer. James noticed, however, that his skin was covered with a film of greasy sweat, and his eyes had grown shiny and glasslike.

"I'm going to have to try and get you on my back," said James, and Miles looked at him as if he were mad.

"Of course," said James, "if you've a better suggestion . . ."

"No."

"Use your good leg and your sticks and see if you can stand," said James.

It was painful to watch, but Miles managed it, wobbling up and standing bent over in the snow. James maneuvered himself into a position a little lower down the slope from him, and he too crouched down.

"Roll onto my shoulders," said James. "Slowly and carefully. If I go over, it's going to hurt."

Miles grunted and tipped onto James's back. James shrugged and pulled him into a more comfortable position, all the while slipping sideways down the slope. He dug his sticks in for support and eventually managed to get Miles firmly in place.

"We'll head across to those trees over there," said James, "try and get well away from that next cliff edge below, then see if there's anywhere we can make a straight run down."

He jerked himself forward, taking as gentle an angle as he could. Too little and they wouldn't budge an inch; too much and they would be heading for the drop.

With a bit of experimentation he found the right line, and at last they were moving gently across the slope. But already his back was on fire, and the muscles in his neck were screaming in protest. It was all he could do to keep his knees together, and they trembled uncontrollably. He and Miles were moving, though, and that was something.

After a few minutes they came to a large tree and James leaned against it, letting it take the weight for a while. He checked that Miles was all right, then pushed off again, gasping with the effort. Just past the tree, however, they hit a patch of loose powdery snow, and James found himself skidding, unable to hold his line. He knew he would have to take a steeper angle or risk falling. With any luck, the extra momentum would hold them in a straight line.

He forced his skis around and they speeded up just enough to regain control. The line was taking them steadily closer to the cliff edge, though, and a few seconds later they hit another loose patch of snow and James spun around until he was sliding backward down the slope.

"Hang on," he grunted, but he couldn't stop himself. He had no idea how near they were to the drop, and he was totally out of control. There was only one thing to do. He collapsed into the snow.

Miles screamed, and in his agony kicked out at James, who got a knee in the face.

"I'm sorry," said James. "I had no choice."

"I can't go on," said Miles. "I can't. I just can't."

"Yes you can," said James. "You'd be surprised how far you can push your body when you have to."

"What would you know about it?" said Miles. "This isn't the steeplechase at Eton."

"Well, maybe it would help if we pretended it was," said James, trying not to let his anger resurface.

"You're going to kill me," said Miles.

"Believe me," said James, "the thought has crossed my mind."

Miles swore.

"Look here," said James. "Arguing isn't going to help us at all. You can't go on like this, and I must say I'm not sure whether I can go much farther, so we need to think of another plan. Maybe I should leave you here and go for help."

Miles suddenly grabbed James's arm, a look of sheer hopeless terror on his white face.

"No," he said. "You mustn't leave me. I couldn't bear it. You'd never find me again."

"It's all right," said James, laughing, and pointing across the snow. "Look, we're saved."

CHAPTER 7—WHITE DEATH

A little farther down the mountain, a wooden hut nestled against the rock face, its steep roof heavy with snow.

Ignoring Miles's protests, James hoisted him onto his aching back once more and aimed for the hut. The pain in his knees and ankles had become so intense that his brain had started to shut it out, and he almost didn't register it anymore. But they reached the hut without any further mishap, and he lowered his charge safely to the ground.

Mercifully, the hut wasn't locked, and James staggered inside, his legs shaking uncontrollably. A little later he re-emerged and grinned at Miles.

"I think it's a mountain rescue hut," he said. "It's perfect. There's a stove, blankets, beds, and some food and water."

The look of relief that washed over Miles was almost comical. James put a hand under one of his shoulders and they hobbled inside, where Miles collapsed onto one of the beds. James lit a lamp and busied himself with getting a fire going in the stove. He then put a kettle of water on top to boil before fetching some chocolate and hard sausage from the larder.

The two of them ate in silence.

"What time do you suppose it is?" asked Miles, once his energy was restored.

"It's hard to know with all those clouds around," said James. "I'd say perhaps five o'clock, maybe later. Whatever the case, it's going to be dark soon."

"Do you not have a watch?"

James shook his head. "I've an old pocket watch, but I hardly ever use it. How about you?"

"I had a wristwatch," said Miles, "but I must have lost it in the fall. Shame. It was rather valuable."

"All I know is it's too late to try and carry on now," said James. "We should rest here for the night. Perhaps the weather will have cleared by the morning. There's some kind of sledge here, large enough to carry a man. I could take you down on that tomorrow. I assume there must be a fairly easy route from here."

"Should we not go now?"

"No." James went to the window and looked out. A fresh snowstorm had settled in, and thick flakes swirled in the air. The sky was completely blotted out by heavy clouds, and it looked for all the world as if it were the middle of the night.

"I'm shattered," he said. "And you're in no fit state to be stumbling around out there in the dark."

"My leg hurts like the devil," said Miles, and James noticed that he still couldn't bear to look at it.

"I'll see if there's anything here to take the pain away," he said, and rummaged through the cabinets and storage boxes. He eventually found a first-aid box that contained, among other items, a tin with the Bayer trademark on it. Inside the tin was a packet of aspirin. He gave two to Miles.

By this time the kettle had boiled and James poured two mugs of beef tea.

When Miles took his tin mug, he was shaking all over,

and despite being wrapped in two blankets, he complained of being freezing cold. James realized that he was cold, too. He stripped off his damp outer layers and hung them to dry on a chair back. His boots were soaked as well. He didn't want to risk taking them off, in case he couldn't get them back on again, so he propped his feet up on a stool near the stove and watched the sodden leather gently steam.

He closed his eyes. His head felt as heavy as a cannonball. It tipped forward and he was out like a light.

The next thing he knew he was being shaken awake by Miles.

"What is it?" said James, momentarily confused. "What's the matter?"

Miles looked wild-eyed and feverish. He was using a broom for a crutch and had taken half his clothes off. He was running with sweat.

"My leg," he said. "It's burning up. I'm in agony. I don't think I can stand it any longer. You have to get me down from here; you have to get me to a doctor."

"That would be crazy," said James, glancing at the window. It was pitch dark outside. The panes of glass might just as well have been coated with black paint. "You'll be all right in the morning. . . ."

"No." Miles grabbed James and shook him roughly. "I've heard of cases, people with broken limbs—they get infected. I might lose my leg. I might die. I can't bear the pain anymore. I want to chew my leg off."

James stood up stiffly and struggled over to the window. It seemed to have stopped snowing at least, but there were no stars visible in the sky.

"If we go out there," he said, "the likelihood is that you will only come to more harm."

"Y-you said there was a sledge," Miles stammered. "Put me on it. Get me down from here, or I swear I shall die."

James stared out the window into the blackness.

What should he do?

Miles was becoming more agitated by the second. James didn't want to risk being cooped up in this cabin with a mad person, and there was no way that Miles could get down the mountain by himself.

But to go out there? Into the night. With the temperature below freezing.

How many people had died on this mountain, he wondered. And what bitter irony it would be to die in the same way as his parents.

Miles groaned like a trapped animal, and when James turned around, he saw that Miles was struggling to get dressed.

"It's madness," said James.

"I'm going," said Miles. "Whether you like it or not."

James realized there was no arguing with him.

James dressed quickly in his damp clothes and found a torch, some climbing equipment, and a rope. He lifted the sledge down from where it was hanging on the wall, took it outside, and laid it on the ground. It felt bitterly cold after being inside the cozy little hut, and James would have given anything to go back indoors, lie down under a pile of blankets, and go to sleep.

Instead, he helped Miles into his jacket and secured one end of the rope around his waist. He tied the other end around his own chest. At least the two of them couldn't get separated now, whatever happened.

James switched on the torch, put on his gloves, and manhandled Miles outside.

"There appears to be a path of sorts," he said as he lowered Miles onto the sledge. "We'll just have to set off and hope for the best."

"Thank you," said Miles, gripping on to James's forearm and trying to smile. James took the silver flask from the other boy's pocket.

"What are you doing?" asked Miles.

"I'm going to need this," said James, and he emptied its contents down his throat. "It's going to be a long night."

There were a few moments of burning, followed by a pleasant glow in his belly. This was it, then. There was nothing more he could do. He made sure that Miles was lying down safely. Then he grabbed the towrope on the front of the sledge and pulled.

The sledge jerked forward.

It was almost harder steering the sledge down the mountain than it had been carrying Miles on his back. It seemed to have a mind of its own and wanted to go everywhere except where James pointed it. He couldn't work out whether it was easier pushing from behind or dragging it from in front, and took turns trying both methods.

The crude track wound backward and forward across the mountainside. For the most part it was covered in snow, but there were stretches of bare rock where James had to haul the sledge along with brute force, its runners squealing and scraping. He forced himself not to think about how tired he was and doggedly plodded on, but all the way down he could hear Miles moaning. Occasionally, Miles's whole body would jerk and he would cry out in pain. He was starting to ramble, spewing out endless random facts and figures. . . .

"The Hahnenkammrennen has been held every year since 1931 . . . The highest mountain on land is Everest, but the tallest mountain in the world is actually Mauna Kea, one of the Hawaiian islands, which is nearly six miles high from the seabed to its summit. Because most of it is underwater, this is not commonly known . . . commonly known . . . The second highest mountain is K2, or Qogir . . . The third highest is . . . is . . . Monte Carlo . . . The first men to try and climb K2 were Oscar Eckenstein and Aleister Crowley, who is known as 'The wickedest man in the world' . . . Commonly known . . . Perhaps he is not as wicked as Attila the Hun and Genghis Khan . . . Genghis Khan came from . . . came from . . . Monte Carlo . . . which is not commonly known . . . There is only one rule if you get caught in an avalanche: get your hands to your boots and grip your ankles, that way you can undo your skis so that you are not trapped under the snow . . . No two snowflakes are exactly the same. . . ."

James felt like he was in some ghastly nightmare, staggering down a mountain in the dark tied to a madman. What bliss it would be to suddenly awake and find himself safely tucked up in his bed at the hotel. He started to laugh, and realized he was becoming light-headed with exhaustion and cold.

He was making some sort of progress, though; with every step he must be closer to the bottom, closer to safety. There were periods, however, when he lost all contact with reality and seemed to be walking in his sleep. He would come around with no memory of what he had been doing. Worryingly, these spells grew longer and longer until finally he came around only to discover that he had fallen over and was being pulled down the slope behind the sledge by the rope around his chest. He was too weak to do anything about it, and tried to keep his face out of the snow, until at last the sledge ground to a halt against some rocks, and he slid down and bumped into the back of it.

They had lost the path.

Miraculously, he was still clutching the torch in his hand, which had become a frozen claw. He stood up and shone the beam around. They were on a rocky outcrop. Below was a wide, clear patch of open snow, but to get to it, they would have to climb about fifteen feet down a cliff face.

That was out of the question. Miles could barely stand, let alone climb. There was only one thing to do: James would have to lower him down.

James sat Miles upright and tried to explain what was happening. Miles looked about himself feverishly. Whether he understood or not, James had no idea, and he yelled and sobbed as James lifted him off the sledge and shuffled him toward the edge.

"Keep still, or you'll only make it worse," said James, dropping the sledge down. It landed soundlessly in a soft cushion of snow, and James hoped that Miles's landing would be equally soft.

Miles eventually worked out what he needed to do and slid feetfirst on his belly, over the lip. James let the rope out through his fingers, which had long since lost all feeling. Inch by inch, Miles scrambled down the rocks, holding his body clear with his good leg.

James was never quite sure how Miles did it, but at last the rope went slack, and James shone the torch down to see the other boy sitting safely in the snow.

Now it was his turn.

Climbing in ski boots with numb hands is not easy, and twice James thought he was going to fall. The god of the mountains must have been watching over them that night, though, because soon James was sitting next to Miles with nothing but clear virgin snow ahead of them, sloping gently down into the valley.

However, as James stood up and took a pace toward the sledge, he felt the snow shift beneath his feet, and he quickly threw himself toward the rocks and grabbed hold.

"Be careful," he shouted to Miles. "The snow's loose."

He tried to pull the boy to the rocks with the rope, but Miles panicked and crawled away from him, his bad leg dragging behind him like a tail.

"Stay still," James yelled. "It could give way at any minute."

It was too late—the whole sheet of packed snow started to move, sliding down the slope like rushing water and taking Miles with it. A terrible thought struck James. They might have started an avalanche. There was no time to take in this information, though, as the weight of Miles's body tore him loose. He was helpless. The snow moved faster and faster, and then, with a sickening lurch, James went over another cliff edge and was falling in a cascade of snow.

He had no idea how far they fell, and was not aware of landing. It was as if time and space had simply solidified around him into a freezing black mass. He thought at first that he had died. He could see nothing and feel nothing. His body seemed to be weightless. He wondered if this was what the afterlife was like—an eternity of nothingness. Then slowly his senses returned and he felt a great weight pressing in on him from all sides, as if he were gripped in a huge fist. He couldn't move at all. It was then that he panicked and tried to shout for help, only to find that his mouth was blocked. He shook his head and struggled to spit, and felt something cold and rough pressing against his face.

It was snow. He had been buried alive by the stuff.

A terrible fear gripped him. He was beyond rescue, alone beneath this weight of crushing white death. He wondered why he didn't feel colder. Either he was too numb or the snow was acting like a blanket and insulating him. He tried to calm his mounting terror and take stock of the situation. He could breathe, at least. Some air must have been trapped down here, but with the snow pressing against his chest it was hard work, and he knew that the more he tried to move, the more oxygen he would use up.

Calm down, James. You've been in worse situations before and got out. You can do it again. Stay sane and think.

His legs were bent, as was his back. One arm seemed to be flung out to one side, the other . . . the other was near his face. He wriggled the fingers in his gloved hand and felt them move against his nose. There was a small gap where his breath had melted the snow.

He flexed his fingers, strained with all his strength, and the hand came free. He clawed at his face, compacting the area around it, then dug the snow out of his mouth. This small victory, though, had cost him a lot of energy. He felt weak and dizzy. The blood was roaring and banging in his ears like an orchestra.

It was going to be one hell of a job digging himself out of this.

Then an awful thought struck him—he had no idea which way was up and which was down. He could be lying on his front for all he knew, or even upside down. There was no point in struggling to escape until he knew for certain how he was placed, or he might only succeed in burying himself deeper. Tears of rage and frustration and helplessness sprang into his eyes. He managed to blink them away and felt them crawling across his skin.

He smiled. He laughed. He gave a small shout of triumph. The tears were trickling over his forehead, toward his hairline. That meant he must be upside down. It was a start. He could use his legs to kick upward.

But how deep was he? He could be under twenty feet of snow. A hundred. He pictured himself as a tiny speck in the side of the massive mountain. *Best not to think about that.* The idea of dying all alone down here, buried alive, was too horrible to contemplate. His body wouldn't be discovered until the snow melted in the summer, and there he would be, perfectly preserved by the cold.

He shuddered. There was only one way to find out how deep he was. He started to apply pressure with his feet, forcing them upward into the snow. At the same time he dug with his fingers, enlarging the space around his head. His legs had made some progress; he could now hammer them backward and forward. He worked his hand toward his belly, hoping to move the snow aside and scoop it out of the way, and it was then that he felt the rope. This was fresh encouragement. He could use it to pull himself up to the surface, and with any luck Miles would be on the other end.

He set to work—wriggling, digging, kicking, clawing— and ten minutes later, he had made a space around himself large enough to turn around in.

Soon he was the right way up, and as he had found so many times before, once he attacked a problem, once he started working hard, his fears faded away and he could shut out everything else until the work was done.

He had a plan, a goal. It didn't matter how long it took, how hard it was, how much it hurt, he had to get it done.

It was either that or die.

He reached up above his head and started to pull down the loose snow with his gloves. As it fell to his feet he stamped on it, creating a solid base to stand on and raise himself higher. This way he could slowly bore a tunnel upward, barely wider than his body. It was backbreaking work, reaching up the whole time in the pitch darkness and shuffling the snow down his body to his boots. He had long since lost all feeling in his feet. They felt like two large rocks attached to the end of his legs. Despite being under all that snow, he was sweating. He could feel rivulets of warm moisture trickling down his skin under his clothes, and the space around his face was filled with stale, damp breath.

Every now and again he stopped and stood still, making sure that he was still going straight up and hadn't gone off at an angle. Once he was sure he was still on course, he would start again, gouging out a handful of snow, dropping it, shuffling it down his body, stamping on it. He worked like a machine and had no real idea of what progress he was making, if any. His little bubble stayed the same size. His body was begging for rest and sleep, but he shut these signals out and just kept the one small part of his brain active, the part that told him to keep moving, to keep digging.

Slowly, slowly, as the minutes turned into hours, he groped his way up through the darkness, his throat sore, his lungs burning, his nostrils filled with the smell of the snow.

And then there was a change.

The rope turned at an angle and went off sideways into the snow wall. He checked. No. He hadn't made a mistake. He tugged at it. It had felt like a lifeline, guiding him to the surface, but now he was confused. Should he follow the rope or go up? And could he even go up if the rope was buried under the snow?

As he yanked at it, his head bumped against the top of his tunnel and a shower of snow rained down on him. Coughing and spluttering, he cleared it away, and it was then that he realized that he could see stars.

A million of them. Sitting in a velvet black sky. He had never seen them so bright.

And this magical, clean, fresh air. He had almost forgotten how good it tasted.

And the smell of pine.

He laughed and howled at the moon, his small voice echoing off down the valley. He was alive. He was free.

But what of Miles . . . ?

What would he find on the other end of the rope?

CHAPTER 8—GOOD NIGHT, VIENNA

James hauled himself out of the hole and slumped onto the snow. He lay there for a long while, feeling the fire in his cramped muscles slowly subside. Gathering his strength.

It was night, which meant that there would be no search parties out looking for them.

The sky was clear, but it could easily start snowing again. He didn't know if he could go any farther tonight. He would have to find Miles and then decide what to do.

"Come on, lazybones," he said, hauling himself onto his knees. "Get up and start looking." All his muscles screamed in protest as he fought to stand, and when he finally managed to get to his feet, he stood there swaying, dizzy, and nauseous.

He took hold of the rope in his trembling hands and pulled. At first it resisted, then at last he felt it shift and spring up out of the snow. He knew that if Miles was buried as deeply as he had been, there'd be no hope of pulling him out. James would simply have to cut through the rope and go to find help. The only thing that gave him any strength was the fact that the rope hadn't been more than about twenty feet long.

He walked slowly forward, pulling the rope up as he went. After a few paces he felt it tighten. He dropped down and started to scoop up handfuls of snow, which was soft and powdery here. He dug down several inches until he felt something hard.

It was Miles's head. He was facedown and utterly still. James cleared more snow away, then used the rope to pull him free.

His body was stiff and cold, but there was a faint pulse in his neck, and he was still breathing.

James couldn't give up now. He had come this far. He had survived the fall. He had gotten out of his snowy grave. He would get down the mountain. And he would take Miles with him.

The snowslide had torn a small tree up from its roots and tumbled it over the cliff edge along with the boys. It lay in a twisted heap of broken branches. James picked out a long straight limb to use as a staff, then braced himself against the rope.

The lights of Kitzbühel looked impossibly far away, but there were a few isolated farmhouses closer with lights showing in their windows. James fixed his gaze on the nearest and started to walk, like a moth toward a flame, dragging the other boy behind him and digging the stick into the ground for support.

The wind tugged at his clothing, searching out every gap. His face was stinging. His eyes were scrubbed raw. His sweat was freezing on his body, which was not a good sign. If his body temperature dropped too low he would pass out. It was hard going on the fresh snow—with each step his feet sank in almost up to his knees, and as his toes were numb, he felt very unsteady. Miles moved like a deadweight behind him, and every now and then his body would get stuck, then suddenly jerk loose, and James would fall, cursing, onto his face.

The worst part was that the lights of the farmhouse didn't seem to be getting any nearer. It was impossible to judge how far away it might be. He remembered the time it had taken them to get up the mountain in the cable car. But surely they had come a long way down already. . . .

He didn't stop, though. He forced his body to keep moving, and was so intent on simply putting one foot in front of the other that he didn't notice when the first flakes of snow began to fall around him. It was only when he put a hand up to brush some off his face that he realized how heavily it was snowing.

Then, as he looked for the lights of the house, they flickered and disappeared. This wasn't good. If he got lost he might wander around in the dark for hours. He groaned and sank to the ground.

It was impossible. He had done all he could. It was time to think of a new plan. He needed to take shelter until the morning.

There was only one thing for it. Although he had spent ages escaping from a hole in the snow, his best chance of survival now was to dig another one and crawl into it. He found where the slope was steepest, checked which direction the wind was coming from, then burrowed into the bank, using the snow he shoveled out to build extra walls as a windbreak and packing it tightly around the top and sides to make it secure. He worked fast, using up his last reserves of energy.

Once it was built he could rest.

Gradually the snow cave took shape. He was too exhausted

to do much more than make a coffin-sized hole, though, and he hoped the two of them would fit.

He tied Miles's scarf to the end of his stick and shoved it into the ground next to the cave mouth as a makeshift flag. It wasn't perfect, but it was the best he could do. Someone might spot them once it was light.

The next thing he had to do was somehow get Miles inside. He knew they ought to keep their heads near the entrance, in case the hole caved in while they were asleep, which would mean going in feetfirst. That was easy enough for him, but for Miles, unconscious and with a broken leg, it was another matter altogether. In the end James lay on his back, rolled Miles on top of him, and shuffled into the hole. Once inside, he tipped Miles off and held on to him so that they could share their body heat. He soon found that it was surprisingly warm in the cave, and as he lay still, he felt the nerves tingling painfully in his fingers and toes as feeling began to return to them. While the wind howled and scraped at the entrance, he fought to stay awake, but it was no use. He felt his consciousness slipping away like melting snow, and before he knew it, he was dead to the world.

Some 230 miles to the east, the Gräfin Frieda von Schlick was sitting alone in her box at the Vienna State Opera, looking down at the stage. A huge blond soprano in a billowing white dress was belting out an aria, her voice filling the whole building.

Frieda was not a fan of opera at the best of times. She found the stories difficult to follow and the acting rather exaggerated, but tonight she was finding it harder than ever to concentrate. She had spent the last few days at her husband's side in the clinic above Westendorf. Not that he had noticed. He had been so badly burned, he was bandaged nearly from head to foot, and he was on such heavy medication that he was barely conscious. She might as well have been sitting beside a sack of potatoes. They were due to operate on him in the morning, in an attempt to save his face with plastic surgery. There was nothing she could do until he came around.

If he came around . . .

The surgeon, Doctor Kitzmuller, had warned her that Otto might not survive. He was very weak. Even strong men could die under the knife.

Poor Otto. Lying there, pumped full of morphine, occasionally shaking or nodding his head. She had done her bit, played the dutiful wife, but it had been so *boring*, and all the while she had longed to be back in Vienna.

She knew she should feel more sorry for her dear Otto, but the man was a fool. He always did drive his precious Bugatti too fast, and she had warned him countless times that he would one day have some ghastly accident. Well, now it had happened. The man driving the other car had been equally badly burned, apparently. They were going to operate on him at the same time as Otto.

The doctor had told her that the two of them were lucky to be alive.

Lucky? She had no idea exactly what damage had been done to Otto's face, and it might be weeks before they could take the bandages off. She couldn't bear to think about it. If Otto *was* badly disfigured, she knew she would never be able to look at him again. She hated ugly things.

He may have behaved like an idiotic child, but he had been *so* handsome.

The fool. The silly, damned fool . . .

There were tears in her eyes. Never mind; if anyone saw her they would assume she was weeping because of the opera. It was the highlight of the whole season. Wagner's *Tristan und Isolde*. And how *long* it was. The fat German singers had been wailing and screeching all night, it seemed. Some silly story about dying for love.

Hah!

Those Germans with their gloomy romantic notions!

She supposed she loved Otto, in her way, but she would never be prepared to die for him. Thank God she hadn't been in the car. He had been all alone, visiting his depressing family *Schloss* in the mountains. If her own face had been scarred . . .

That was what would make a woman kill herself. Not love.

Isolde seemed to be working herself up into quite a state onstage now, and Frieda wondered if she ought to be expressing her own emotions as strongly.

No. That just wasn't done in polite society.

And keeping up appearances was the main reason she was here for the opening night of the opera. She hated the music, but she loved the occasion. The dresses, the gossip, the sense of being at the heart of things.

She wouldn't have missed this for the world. There was nothing more she could do at the clinic until Otto came out of surgery tomorrow. So she had been driven home to Vienna this afternoon.

Ah, Vienna . . .

Tonight there was the opera, followed by a proper meal,

not that heavy Tyrolean muck she had been putting up with in the Alps, then home to sleep in her own bed. A long lazy bath in the morning, then back to the hospital to see Otto, refreshed and fragrant.

Ready for the worst.

The door to her box opened and an usher came in carrying a silver tray on which stood a bottle of champagne and a cut-glass goblet. Frieda didn't even bother to turn around.

"Put it on the table," she hissed, waving a gloved hand.

Had she looked around she would have seen a large, bulky man with puffy eyes.

Frieda didn't bother to check whether the man had gone out. Why should she? So she didn't see him standing in the shadows at the back of the box, still staring at her through the narrow slits in his swollen eyelids and listening carefully to the music.

Wrangel had studied it well. All week he had attended rehearsals, sitting out of the way up in the gods. At first he had found the music overlong and overblown, but he had grown fond of it the more he listened, and now he even found it quite moving.

This was the moment he had been waiting for, the climax of Act 3, when Isolde dies of grief over her dead lover, Tristan. The music slowly built in a relentless rising pattern, louder and louder, until the whole massive orchestra was pounding away like huge waves crashing against rocks.

He stood there, counting the beats, following the music in his head, waiting for the final peak, when the orchestra seemed almost to explode. Up it went, up and up and up, Isolde's voice soaring majestically over the top of it.

Now at last he quietly stepped forward, his soft shoes making no sound. If anyone had happened to look up at the *Gräfin*'s box, they would have noticed him quickly slide behind her, slip one hand over her mouth and the other across her chest, and lift her effortlessly out of her chair. But nobody did look up. All eyes were on the stage, as he knew they would be.

Frieda struggled briefly, then was still. Nobody saw her as she fell from the box. The first they knew of it was when she crashed to the floor of the auditorium.

A gasp went up. Now all heads turned.

What had happened?

Had she slipped? Had she deliberately thrown herself off? Nobody had heard her scream.

What they could not have known was the reason why Frieda hadn't screamed. The *Gräfin*'s neck was broken long before she hit the ground.

There was a patch of sky. It had a curious shape. It became an island, a cloud, a monster, a human face, and finally a window into another world. James could look through it and see angels, all in white, moving around slowly. He closed his eyes, and when he opened them again the patch of sky had become a stain on a ceiling. This was the most vivid vision of all. He could see every crack and bump on the paintwork. The stain was a yellowish brown, as if from some old leak. He turned his head. There was another window with its own view through to another world. This window, though, was square and the view was of mountains. . . .

He fought to take control of his senses.

Come on, you fool; if you can see mountains it's because you are halfway up the side of one. That's not a view through to another world; it's simply the view out of your snow cave.

Then why was the window square-shaped, and not round?

That was too much for James's tired brain to work out.

He closed his eyes again.

Why was he not colder? And wetter? How was it he could wriggle his toes?

"James?"

There *was* an angel standing there . . . No, not an angel. A female doctor. In a white coat.

He smiled with relief.

He remembered now. . . .

The faces of the men who had found him in the snow. Hannes Oberhauser and the others. And being loaded onto a stretcher. The men skiing down the mountain holding the stretcher between them. A drive in an ambulance. Then the paradise of clean sheets and warmth and dry cotton against his skin.

"You are awake?" said the doctor in halting, heavily accented English. She had a kind face.

"It's all right," said James in German. "You can speak in your own language. I'll understand."

"That is good." The doctor smiled. "Do you know where you are, James?"

"I don't really mind where I am," said James. "Just so long as I'm alive."

He looked around the ward. It was nighttime, and what he had taken to be a window was a poster hanging on the wall.

"It is something of a miracle," said the doctor. "You must be made of pretty strong stuff. We feared frostbite, exposure,

God knows what. But apart from some minor skin damage, you seem to be in one piece."

James sat up suddenly.

"The other boy," he said anxiously. "Miles Langton-Herring? Is he all right?"

The doctor put a comforting hand on his arm.

"Do not agitate yourself," she said. "He is alive. His leg is bad, but we have saved it."

"Thank God," said James, sinking back onto his pillows.

"He will need to stay here for a while, though," said the doctor.

"But I can leave?" said James.

"We would like to keep you in for observation. And we need to treat your skin. The cold can burn as badly as a fire. You have come to the right place, though. This clinic is the leading hospital for plastic surgery in Europe. We are high in the mountains here, and the air is sterile."

"I'll remember that," said James. "The next time I'm badly bashed about, I'll know where to come."

The doctor laughed and went on her way, seeing to the other patients.

James closed his eyes and was soon fast asleep once more.

He was woken by a noise. Someone was shouting. He was sure of it. But as he woke, the sound ceased, so that he began to wonder if he had only dreamed it.

He tried to swallow and winced. His throat was raw and dry as dust. He felt like he was being strangled, and he had a raging thirst. The clock on the wall read 4:27 a.m.

A dim night-light showed him that the jug and glass on

his side table were both empty. His throat hurt too much to call out, and besides, he didn't want to wake anyone up, so he climbed out of bed and slid his bare feet into a pair of felt slippers that had been left out for him. He winced as he stood up. His leg muscles felt stiff, and his sore skin rubbed against his pajamas. It was a pain he could deal with, though—at least it meant that he was alive.

He put on a dressing gown and shuffled down the gap between the beds, rolling his head and shoulders to loosen himself up. It was only when he was halfway down the ward that he properly noticed the state of the other patients. Most were heavily bandaged, though some showed horrific wounds on their faces and hands. James tried not to stare, but he still caught glimpses of skin covered in blisters, scars, and deep gashes, or looking horribly like cooked bacon. There were men missing fingers, hands, legs; one had a hole in the middle of his face where his nose should have been.

James felt embarrassed to be here; there was really nothing wrong with him. He was a fake, an intruder. He kept his head down and carried on walking.

There was no sign of any nurses, but he spotted a notice pointing toward a bathroom and headed for it.

It was then that he heard the voice again, crying out from behind a half-open door. He looked left and right but could still not see any hospital staff. He pushed the door open and went in.

There were two beds in here, and the bodies lying on them looked identical. They were both wrapped in so many bandages there was not an inch of skin showing. All that was visible of the men beneath were their eyes.

One of the patients was moving feebly, as if trying to sit up, and he was muttering and calling out, his voice slurred so that James found it hard to understand what he was saying. One phrase kept repeating, though . . .

"*Mein Vetter Jürgen . . .*"

My cousin Jürgen.

The man was raving. His eyes were staring mindlessly into the distance.

"Are you all right?" said James. "Can you hear me?"

The eyes still would not focus.

"*Mein Vetter Jürgen . . . Sie werden meinen Vetter Jürgen töten. Eine Donnerkugel. Es wird Donner geben. Es gibt einen mächtigen Knall . . . Schneeblind! Schneeblind!*"

"You're dreaming," said James, trying to make sense of the garbled ranting. The man seemed convinced that someone was trying to kill his cousin Jürgen. And there was something about thunder and being snow-blind.

"Don't worry," James said. "I'm sure your cousin is safe. . . ."

He glanced over at the other bed and saw that the man in it was watching him intently. His eyes were shining in the half-light, fixed on James, wide and staring.

"I'll go and get help," said James. "Don't worry."

As he turned to leave, he found himself face-to-face with a very solid-looking man. He had the broad-shouldered build of a boxer, although he was carrying a lot of weight and some of his muscle had turned to fat. He was wearing a damp overcoat and hat, and had obviously just come in from outside. At first James thought he was wearing goggles, and then he realized the man had very heavy eyelids that were thick with puffy, scarred flesh. Like two black eyes but without the discoloration.

"What are you doing here?" he grunted in Russian-accented German.

"He was crying out," said James. "I thought he might be in some kind of trouble."

"He is all right," said the man, opening a leather attaché case and taking out a syringe. "I will look after him. I am his manservant. You should not be here."

"I was only trying to help," said James.

The man looked over to the other patient, then quickly back at James.

"Leave now," he said, raising the syringe and checking its contents.

James went out. As he turned to close the door, he saw two pairs of eyes staring back at him. One pair hidden by swollen eyelids, the other by bandages.

The man who had been making all the noise lay still.

CHAPTER 9—THE MAN WITHOUT A FACE

"It is my fault, James. I should never have tried to bring you all down the mountain on your skis that afternoon. The weather was too bad. We should have taken the cable car."

"It wasn't your fault."

Hannes Oberhauser had come with Mr. Merriot to collect James from the clinic in his horse and carriage. He calmed the horse as James climbed aboard, the carriage rocking from side to side.

"If anyone is to blame," said James, settling on a bench opposite Mr. Merriot and arranging a blanket over his knees, "it's Miles Langton-Herring. If I hadn't gone after him, I wouldn't have ended up in the clinic."

"If you hadn't gone after him, he would probably be dead right now," said Merriot, puffing out a cloud of smoke from his pipe. He very rarely lit it, and James wondered if it was offering him some small warmth on this bitterly cold morning.

"Who knows," said James. "But it's not going to help anyone handing out blame left, right, and center. I don't really blame Miles and I certainly don't blame you, Herr Oberhauser. Everyone else got safely down, and it was you that led the search party that rescued Miles and me. So I think we're quits."

Hannes smiled and shook the reins. The horse walked slowly forward, placing his hooves carefully on the slippery road. The sturdy open carriage jingled and rattled.

"Nevertheless," said Hannes, once they were under way, "I feel responsible, James, and I would like to make it up to you. We have spoken about it, Herr Merriot and I, and I would like to offer you my hospitality."

"What do you mean?" said James, his breath coming out as a white fog.

"As you know, the doctors were not happy to let you out of the clinic so soon—"

"Oh, but I'm quite all right," James interrupted. "If I'd spent another day in there, I would have—"

"Let him finish," said Mr. Merriot.

"They asked if there might be someone who could look after you for a few days," Hannes went on. "Until we are all sure that you are not suffering any aftereffects from your adventure."

"As I say," James insisted, "there's nothing wrong with me."

"Hannes is offering to put you up at his house," said Merriot. "Just for a few days. It was the only way we could pry you out of the doctors' claws."

"I could give you some extra help with your skiing," said Hannes. "That is, if you can face getting back on the snow."

"I can't wait," said James. "But, really, I don't want to be any bother."

"It will not be any trouble," said Hannes, urging the sure-footed horse down the narrow road. "It will be my great pleasure. My wife, Helga, is dying to meet you."

The Oberhausers' farm lay on the lower slopes of the

Hahnenkamm. They had an orchard, as well as twenty cows, which were laid up for the winter in a large barn underneath the back of the house. They were kept warm there, and in turn warmed the house. Hannes explained that in the summer Helga looked after the cows while he made a good living as a mountain guide for the many walkers and climbers who came to the area.

The farmhouse was built into the side of the mountain and had a raised veranda at the front reached by wooden steps. It was entirely built of pine, stained almost black by preservatives, and cut into pretty shapes around the doors and windows and along the eaves. There was wood for the fire neatly stacked along one side beneath the wide, pitched roof.

Inside it was cozy and warm. Two wood-burning stoves heated the main living area, which was filled with blankets and rugs and painted pine furniture. When James arrived, there was a big pot of stew bubbling on the range in the kitchen, and it filled the house with delicious cooking smells.

Helga was a jolly, plump woman, who greeted James with two shy toddlers clutching her skirts and a tiny baby in her arms. Once she realized that James spoke German, she bombarded him with questions as she busied herself about the place.

There were more questions over supper, and James felt finally that he was thawing. It was as if he'd been turned into a solid block of ice and was only now beginning to melt. He felt his tight muscles relax, his breathing slow and deepen, the knotted tension in his spine work loose.

He found himself opening up to these kind, honest people

more than he had opened up to anyone since his parents had died. He wondered if it was because he was using a different language; it was almost like being a different person. He talked about his life, his Aunt Charmian, his friends, his problems at school, the fact that all his trousers were getting too short for him, how nice the food was—all the ordinary little things that he normally never bothered with.

This must be what it's like, he thought. This must be what it's like to have a mother and father. He had to force himself not to cry. It wasn't the sad things that made him emotional, or the hurtful, and it certainly wasn't fear . . . it was simple kindness. It was the decency in the hearts of ordinary people.

After supper they played cards and chatted until James felt his eyelids growing heavy.

Helga showed him to his room, which was at the back of the house, tucked up under the roof. It reminded him of his room at Eton, which also had a sloping ceiling. But this was much more welcoming.

He smiled as he slipped under the fresh clean sheets. He was going to like it here.

As he drifted into sleep, however, a voice came back to him, crying in the darkness. . . .

"Schneeblind! Sie werden meinen Vetter Jürgen töten. . . ."

Snow-blind! They are trying to kill my cousin Jürgen. . . .

The rest of the week passed without incident. There was skiing during the days, and supper and cards with the Oberhausers, or a meal in town with the boys, in the evenings. In a way James preferred the calmness and solitude at the Oberhausers. They never pried or probed too deeply if they felt that James didn't want to talk about something. With the boys it was different. All they wanted to discuss was James's escapade with Miles.

James was miserly with his responses. He would rather forget all about it. He hated being the center of attention and felt, in a way, that he had failed. He wasn't a hero.

Far from it.

The truth was that they had got lost, Miles had broken his leg, and James had failed to get him safely down off the mountain.

One night the boys were sitting in a coffeehouse on the Hinterstadt in Kitzbühel, once again discussing what had happened. They were drinking creamy hot chocolate and all shouting at once and laughing noisily.

"You should have left mouthy Miles up there," said Teddy Makereth. "It's been blessedly, blissfully, beautifully quiet since he's been in hospital."

Miles was still in the clinic. His leg had been very badly broken, and his parents would be arriving the next day to take him home to England.

"You should have broken his other leg," said Gordon Latimer.

"He's not so bad," said James, forced to defend the boy, even though he, too, had found him intensely irritating.

"He thinks he knows it all, but he didn't know enough to come the right way down the mountain," said Teddy. "*We* all managed to get down in one piece. Why couldn't he?"

"Keep it under your hat," said James, lowering his voice to a stage whisper. "But he was drunk."

"No."

"Yes."

The boys all burst out laughing, and their noise grew noticeably louder.

The events were already fading into a bad memory, and James could see the funny side. He hadn't mentioned Miles's drinking to anyone else before. He reckoned the poor boy had enough on his plate. Obviously his two cronies knew what had happened—they had shared the schnapps after all—but until now James had thought it best not to say anything about it. He trusted the others not to blab to any masters, though, so Miles shouldn't get into any trouble over it.

When the boys left the coffeehouse in a rowdy gaggle, they passed a darkened archway that led to the Sport Hotel. Had they looked down it they would have seen a man in a trilby writing something in a notebook. And had they looked in that notebook, they would have found a record of exactly what James had been up to since he had left the hospital. Provided, of course, that they were able to decipher the code it was written in.

It was all there in minute detail. The precise times James had left the Oberhausers' chalet in the mornings, where he went skiing and for how long, what he did at the end of each day, who he spoke to, who he seemed to be friends with, who he avoided. The man hadn't missed a thing. And he had stayed hidden all the while. Hanging back. Keeping his distance. Watching.

It was only on those few occasions when James was by himself that the man had moved closer, becoming even more alert and cautious.

One time James had visited the shops to find a gift for his

Aunt Charmian. The man had never been more than a few feet away from him the whole time, waiting to see if James strayed into a deserted part of town. But James had stayed on the brightly lit main shopping street.

On nights like this, James would walk back to the Oberhausers' and the man would shadow him every step of the way, watching him like a cat watches a mouse. The boy always looked so innocent, so careless of danger, so unaware of what might be lurking in the night.

For now, the man's orders were to watch.

He didn't mind watching, though. It was his job, after all, what he had been trained to do. He was patient. He knew that in the end all this careful waiting would pay off. There would come a time when he would make his move, and make it count.

That night James talked to Hannes about leaving. The holiday was nearly over and James would shortly be on his way back to England. Hannes insisted that he must return sometime, and sometime soon.

"But don't wait until the winter," he said. "The Alps are beautiful in summer. There is walking, climbing, swimming in the Schwarzsee."

"I *do* like it here," said James. "And I should love to see the mountains all covered in green. I don't know if my aunt has plans for the summer holidays, though."

"You must both come," said Hannes. "I have grown very fond of you since you have been here. There will always be a bed for you in Kitzbühel, and if there is ever any way I can help you, then do not hesitate to ask."

"You are much too kind," said James. "You and Helga. I shall definitely return one day."

"See that you do."

The next morning Andrew Carlton met James as he came out of the farmhouse. They had arranged to say good-bye to Miles and see him off. The weather had turned. It was warmer and the snow was beginning to melt. There was still some skiing to be had on the upper slopes, but the season was nearly over. The roads were all open, so Andrew had arrived in a taxi to take them up to the clinic.

There was a grayness to the day, a light drizzle was speeding the thaw, and the snow in the valleys was changing to slush. It was piled up at the edges of the roads in dirty heaps. The car sent up a fine spray as it hissed along.

"We'll soon be back at school," said Andrew glumly, writing his name on the steamed–up taxi window.

"It won't be so bad," said James. "I'm looking forward to catching up with old friends."

"It's all right for you," said Andrew. "You missed the entire last half. Some of us were chained to our desks."

"At least summer is coming," said James. "Things always seem better in the sunshine. Eton in winter is pretty grim."

"Well, that's just it," said Andrew. "Summer may be coming, but autumn will follow summer, and winter will follow autumn, on and on forever and ever, amen."

"You're sounding like an old man," said James with a laugh. "Boys aren't supposed to think that far ahead."

"I know," said Andrew. "But can you really imagine all the long years of your life you're going to be spending at Eton?"

"I'm not like you," said James. "I don't look much past next weekend. I try to enjoy today and not worry about what tomorrow might bring."

"I wish it were that simple," said Andrew. "But I'm afraid my father has my whole life already mapped out for me. Eton, then Cambridge, study hard, but not too hard, leave plenty of time for rowing, maybe a blue, then I'm to join the family firm, settle down with a nice little wife, and start breeding the next generation of Carltons so that they can do the same thing all over again."

"It must be a pleasant feeling in a way, though," said James. "Knowing what your future holds. Not having a mother and a father, my future is a little more uncertain. There's no family business. There's nobody who really expects anything of me."

"You're free to make your own life," said Andrew.

"But who knows what might happen?" said James. "Think of all those young men, before the Great War, who were just like you. They thought they knew the exact paths their lives would run along, but they ended up getting blown to bits in muddy trenches."

"When you put it like that," said Andrew, suddenly rubbing his name out and clearing the window, "then my life doesn't seem quite so bad."

They arrived at the clinic to find a large black Rolls-Royce parked on the forecourt, with a uniformed driver standing proudly next to it under an umbrella.

"That'll be Miles's people," said Andrew as they climbed out of the taxi. "His father's rolling in it."

Once inside the clinic, they were directed to the sun

terrace to wait for Miles. Despite the cold weather and the drizzle, several patients were sitting out under umbrellas in bath chairs, wrapped in blankets. By himself, off to one side, sat a man with a shaved head, his back turned to the others, staring out at the mist-shrouded mountains. He was wearing a high cravat tied around his neck, and white leather gloves, presumably to hide scars.

As James came out onto the terrace, the man turned and looked at him.

He had had extensive surgery to his face. There was livid purple and yellow bruising around his ears and neckline, dotted with nasty black scabs, but the skin on his face was smooth and tight so that he appeared to be wearing a mask. The surgeons had done a very good job—if James hadn't known that the man must have once been disfigured in some way, he would not have been able to tell. He looked bland and incurious. Even his eyes showed no emotion.

One learns so much about a person from their face. One can read every line on it. Yet it was almost as if this man had no face at all. It was impossible to read him.

James turned away, unnerved by the direct stare, and when, a few moments later, he glanced back, the man was still looking at him. He sat very still. He might have been a mannequin, a dummy in a shop window, for all the animation he showed.

James was relieved when the uneasy mood was broken by the arrival of Miles, hobbling awkwardly out onto the terrace on his crutches accompanied by his parents. His mother was wearing a long fur coat; his father sported a gleaming top hat and a magnificent set of bristling whiskers. If *he* had been wearing the fur coat, he would have looked like some sort of exotic wild animal.

"James," Miles shouted, smiling broadly. "I'm so glad you came."

Miles tried to shake hands without falling over, and then introduced his parents. His mother was a little distant, but his father seemed genuinely pleased to meet James and shook him briskly by the hand.

"I was worried I'd be leaving without seeing you again," said Miles. "I never properly thanked you for saving my bacon. I behaved like an ass, I'm afraid, but I was very scared and trying not to show it."

"Well, it *was* all rather terrifying," said James.

"Come off it," said Miles. "You don't fool me; you weren't scared for a moment."

Before James could protest, Mr. Langton-Herring slapped him across the back.

"You must look us up when you are back in England, young man," he said. "I should very much like to show you our appreciation for looking after Miles."

"Thank you," said James. "But you really don't need to go to any trouble."

Mr. Langton-Herring leaned close to him.

"Let me give you a word of advice, young fellow-my-lad," he said with a friendly wink. "Learn to accept praise when it's sent your way, and be gracious when someone offers thanks. Nobody likes false modesty, eh?"

"I shall remember that," said James.

"See that you do," said Mr. Langton-Herring, and he led the little group back through the clinic to the front entrance.

On the way, James asked Miles who the man on the terrace with the shaved head was.

"Oh, that would be the Graf von Schlick," said Miles. "They operated on him the other day. It all went very well, but he's had a bit of bad news. His wife died in some sort of an accident in Vienna."

"Poor chap," said James.

"He was in a motorcar smash," Miles explained. "Pretty badly burned. They operated on the other driver at the same time. Sadly, he didn't make it."

"I think I saw them," said James. "Before the operation. It must have been them. One of them was raving about his cousin Jürgen."

It was still drizzling when they came back outside. Miles was helped into the Rolls-Royce. There were waves and shouted farewells, and then the car slid almost silently out of the forecourt. James noticed for the first time another car that had been hidden behind it, a black Lagonda. A driver was sitting at the wheel cleaning his nails with a penknife. Miles was obviously not the only patient being let out today.

As he walked back toward the taxi with Andrew, James glanced up to see the Graf von Schlick emerging through the big brass–studded double doors of the clinic. He was wearing a long black astrakhan overcoat that came almost down to the ground, black leather gloves, and a black fur hat covering his bald head. Once more he stared at James with that disconcerting blank look.

A second man came out and muttered something. It was the manservant with the swollen eyelids. He took hold of the *Graf* by the elbow and led him down the steps.

So it must have been the *Graf* ranting about his cousin that night in the private room, and now his manservant was taking him home.

It wasn't clear, though, if the servant was supporting him or leading him.

The man in the astrakhan coat kept his eyes fixed on James all the way to the Lagonda. He got in, the doors slammed, and the car sped off in a spray of dirty water.

"Does he know you?" asked Andrew as they followed in their taxi.

"The *Graf*? I don't think so," said James. "That is, I mean to say—no, he doesn't know me at all. Or at least I don't know him. I saw him once before when I was at the clinic. It was nighttime; he was delirious."

"Well, he was certainly giving you a look," said Andrew.

"Yes," said James. "It's strange. I can't help thinking that he's somehow familiar. That I knew him before I came here. I'm confused, to tell you the truth."

"He spooked me a little," said Andrew.

"I wouldn't worry about him," said James. "We're never going to see him again. In a few days we'll be back at Eton."

Andrew made a strangled noise. "Damn you, James," he said. "I'd managed to forget all about school."

PART 2—ETON

CHAPTER 10—BLOODY BENTINCK

"**I** don't see you for four months, James, and you come back looking older. Older but no wiser, I might add. I hardly recognize you." James's messmate, Pritpal Nandra, was sitting by the fire in his room, warming his feet.

"Well, you haven't changed a bit, Pritpal," said James, sitting down opposite his friend. "Except you're perhaps a little fatter."

"Less of your cheek," said Pritpal. "I'll have you know that I have actually lost some weight. I have taken up Ping-Pong, and I am becoming quite a master at it. For once there will be something that I am better at than you."

It was James's first evening back at school. He had arrived an hour earlier and gone straight to his room to unpack before meeting his housemates. Everything was very familiar and yet somehow slightly different at the same time. He was conscious that he had been away and missed part of the year. There were subtle changes. Pritpal had some new pictures on his wall and some new furniture. He was at home here, settled nicely into the routine at Eton, and James felt slightly awkward, like an outsider.

In a moment, though, James's other messmate, Tommy Chong, came in, swearing loudly as he launched into a story about being attacked by an overfriendly dog in Judy's Passage.

Soon all three were eating toast and drinking tea, and it was as if James had never been away.

"I am most upset that you never received any of my letters in Mexico," said Pritpal.

"It doesn't matter," said James. "I think I caught up on most of the gossip in Austria. You know, when you're here at school, everything seems hugely important, but when you're away it doesn't seem to matter so."

"Ah, the great globe-trotter is sneering at us feeble, provincial stay-at-homes," said Pritpal.

"I didn't mean it to sound that way," James apologized. "I suppose it's the same anywhere. You get caught up with the small things."

"And I suppose your time in Mexico was all fighting crocodiles and finding lost treasure," said Pritpal with a snort.

James shrugged. He had said enough. "So what's so important that I might have missed out on here?" he said, changing the subject.

"There's Roan, the new boys' maid, for one," said Tommy Chong, smiling broadly.

Before Christmas there had been a fire in the house, and Katey, the previous boys' maid, had never recovered from the shock. She had left while James was away, and Roan had replaced her.

The two messmates suddenly came alive, stumbling over each other in their efforts to sing Roan's praises.

"She is very young—"

"I think she is eighteen—"

"Teddy Makereth says she is sixteen—"

"Much younger than Katey—"

"Much prettier, too—"

"All the boys are in love with her—"

"She calls us all darling—"

"She's Irish, and knows all the folk songs—"

"You feel that she really cares about us boys—"

"All right, all right," said James, holding up his hands for them to stop. "I think I get the picture. You quite like her. Yes? So life at Codrose's is perfect."

"It would be if it wasn't for Bloody Bentinck," said Tommy in a hushed tone.

"The new house captain?" said James. "He was here before I left. I remember him as being strict, but he didn't seem that bad. Surely he can't be as bad as Bloody Bill Marsden; he's the worst teacher in the school."

"Why do you think Theo Bentinck has been named after him?" said Pritpal. "He is even more fond of beating boys than Bloody Bill."

"You were so busy playing the great detective before Christmas you didn't realize what was going on," said Tommy. "Bentinck has got worse and worse."

"Oh, come on," said James. "He can't be as bad as everyone makes out."

Tommy let out a harsh grunt. "You don't know the half of it," he said.

Pritpal cast a nervous glance toward the door. "Maybe he didn't dare do very much while you were around, James. You may not know it, but a lot of boys here are scared of you. Even the older ones. You have a reputation of your own."

"Me?" said James.

"Yes, you," said Pritpal. "Don't look so surprised. You have always known how to look after yourself. Even in your first year here you knew how to deal with bullies and cheats. But while you have been away, Bentinck has got himself into a position of power, and nobody dares stand up to him anymore."

"Well, don't look at me," said James, holding up his hands in surrender. "I don't want any more trouble. I aim to keep my head down and get on with it. There's rowing to look forward to, and cricket, running, fives . . ."

"Not to mention Latin, science, French, art . . ." said Tommy with a grin.

"Yes," said James wearily. "And that."

"Well, don't say you haven't been warned," muttered Tommy darkly. "You may not find it so very easy to keep your head down. We all try to stay out of trouble, but Bentinck has a genius for catching us at crimes we never even knew we were committing. The other day he beat me for laughing at breakfast."

"There's nothing wrong with that," said James.

"He accused me of laughing at M'tutor."

"At Codrose? Were you?"

"No, I was laughing at a joke, but I couldn't prove it."

"And what about Codrose? He must know what's going on."

"Bentinck sucks up to him," said Pritpal. "And, besides, Codrose likes it this way. The house is quiet, the boys shuffle around staring at the floor, scared that if they so much as breathe loudly they will be punished. Codrose likes the rule of law."

There was a knock, and a moment later, almost as if

he had been listening outside the door, Bentinck himself came in.

James had barely been able to remember what the boy looked like. He'd been built up into such an ogre that James was mildly surprised to see that he looked quite normal. He was of average build and height with dull brown hair and wire-framed spectacles. He had peach fuzz across his top lip, pale skin spotted with pimples, a small, slightly pinched mouth, and a pointed chin.

He wouldn't stand out in a crowd. His face would never be used to frighten small children. To James he was just another boy.

But it still wouldn't do to get on the wrong side of him now.

"Ah, Bond," he said. Traditionally, everybody at Eton addressed each other by their first names, but with Bentinck it was obviously different.

If that was the way he wanted to play it, James would follow suit.

"Hello, Bentinck," he said. "Did you enjoy the holidays?"

"That is no concern of yours," said the older boy dryly. His voice had a grating, nasal quality to it, almost as if it had never properly broken.

"I was only being polite," said James. "Is that a crime?"

"It is not," said Bentinck. "But cheek is."

"I wasn't aware that I was being cheeky," said James. "I certainly didn't mean to be."

Bentinck stared at James. Sizing him up. "You think you're something, don't you, Bond?" he said, and walked farther into the room as if he owned it. "Quite the little hero. Well, it means nothing to me, do you understand?"

James shrugged. Kept his mouth shut.

"I gather you were showing off again in Austria," Bentinck went on. "If you try and show off around Codrose, I'll take you down a peg or two and make you regret it. I am top dog here. Don't ever forget that."

"I won't," said James, and he smiled affably at Bentinck.

"I want you to tidy my room for me."

"All right," said James. "I'll come as soon as I have finished my tea."

"No," said Bentinck, turning on his heel and marching out of the room. "You will come now."

The door slammed shut and Pritpal jumped up. "Are you going to let him talk to you like that, James?" he said, flapping his hands in the air.

"Yes," said James. "Why not? He's quite within his rights. Us younger boys have to do whatever the older boys ask of us."

"He's trying to make you feel small."

"He can try as hard as he likes," said James. "But right now I don't feel small. If anyone's small, it's him. He's the one wasting all his energy. It'll take more than a silly schoolboy tyrant to get to me, Pritpal."

"But we were hoping . . ."

James stood up. "It's boring, Pritpal. Nothing worse. He can't hurt me."

"He *will* hurt you," said Tommy. "You can see he wants to."

"He can try," said James. "But he'll fail."

He turned his back to the fire to soak up a little more of its warmth and then set off for Bentinck's room.

It was chilly in the corridor and James shivered. He decided to get a jumper from his room and quickly ducked in. He was expecting the room to be empty and nearly crashed into someone as he came through the door. He tottered to an abrupt halt inches away from a girl.

James was very aware that he was standing too close to her, but when it became quickly obvious that she wasn't going to move, he shuffled backward.

"You must be James Bond," she said, looking him up and down with a raised eyebrow. "I've heard a lot about you."

"And you must be Roan, the new boys' maid," said James. "I've heard a lot about you, too."

And his messmates hadn't been making it up.

Roan was indeed a lot prettier than the previous maid.

She was about the same height as James, but two or three years older, with wavy black hair and skin as white and smooth as a marble statue. Her huge eyes were deep and dark, but they shone with an intense brightness, like polished glass. Her wide mouth was curled up at one end in a slight, mocking smile.

"So you've heard a lot about me, have you?" she said with a singsong Irish accent. "All good, I hope."

"We're not used to having young, pretty maids here at Eton."

"Would you listen to him?" said Roan, shaking her head. "Young and pretty, am I? Well, I'm older than you, darling, and as to *pretty*? You shouldn't be thinking about such things. Your mind should be on your schoolwork, all that Latin and cricket."

"I didn't mean anything by it," said James. "I was just

stating a fact. You *are* pretty. In the same way that the sky is blue and ice is cold."

"It wasn't very blue today," said Roan. "I'd say it was gray. Now, I suppose you'll be wanting your room back."

"It's all right," said James. "I'm not staying. I have to do a chore. If you're busy . . ."

"Truth be told," said Roan, picking up a dustpan and brush, "I wasn't sure you were definitely coming back this half. I've not touched anything in here. It's all just as you left it, though a bit tidier, mind. I think Katey must have been a bit shortsighted. She never saw all the dirt and the dust. And, my, you boys sure can create a lot of dirt."

As she talked she was constantly moving, busy, alive, every few seconds flashing her eyes at James and turning the full power of her gaze upon him, like a mythological creature who could cast a spell on someone just by looking at them. She seemed to fill the whole room with her energy, and James was rooted to the spot.

At last Roan stopped what she was doing and stood with one hand on her hip.

"And just what are you staring at?" she said. James blushed and looked away, painfully aware that he had been unable to take his eyes off her.

Roan laughed, crossed the tiny room, and poked him in the chest with a finger.

"Just you watch yourself, James Bond," she said. "There's magic in me. I come from a family of witches. My ancestors were burned at the stake. They don't burn us anymore. They're too scared. So tread carefully or I'll turn you into a fat, ugly toad."

So saying, she pushed past him out of the room.

James let out his breath, and realized he must have been holding it for some time. He smiled to himself. This half was going to be interesting.

As he walked down the corridor two minutes later, he found that he was already wondering when he might see her again.

At that moment two men were standing on Windsor Bridge looking down at the rushing black waters of the Thames. They were leaning on the side, their backs to the passing cars and pedestrians. They wore dark coats and their hats were pulled down on their heads against the cold.

"The cell in Lisbon has been closed down, comrade," said the larger of the two, known only to the other man by his code name, Amethyst. "From now on Operation Snow-blind will be run directly by Obsidian from our European headquarters."

"I understand," said the second man.

"All the details are on this piece of paper," said Amethyst, slipping a note along the parapet of the bridge. "As usual you must burn it as soon as you have memorized it."

"Don't worry. I haven't slipped up yet."

"No. You are a good agent, Emerald."

"I know."

"You will not see me again until after your mission has been successfully completed," said Amethyst. "From now on you are on your own. Do you have everything you will need?"

"Almost. I'll be ready in days."

"You will not need any more money?"

"Not for now. Afterwards maybe."

"And the boy? You understand that now it is even more important that he dies."

"I understand," said Emerald. "Do you want it done before or after I complete Operation Snow-blind?"

"You will find the right moment. Perhaps his death should be a part of it? We need to destroy not only his living body but also his reputation. He must be nothing when this is finished. It would be pleasing if he were connected to Snow-blind in some way."

"I'll see what I can do," said Emerald. "But if the opportunity arises sooner, I'll deal with him then. You can sleep easy, though, Amethyst. He won't be seeing another Christmas."

"Good. And now . . . good-bye and good luck."

"I shan't need any luck. It's down to skill and art, my friend. That's why you chose me. Because I'm the best there is."

"We shall see. If anything goes wrong, if you do not succeed, then it is you who will not be seeing another Christmas, Emerald." The man turned to his companion and spoke briefly in his native Russian. "*Do svidanja.*"

"*Do svidanja.*"

At that the two men parted without another word and walked off in opposite directions, each lost in his own thoughts.

CHAPTER 11—CONSORTING WITH A COMMON MAID

James thought about Roan often as he sat through his lessons at the beginning of the half. It certainly helped to take his mind off the dreariness of his schoolwork, but it also made the days seem longer, as he couldn't wait to catch a glimpse of her again.

A glimpse was all that he could hope for. She hadn't said one word to him since that first meeting. She filled his washbasin in the mornings, but she was always gone before he was properly awake. For the rest of the time she was busy about the house. Sometimes he passed her in the corridor, or on the stairs, and she would nod at him and then pass quickly by. He wondered if she was avoiding him on purpose, or, as seemed more likely, she simply didn't give him a second thought. To her he was probably just another boy.

One warm May afternoon, with the sunshine blazing through the dusty windows of his classroom and creeping across the desktop as he worked, he made a decision.

He would stop thinking about her.

After the 2:45 p.m. absence, he joined the flood of boys heading down to the river over South Meadow. Ahead of him was the castle, its stones glowing honey yellow against the blue sky, but James was so used to the view that he barely even noticed it was there. He didn't join in with the excited chatter of the other boys. He wanted to get out onto the river, alone, and work his body. It would clear his brain and wake him up.

When he got to Rafts, Croaker helped him get his boat down, under the watchful eye of Alf, the boss of the watermen. Croaker was ancient, red-faced and watery-eyed, his face half hidden by a huge mustache. He had been working here on the river for years, and not even the older masters could remember a time when he had looked any younger.

The two of them slid the dodger into the river and then Croaker held it still while James carefully climbed aboard, making sure he didn't capsize it. Croaker then handed him the oars and he was off, pulling steadily upstream toward Boveney Lock.

He enjoyed sculling. It was hard, physical exercise that used his whole body. He always felt a deep, warm glow after being on the river, and there would be a pleasant ache in his back and shoulders. With the water flowing fast in the opposite direction, there was a tremendous sense of speed. He passed several slower rowers and had to keep turning around to make sure he didn't collide with anyone else on the busy river.

The locks were even more crowded, with rowing boats of all shapes and sizes—riggers, whiffs, gigs, perfects, pairs, and fours—crewed by boys of all shapes and sizes. There was a good deal of jostling and name-calling, not all of it friendly, but once James was safely through, he was out onto open water, with grassy meadows on one side and, on the other, large houses with lush green lawns rolling right down to the water's edge.

He sculled on, tugging mechanically against the oars,

and was just starting to feel stiff and cramped when he turned around to see the trees of the small island known as Queen's Eyot six hundred yards away at the end of the reach.

The island was owned by the school and was a popular destination on summer afternoons.

James negotiated his way to a mooring, and ten minutes later he was enjoying a large tea on the veranda of the summerhouse that stood on the island, watching a group of boys play rounders on the lawn.

Feeling suitably refreshed, James got back into his dodger and was about to head back to Rafts when he decided to go farther upstream and really stretch himself. There would be less river traffic up this way and he wanted to see how fast he could go. He made his way slowly around the island and pulled hard on the sculls, smiling as the dodger picked up speed and cut through the water like a knife blade.

A shout from the bank caused him to stop, and he looked over to see a girl waving and calling his name. He started over to her, and as he got nearer he realized it was Roan, wearing a plain green summer dress.

"That looks fun," she said when he was near enough.

James shrugged.

"Would you care to take a girl on a trip?" she added, flashing him a smile.

"I'm not sure if it's allowed," said James.

"Not sure if it's allowed?" Roan scoffed. "I didn't have you down for a sap, James Bond, always worrying about the rules and being a good little boy. Are you scared of getting into trouble, then?"

"Not particularly," said James, trying to act nonchalantly. "I just said that I wasn't sure it was allowed. I don't want to get *you* into trouble."

"Ah, I can look after myself, thank you very much."

"Climb in, then," said James. "And be careful or we'll be swamped."

Roan was sure on her feet and obviously used to boats, and she skipped lightly aboard, barely rocking the dodger. She sat in the stern, facing James, and offered him a wide, open smile.

James carried on upstream, away from the other boys. It was harder work with an extra body on board, but he soon had the dodger flying smoothly across the water. Roan settled back, closing her eyes and letting the sunshine fall on her upturned face.

"Is that as fast as you can go?" she said, and James strained harder at the sculls.

After a while Roan opened her eyes again.

"You make it look easy, so you do," she said. "But I know it's not."

"What were you doing up this way, anyway?" said James.

"I was just out for a walk," said Roan. "It's my afternoon off. It was such a lovely day, and it would have been a shame to waste it sitting around indoors. I like to be out in the sun and the wind and the rain. You look like an outdoors sort of a lad yourself. I'll bet you'd rather be out in the fresh air than stuck in some stuffy schoolroom learning all about why the map of the world is all covered in red. The great British Empire. God save the King."

"You don't like the British Empire?"

"I'm Irish, darling—what do you expect?"

"Well, I'm half Scottish and half Swiss," said James. "So you can't blame me. Do you think I should be up in arms over the English invading my country—well, one of them?"

"You're full of surprises, aren't you?"

"Am I?"

"There's a way about you, James, like you've seen more than a boy your age should have done. Do you think about things more than other boys, I wonder."

"I don't spend a lot of time worrying about history, if that's what you mean," said James. "It's like you said. I'd far rather be outside, running or rowing or playing sports, than sitting inside pickling my brain."

Roan laughed. "Yes, but sooner or later, darling, you're going to have to live in the real world."

"Oh, I get it," said James. "Your world is the real world, and my world is somehow not, is that it?"

"Look around you," said Roan, dangling her fingers in the water. "You're in a very privileged school, James. . . ."

"As if I could ever forget. But it's no less real than the backstreets of Dublin, or wherever you are from."

"Isn't it?"

"To a tribe of Pygmies living in the Congo, I doubt that your world would seem very real," said James.

"Point taken." Roan nodded her head. "But—'

"I've finished with lessons for the day," James interrupted. "So I'd rather not listen to another lecture, thank you very much."

Roan stared at him for a long while, then burst into laughter and clapped her hands.

"I like you, James Bond," she said. "You've got spirit. I can see you're not one to go down without a fight."

"It's getting late," said James, trying to hold back a self-satisfied smile. "We should be heading for home. I'll drop you off somewhere near where I picked you up, before we get to Queen's Eyot."

"Why? Are you ashamed to be seen with me?"

"No, I just thought . . ."

"We've been through this, James. I want to be dropped off in town, and if you were a proper gentleman you'd take me all the way."

James sighed. *What the hell.* If that's what the lady wanted, then that's what the lady would get.

He endured the catcalls, whistles, and banter at Locks. He ignored the shouts from the banks. He sculled past jeering boys in boats without saying a word. And when he got to Rafts, he paid no attention to the looks he was getting from Croaker, Alf, and Charlie, the other boatman.

That night, however, back at Codrose's, Theo Bentinck called him up to Library, where the senior boys who ran the house spent their evenings.

"I hear you were seen on the river with a boys' maid," he said, his tight little mouth squeezing out the words and icing them with disgust.

"It was Roan Power," said James, standing straight-backed and unashamed.

The other boys in Library were lounging in their chairs pretending to read newspapers or play cards, but James knew that all their attention was on him.

"Was it your intention to bring shame on your house?"

"No," said James casually. "She was out walking and asked for a lift back to town. Where's the shame in that?"

"Where's the shame in that?" sneered Bentinck, who was walking slowly around James and inspecting him as if he were something nasty that had been dumped in the middle of the floor. "An Eton boy consorting with a common maid? You are more stupid than you look."

"Consorting?" said James. "That's a fancy word, isn't it? I'm not sure I know what you mean by *consorting*."

"I mean—we do not give boat rides to servants. We do not talk to them or meet with them socially. We do not consort with them."

"You might not," said James, "but I do. Is there a rule that says I can't? If so, I'd like to see where it's written down."

"One does not need to write such things down," said Bentinck, and he laughed in a superior, mocking way. "It is understood."

"Not by me it isn't," said James.

"Well, I suppose you are not from a good family," said Bentinck. "But I would have thought that even you would have understood that servants are beneath us. They need to know their place, and their place is not sitting in the back of an Eton boat like Lady Muck."

"She was doing no such thing," said James, who was growing bored of Bentinck. "She was merely getting a lift back to Rafts."

"In full view of boys from other houses," said Bentinck, his voice getting louder and louder. "We might never live this down."

At this, James couldn't help but burst out laughing.

"Do you suppose the reputation of Codrose will ever recover?" he said, looking around at the other members of Library, who were all trying not to smile. "Why, I should expect it'll be on the front page of the *Times* tomorrow— 'Codrose boy seen talking to a servant.' Don't be ridiculous, Bentinck."

Bentinck colored a deep scarlet, and he jutted his chin forward bullishly.

"How dare you speak to me like that," he said.

"Oh, come on, Bentinck, don't you think you're going rather over the top?"

"Don't question me," Bentinck thundered. "I am head of house. I will not have my authority questioned. You have earned yourself a beating, Bond."

"Of course," said James. "I was wondering how long it would take you to come to that."

"Perhaps after this you will know your place a little better."

"And just what is my place?" said James.

"Your place is where I damned well say it is!" screamed Bentinck, and he stalked across the room to a cupboard from which he took out a thin cane, a little shorter than a walking stick, with a curved handle.

James knew there was no point in protesting any further. Bentinck was in charge, and he could write the rules. James wondered if he should have held his tongue, but guessed that Bentinck had been lining him up for a beating from the start and had just been looking for an excuse. James wasn't worried about the pain—he could cope with that; what made him furious was the pleasure that Bentinck was going to get from this little victory, and the pleasure he would obviously take from inflicting pain on him.

James knew all too well that there were people in the world who enjoyed causing hurt to others.

Well. He would make it as unpleasurable for the sadistic brute as he could.

He took up a position, leaning over the table in the center of the room, and heard Bentinck walk around behind him. He tried to relax. He knew that if he tensed, the pain would be greater. He put his mind outside his body and pictured himself back on the river. Whatever was going to happen was going to happen to someone else.

Then there was a grunt, a quick swish, and the cane lashed into his backside with a loud thwack that filled the room.

James clenched his teeth so as not to make any sound, though the pain was more intense than he had been expecting.

He had to admit: it hurt like hell.

All the muscles down his legs jumped and spasmed, and there was already a deep ache in his buttocks and a stripe of fire across them. A second blow came quickly on the first, and the force of it rocked James forward. Bentinck had done this before; he was an expert at it, and he made sure that the second lash landed in exactly the same place as the first.

Thwack!

A third lash. Once again hitting the same spot.

The pain was spreading from the red-hot center along all his nerves so that it went right through him.

Bentinck slowed down for the final three lashes, letting James wait for them. Allowing the pain to die away just enough each time so that when it came back it was a worse agony than before.

In a way, the pain grew so great that it became unreal, and James found that he could easily take his mind back to the river. He was with Roan now, looking into her smiling, happy face, and the sun was glinting on the water, making it sparkle with shards of silver. And there was silver and gold glittering in Roan's eyes. . . .

He smiled. The image of Roan's face was enough to make the last blows feel like they were landing a thousand miles away.

Finally it was over.

Bentinck must have hit him especially hard. James could feel blood trickling down his legs. He took a deep breath and set his face into a bland mask, then straightened up and turned to face his tormentor, who was sweating and panting from the effort.

James knew the etiquette was for him to thank the boy, but he wasn't going to do it. Let him beat him again if he wanted. Instead he looked Bentinck straight in the eye and held his gaze until the older boy was forced to look away.

James now turned to the other boys in the room, who were all watching closely in dead silence.

"Good night," he said. His voice loud and clear and firm. Then he walked steadily out of the room, being careful not to limp.

Once safely outside, he groaned and leaned against the wall, his legs wobbling uncontrollably. He grimaced as he tenderly felt his wounded flesh with his fingers.

He stayed like that until he was sure he could walk, and then hobbled down the stairs, along the lower passage and up again to his room, where he threw himself facedown on his bed. He would get his revenge on Bentinck one day. When the time was right.

Pritpal knocked on the door a few minutes later, but James said nothing, and after a while he heard his retreating footsteps.

He didn't want to see anyone. He wanted to be alone with his dark thoughts. But the more he brooded, the more the image of Roan in the boat kept coming back to him, until it banished all the darkness and he found that he didn't really care one jot about Bloody Bentinck.

He fell asleep in his clothes, dreaming of the girl.

"**Y**ou've been looking rather uncomfortable these last few days, James. Ants in your pants?"

"No, sir. I'm all right, sir."

"Yes, sir, no, sir, quite all right, sir!" Mr. Merriot was packing away his books after private business and had held James back.

If James had been squirming in his seat, it was because he still found it difficult to sit down after his beating. The bleeding had stopped and the wound was healing, but it was still very sore and he was covered in purple bruising. He had had to be careful around Bentinck, because he knew the boy would relish the chance of giving him another beating and opening up the wound again.

"You are quite sure there is nothing the matter?" said Merriot. "Nothing I can help you with?"

"I'm quite sure, sir."

"Your mind hasn't been on your work lately, has it?"

"I suppose not, sir. I *do* try . . ."

Mr. Merriot stuck his unlit pipe into his mouth and studied James's order-card. The card showed how well James was doing in his lessons.

"This is showing a distinct downward trend," said Merriot, the words muffled by the pipe. "If you don't pull your socks up, we might have to prepare for squalls ahead. How many rips do you have at present?"

"Six this month, sir, and two yellow tickets."

"Hmm. Not good, not good." Merriot signed the order-card and handed it back to James before walking him to the pupil-room door.

"I can't say that I really blame you, James," he said, opening the door. "It must be difficult getting back into the swing of things after your time away, and all that has . . ." Merriot paused, searching for the right words. "All that has *happened*."

Merriot was one of the few people in the school who knew what James had been through.

"I try my hardest to keep your life here at Eton as straightforward as possible," he went on. "So that you can lead something approaching a normal life."

"I know, sir," said James. "But I suppose I'm just not that excited by Latin and Greek. I like the stories, but . . ."

"He likes the stories, does he?" barked Merriot, leading James out onto the street. "Well, that's a start. The bloodier the better, I suppose?"

"Maybe, sir," said James, and they both smiled.

They set off down Common Lane toward the High Street, walking side by side. It felt good to be out in the fresh air and the bright sun. James liked Mr. Merriot. He was clever, he had a sense of humor, and he taught well. He also knew when not to push a boy too hard. He tried to make the boys' lives at school fun and interesting and not too taxing. He was one of the few masters who seemed to realize that there was more to life than school.

"You must thank your lucky stars you were not a pupil here in the early days," said Merriot. "Way back in 1440, when the school was built by good King Henry, you would have had to get up at five o'clock in the morning for prayers, then lessons at six—Latin. That's all they taught: Latin. Latin in the morning and Latin in the afternoon and Latin at night."

They crossed the road by the Burning Bush, and as they stopped by the entrance archway under Upper School, a cloud passed over the sun. James shivered in the sudden chill. Summer was approaching, but the air was still cool.

"And you were only ever allowed to speak in Latin," Merriot went on. "Woe betide any boy caught speaking English! He would have been soundly thrashed. Lessons finished at eight o'clock at night, and there was one hour for play."

James wasn't really listening. Something had caught his eye on the other side of the road. Someone was standing in the shadows between Durnford House and Hawtrey. James hadn't noticed him before because in contrast to the bright sunlight on the pavement, the shadows had been deep and black, but now that the sun had gone in and his eyes had adjusted to the lower light levels, he clearly saw the familiar shape of a man wearing a trilby and overcoat. It was only for an instant, and then the man sank back into the darkness and was gone.

James had only seen the man for the briefest of moments, but it was enough to unsettle him. He could have sworn that it was the same man he had glimpsed before.

Mr. Merriot was still filling James in on a bit of Eton history. "There were two meals a day back then, and nothing on Fridays, which were fasting days. And do you know how many weeks' holiday they had a year? Six! Not the luxurious sixteen you pampered lot get these days. Six weeks a year. Imagine! Three in the summer and three at Christmas, although they were only allowed to go home in the summer. So, Mr. Bond, aren't you glad you don't live in the fifteenth century?"

James mumbled a yes.

"Me too."

Merriot winked at James and strode off through the archway, his pipe jutting out in front of him like the bowsprit of some great sailing ship.

James turned and looked toward where the man had been.

Could it be the same person? And why on earth would he be watching James? Following him? His life had been settled and happy lately, with nothing to worry about except Bentinck and his schoolwork. Was that it, though? Deep down inside, he knew that he needed excitement and danger to give flavor to his life. Was his bored brain inventing imaginary enemies and trying to create a fresh adventure for him?

There was one way to find out.

James checked that there was no traffic and sprinted back across the road and into the shadows. He looked in vain for the man as he worked his way through the warren of back alleys and gardens behind School Hall. He came out eventually onto the Eton Wick Road and looked left and right. The sun came out again and glinted off an open window, catching his eye.

There he was.

On the corner of Keate's Lane.

James ran after him as he crossed the road and entered the

gardens by Queen's Schools. He had to dodge between some cyclists and momentarily lost sight of his prey, but he worked out that he must have gone into Jourdelay's Passage, which ran along a row of masters' houses.

As James entered the alley, though, he found it empty. There was no sign of the man. Surely he couldn't have made it to the other end already? Maybe he'd gone into one of the buildings?

James walked slowly along, his senses alert to any noise or movement.

Nothing. It was just a normal spring day in Eton.

Unless the man hadn't come this way at all?

James set off back the way he had come, but just before he came to the end of the passage, he heard running footsteps behind him and turned to see someone dashing out the other way onto the High Street.

The man must have been hiding in a doorway.

James wasn't going to let him get away again. He was onto him in a flash, pumping hard over the flagstones, and he burst back into the sunlight at full pelt, skidding to a halt as a big coal lorry thundered up in a cloud of smoke and grit. James just had time to register that he couldn't see the running man before someone barged into him from behind, and he was spilled into the road, directly into the path of the speeding lorry.

He was aware of several things at once. A sharp pain in his knees and elbows as he landed on the tarmac. The squeal of tires and hiss of the lorry's brakes. A woman's scream. A man's shout. The roar of an engine . . .

But no terrible crushing blow. No hideous impact of hot metal on soft flesh.

Some deep-rooted animal part of his brain had made him move fast, without thinking. He had rolled between the wheels of the lorry and then flattened himself against the road surface.

He was lying there, eyes closed tight, holding his breath, every muscle tensed, his nerve endings tingling, ready for the awful pain that must surely come.

He opened his eyes and twisted his head to look up at the underside of the lorry, which was rumbling and smoking. There was just enough space for him to lie there, unharmed.

Shouts came from the pavement.

"Is he all right?"

"Can you see him?"

"What happened?"

James shuffled sideways and crawled out from under the lorry.

"It's all right," he said. "I'm not hurt."

Someone helped him to his feet. Miraculously, there was not a scratch on him. The lorry driver climbed down from his cab, white as a sheet, half angry, half terrified.

"You scared the living daylights out of me, son. What did you want to go and play a trick like that on me for?"

"Someone knocked into me," said James, searching around for the man he had been following.

"Come along, it's not his fault," said a short, plump woman, and she was backed up by a babble of voices, all talking at once.

James wasn't listening. He had spotted, on the opposite side of the road, near Tom Brown's, a familiar coat and trilby hat.

He tried to move off, saying he was unhurt, turning down offers of help, pulling away from hands that tried to hold his sleeve.

He apologized to the driver, said he didn't need a cup of tea, and at last managed to break free. By the time he got across the road, though, the man was already past the barber's and walking briskly off in the direction of Windsor.

"Hey," James shouted, and sped up, but he was suddenly pulled to the side as someone grabbed his arm.

"Please," he shouted angrily, ready to lash out if needs be. "I don't need any help!"

He was confronted with the startled face of Miles Langton-Herring.

"James," he said, propping a crutch back under his armpit. "It's me."

James looked quickly down the road. The man had disappeared.

He sighed. This time he would let him go.

"What is it, Miles?" he said.

"I'm back," said Miles.

"I can see that."

"You don't seem very pleased to see me."

James shook his head and offered Miles a sour smile. "I'm sorry," he said. "I was going somewhere. I was late."

"You certainly seemed in a bit of a hurry. If I'm holding you up . . . ?"

"No, it's all right. It doesn't matter now. How's the leg?"

"Mending. I still have a cast on, as you can see—will for a good few weeks—but I'm up and about. I was coming to see you later, actually; you've saved me a trip."

"What's it about?"

"I've an invitation for you. My father wants to ask you over to our place for a small celebration."

"Celebration of what?" said James.

"Celebration of me not being dead, I suppose," said Miles. "It's a sort of party. We only live in Virginia Water, so you won't need a leave ticket, just a house ticket for the evening."

"I don't know, Miles."

Miles's face fell and he looked at the ground. "I know you don't like me very much, James," he said quietly. "But it would mean a great deal to me if you could make it. I've changed since my accident; it's brought me down a peg. I realize I don't know everything and maybe I should listen to what other people have to say more often."

James sighed and took the invitation from Miles.

"I'm sorry," he said. "I'm being ungracious. Of course I shall come. Will you tell your father for me?"

Miles smiled broadly. "Good man."

That evening James fetched his suit from the slab by the back door at Codrose's. He had had to have it cleaned and pressed after the beating, and it had been sent back wrapped in brown paper and string. As he was picking it out from the other parcels on the slab, Roan appeared. She wasn't her usual lively self and had a concerned look on her face.

"I've been looking for you," she said.

"Oh, yes?"

"Bentinck beat you, didn't he?"

"That's hardly news," said James. "He beats everyone."

"He was particularly hard on you, though, James."

"It wasn't so bad."

"I saw the blood," said Roan. "On your clothes. He hurt you."

"It's not your problem," said James, embarrassed. But Roan wasn't about to let it go.

"I've heard the gossip, James. I know it was because of me," she said.

"Not really," said James. "If it hadn't been for you, it would have been for some other reason."

"All the same, I feel responsible."

James tried to leave, but Roan held him back.

"You don't have to be a hero," she said. "It's not weak to admit that something hurt you. It's not weak to allow other people to help you. You don't have to carry the world on your shoulders all the time."

"You wouldn't understand," said James.

"Wouldn't I? Listen. This Sunday I'm going to the park for a picnic. Why don't you come along? It'll be my treat. And don't worry—I'll make sure nobody sees us together. We won't give Bloody Bentinck any reason to thrash you again. What do you say?"

James shrugged. Roan put her hands on her hips and cocked her head to one side, turning the full power of her gaze upon him.

"What are we going to do with you?" she said. "It's not every day a pretty girl asks you to go on a picnic."

"Do I have any choice?" said James.

"No," said Roan. "It's not an invitation, darling, it's an order."

"In that case I'll come," said James.

"Good lad. Oh, and I nearly forgot. I've this for you."

Roan passed him a small glass jar with a white paste inside it.

"What is it?"

"Didn't I tell you I was a witch?" said Roan. "It's a healing ointment I made up. It'll help. Just don't ask me to rub it on for you."

Roan laughed and walked away. When she had gone, the corridor seemed smaller and colder and darker.

James went up to his room, confused.

He was finding everyday life a lot harder to cope with than he had expected. Dangerous adventures were fine. Back in Mexico all he had had to worry about was trying to stay alive. True, he had needed to take terrible risks, but he'd found that pretty simple. Coping with people was different. Understanding their emotions, understanding his own emotions, was a lot harder. Nearly dying under the wheels of the coal lorry had shaken him up a lot less than Roan Power had.

He punched the back of his armchair. Why did he feel so foolish in her presence, like a small child? Why did he feel a compulsion to be rude and offhand with her, when what he really wanted was to make her smile?

It wasn't as if he hadn't spent a lot of time with girls before. He got on well with them usually, and easily felt their equal, so why now did this one make him feel so utterly useless?

He wondered if this was what it felt like to be in love.

"No," he said, dismissing the thought instantly. Love was for saps.

* * *

Before bed he rubbed some of her cream onto his tenderest parts, and, although he felt faintly ridiculous doing it, he had to admit that it did soothe the pain.

CHAPTER 13—THE INVISIBLE MAN

James was sitting in the light by the open window in his room. It wasn't the largest room in the world, and tucked up here under the eaves it was made even smaller by the sloping roof beams. But at least it was bright, and the extra height gave him something of a view. Lately he had felt the need of a view. Like a guard in a watchtower, he could see everything that was going on outside.

Every once in a while he cast a glance down into Judy's Passage, the alleyway that led to Codrose's. He did it almost without thinking, and would look just long enough to make sure that nothing was happening, before he returned to the job in hand.

If anyone had seen him they might have laughed.

James Bond was sewing.

He had borrowed a sewing kit from Roan and had been busy since breakfast.

He had opened the seam of one of his coattails, carefully unpicking the stitches with his penknife, and was now busy sewing a small pocket into it.

James wasn't laughing, though. This was serious business.

He couldn't prove that he was being followed. He couldn't prove that someone had pushed him into the path of the coal lorry. He couldn't prove that it wasn't an accident. But he knew in his gut that something was wrong, and he didn't intend to sit around on his backside waiting for something worse to happen.

If the man in the trilby came after him, he was going to be ready.

He cursed and looked out of the window for the hundredth time.

This was ridiculous. He couldn't keep on calling him "the man in the trilby." He needed to give the stranger a name. Once you gave a name to something, you took the first steps to controlling it. But how did you give a name to a man you had never properly seen? A man who might not even be there, a man who was, to all intents and purposes, invisible.

Well, there was his answer. From now on he was "the Invisible Man."

Yes.

James already had a secret compartment in the heel of one shoe, inside which he kept his penknife. It would be next to useless in a fight, but it had saved his bacon on a couple of occasions.

Now he had another plan.

Once he had finished sewing the pocket, he removed a razor blade from its cardboard packet and slipped it inside. He held the jacket up to the light to inspect his handiwork. He was satisfied. You couldn't tell that the razor blade was hidden in there, and James was confident that there was no danger of cutting himself, as the tail would always hang safely down below his chair.

This was the fifth secret pocket he had made today. In one he had hidden a book of matches and a set of lock picks he had been given by his friend Red Kelly. In another were a pencil stub and some slips of thin paper. And there was a long metal skewer down his other jacket tail, where there was also a second razor blade sitting in its own pocket.

Just in case.

There was a long tradition at Eton of using your coattails to smuggle items in and out of school, and much larger objects than these had been secreted in boys' jackets before now.

Satisfied, he slipped the jacket on and studied himself in the mirror.

No one would ever have known what the tails contained. He smiled. It was like a stage magician's jacket, full of secrets. He wondered if he should try to hide a white rabbit or a dove inside it. Maybe a length of silk handkerchiefs tied together . . .

Actually, that might not be such a bad idea. Silk was surprisingly strong and he could use it like a rope.

James looked at his clock. That would have to wait for another time. It was getting late. Making the alterations to his jacket had taken longer than he had expected.

He packed away the sewing kit and grabbed his hat.

Earlier that morning he had received a note from Andrew Carlton, telling James to meet him in Windsor at their lock-up. The boys in the Danger Society had maintained a small garage there, and since the society had been disbanded, James had pretty much forgotten all about it.

He left the house, then walked briskly through Eton and across the bridge into Windsor. It was a warm and sunny day, and James was pleased to find that the pain of Bentinck's beating had almost disappeared. It didn't affect his movement at all beyond a slight tightness.

He made his way to the backstreets behind the Victoria Barracks. The garage was in an old mews building in a little courtyard, and as James approached he saw Andrew waiting.

"We wanted to keep it a secret until it was finished," said Andrew as he unlocked the padlock on the garage doors. "Not that it really is finished. Not sure it ever will be."

"The Bentley?" said James as Andrew pulled the doors open. And there it was.

James had bought the car last year with money he had won at an illegal casino. She was a 4½-liter Bentley Blower. A big, powerful, open two-seater, built for racing. She had been a near wreck when James had got her, and so much had happened since then, he had all but forgotten about her.

His friends from the Danger Society hadn't, though. They had been busy.

"We've worked on her every available moment," Andrew explained. "It was Perry's idea, and he was pretty cut up that he couldn't be here to help out after he was sent down. But he's still been helping, in his own way. In fact I doubt we could have finished it without him. He visited me in London just before the start of the half with a big pile of one-pound notes. The only thing not finished is the paintwork."

The car was painted a flat gun-metal gray.

"It rather suits her," said James, running a hand along the car's flank. "It shows her history. We should leave her just as she is."

"So you like her, then?"

"She's beautiful," said James. "If that's the right

word for such a brute. Does she run?"

Andrew shrugged. "None of us has been able to take her out on the road. Though the man from the workshop who finished her off drove her around here for us."

"I don't know how I can ever thank you all for this."

"Being allowed to work on her has been all the thanks we need," said Andrew. "Although I'd dearly love to take her out for a spin one day."

"It'll be my pleasure," said James, trying not to grin from ear to ear like an idiot as he inspected the magnificent car, going over every detail. The work was crude and not finished to the usual high standards of Bentley, but somehow it made the car seem more powerful, more rugged. She was a working machine and not a gentleman's plaything. The leather seats didn't match, but at least the wheels did. The controls were scrounged from spare parts, mostly from other makes of car. In fact some were not even from cars at all, by the looks of them. There was an odd assortment of knobs and dials and levers.

James climbed into the driver's seat and started her up. The noise of the engine was music to his ears as it coughed and growled and rumbled into life, shattering the peace and quiet of the sleepy mews. The whole car shook on its springs, like an animal eager to be off and running.

Reluctantly, James cut the engine and silence returned.

The smell of hot oil and petrol filled the garage, but as far as James was concerned it was the sweetest perfume.

He got out of the car and walked over to Andrew.

He couldn't think of anything to say, but the expression on his face told the whole story.

* * *

He was still thinking about the car half an hour later as he entered Windsor Great Park to meet Roan for her picnic. She had drawn him a map of where they were to meet, a secluded spot among some trees. She had also drawn little stick figures of the two of them enjoying the picnic together, and he couldn't wait to act out the scene.

As he marched along the wide tree-lined track known as The Long Walk, all thoughts of school and Bloody Bentinck and the Invisible Man drifted away.

The park was busy with families enjoying the sunshine, walking, sitting on the grass, riding horses. Deer wandered on the fringes of the forested areas, where the oaks and elms and chestnuts were in full leaf. James was overcome by a sense of how good it was to be alive.

He wished he could have driven over in the Bentley. It was the perfect day for a drive. He pictured himself at the wheel, flying around a bend with the wind tugging at his hair. He could almost hear the throaty growl of the engine.

He broke into a run and dashed past Snow Hill with its statue of King George III dressed as a Roman emperor sitting on his horse looking regally toward Slough. The royal family had always owned the park and it was impossible to forget their presence. There were the towers and turrets of Windsor Castle to the north, the Frogmore mausoleum to the east, where Queen Victoria was buried with Prince Albert, and King George up on his hill in the middle. He remembered what Roan had said to him about not living in the real world, and he wondered if the royal family ever looked out of the windows of their huge castle and thought about what life must be like for the ordinary people out here going about their everyday business.

He followed the map until he identified the patch of woodland Roan had marked with an X. He soon found the path that led away from the open grassland in among the trees.

A minute later, there was Roan, sitting on a blanket in a clearing, lit by broken sunlight filtering down through the leaves and branches overhead. He stopped for a moment to look at her, while she was still unaware that he was there.

She was eating an apple and looked utterly at peace with the world.

James took a moment to pull himself together. He slowed his breathing and adopted a casual expression, and then, when he was sure that he would appear as relaxed and untroubled as she did, he sauntered into the clearing.

As soon as he stepped out of the shadows, however, he realized that Roan was not alone.

A young man was there. He had been hidden from James's view, sitting with his back against a tree stump. When he saw James, he tossed a chicken bone aside, sprang lightly to his feet, and bounded over to greet him.

"You must be the famous James Bond," he said with a broad Irish accent to match Roan's, and he slapped James hard on the shoulder.

James fought not to show his disappointment. He had assumed that he and Roan would be alone. There had only been two stick figures in her drawing. . . .

Don't be a fool. Why shouldn't she have asked someone else on her picnic?

The young man was as handsome as Roan was beautiful,

with a glamorous mop of wavy fair hair and dark blue, almost black eyes. He was dressed in an olive green moleskin suit with a bright orange waistcoat and a red scarf knotted loosely around his throat.

Roan stretched out on her back on the blanket and called over to James.

"This is my pal, Dandy O'Keefe," she said. "Us Paddies need to stick together, you know. When we're so far from home."

"Is there anyone else joining us?" said James, with a brave attempt at sounding unconcerned.

"No, it's just the three of us," said Roan, closing her eyes and letting the sunlight fall across her face. "I bumped into Dandy this morning in town, and he sort of invited himself along."

"Roan told me you got into a whole heap of trouble last time she was out with you," said Dandy, grabbing a fresh chicken leg and passing it to James. "I hope you've not told anyone you were coming here today, bucko."

He winked at James, who shook his head.

"It's our secret, isn't it?" said Roan.

"Well, it's safe with me," said Dandy.

"Dandy's a gardener," said Roan. "He works for the school as well. Looking after the grounds. He's the greenest fingers of any man I know."

"Ah, it's all fertilizers and chemicals these days," said Dandy.

"Dandy used to work on one of the big estates back in the old country," said Roan.

"I've come over here to make me fortune," said Dandy.

"Though, between you and me, it's going to take the devil of a long time. I'll be a hundred years old with a beard around me ankles by the time I make me millions. Too old to enjoy them. Now come along, let's get stuck in here; I'm starving."

"You're always starving," said Roan as she handed out plates of food.

James was amazed at the spread. There was bread and cheese and ham, cold pies and chicken, pickles and hard-boiled eggs. She had brought water and lemonade and some bottles of beer for Dandy, who gave one to James.

"This is quite a feast," said James.

"I've made great friends with the kitchen staff at Codrose's," said Roan with a wink.

"Roan could charm the crown off the King's head," said Dandy.

"You should see Codrose's pantry," said Roan. "It's fit to bursting with food. And he's miserly with it. You're a Codrose boy, James, so by rights this food is yours."

"*I've* no right to it at all, of course," said Dandy, taking a swig of beer. "Which makes it taste all the sweeter."

Dandy went on to tell a long story about getting into an argument in a pub in Virginia Water, which had Roan crying with laughter. He was great company, always talking, joking and telling stories, but all the same, James wished that he hadn't come along, that it was just him and Roan.

"Dandy's always in trouble," said Roan. "He loves a drink and he can't walk away from a fight."

"Listen to her, James," said Dandy. "As if butter wouldn't melt in her mouth. To hear her talk you'd think she was a saint, but I'm sure you know her well enough to know she's no shrinking violet. I've seen her deck three men with one punch."

"Ah, now you're exaggerating, Dandy. It was one punch and a kick."

"She's got a wicked kick on her, James. You don't want to get on the wrong side of her."

Dandy took a big folding knife out of his pocket and used it to cut himself some slices of hard cheese. The knife put James's penknife to shame. It looked like a hunter's weapon, big and powerful, with a blade that had been lovingly sharpened. Suddenly, all his preparations, stitching the razor blades and tools into his coattails, seemed pathetic.

"You're staring at me knife, I see, bucko," said Dandy, eating the cheese off its blade. "What is it with boys and knives? Are you wondering if I know how to use it, perhaps?"

"Well . . ."

Without another word, Dandy suddenly flipped the knife expertly in his hand so that he was holding it by the tip of its blade then tossed it hard at James.

James froze, but the knife flew harmlessly past his ear, and he heard a dull thud as it embedded itself in a tree.

He looked around; the knife was gently quivering.

Roan laughed.

"He didn't even flinch," she said. "You'll have to try harder than that to put the wind up this one, Dandy."

Dandy laughed as well and went to fetch the knife.

"Don't pay him no never-mind, James," said Roan. "He's never hit anyone yet. That's his party trick. You were supposed to yell and duck."

"You gave me the old stone face," said Dandy, wrenching

the knife out of the tree with a grunt. He wiped it on his sleeve and passed it to James.

James felt the weight of it in his hand. If he had someone like Dandy by his side, the Invisible Man would be no threat.

"That was a good shot," he said.

"Maybe I should join a circus, eh?" said Dandy, and he sprang onto his hands and walked upside down across the clearing while Roan clapped and laughed.

James felt a pang of jealousy. Why couldn't he make Roan laugh like that? He knew better than to try right at this moment, though—that would only make him seem desperate. The last thing he wanted was to look like he was trying too hard.

Besides, there was no competition. Dandy was older. He was a man. James was just a boy.

Dammit. Sitting in the Bentley, revving the engine and dreaming of the open road, he had felt grown-up, on top of the world, ready to face anything.

He passed the knife back to Dandy, who put it in his pocket.

"I don't suppose they teach you knife throwing at school," Dandy said.

"No," said James. "But there is the Corps. We train to be soldiers. There's shooting . . ."

"Sure, and marching and saluting and polishing your boots," said Dandy. "I know all about the army. I know all about training you boys to be good soldiers, to be able to march to some foreign land and shoot the natives. To die for King and country."

"Leave him alone, Dandy," said Roan. "Don't tease the boy."

"Who's teasing?" said Dandy with mock indignation. "Besides, he's old enough to stick up for himself. Isn't that right, bucko?"

"I suppose so," said James. Though he didn't feel very old right at that moment. He looked away, trying to hide the confused emotions that he was sure were playing on his face.

And that was when he saw him. Ducking behind a tree.

The Invisible Man.

CHAPTER 14—BY ROYAL COMMAND

James tensed, becoming alert, like a dog that had caught a scent.

"What is it?" said Dandy, who had noticed the change in him.

"It's probably nothing," said James, peering into the gloom beneath the trees. "I just thought there was someone there for a moment."

"It's a public place, bucko; there's lots of people about."

"No," said James. "It'll sound ridiculous, I know, but I think someone's been following me. Spying on me."

"A boy from the school, you mean?"

"No . . . I don't know. A man."

"Spying on you? Now who would want to spy on you?"

"I'm probably just imagining it," said James.

"Well, let's go and find out," said Dandy, and he was up on his feet before James could say anything else. "Which way did he go?"

"There . . . among the trees . . ."

Dandy stalked off in the direction that James was pointing. James ran to his side and kept pace with him.

"And just what are we looking for?" said Dandy.

"A man," said James. "He wears a trilby."

"Most men do," said Dandy. "Can you narrow it down a little?"

"Not really, no," said James. "I've never seen him up close."

A movement caught James's eye and he turned to see a figure flitting from tree to tree some distance away.

"There he is!" he shouted, and set off at a run.

The two of them pounded deeper into the woods, their footsteps dulled to muffled thumps by the thick carpet of leaf mold on the ground. They split up and crashed through the undergrowth, keeping watch for any movement.

They could find no sign of the man, however, and both soon slowed to a walk.

James headed over to Dandy. It was dark under the closely planted trees, and very quiet. James was about to say something when Dandy put a hand on his arm.

"Hold still," he whispered. "Listen . . . we might hear him."

They stood there, unmoving. James was aware of the deep stillness in the woods. There seemed to be no birds or wildlife of any kind here. All he could hear was Dandy's breathing.

He took a couple of paces away from the Irishman, peering between the gray tree trunks.

Nothing.

Eventually he shook his head and turned around.

Dandy was standing with his knife open in his hand. There was an animal intensity about him, and James saw him in a very different light. He looked as if he could have stepped out of a history book; he was every inch the wild Irish warrior, stalking the forest for deer. Roan had said he liked to fight, but what exactly was he intending to do with that long blade of his?

There was a heavy, expectant mood. The air hung lifeless in the branches of the trees. Dandy stepped closer to James.

Then there was a shout and the mood was broken. It was a girl's voice, calling for help, and James's first thought was that it must be Roan.

"Who was that?" he said, and headed toward the sound.

He came to a thicket of brambles, then some densely packed rhododendrons. He fought his way through. There was a stand of oak trees on the other side, and past them a straggly hedge. Beyond the hedge he could see a large, square house, painted pale pink. He stuck his head through the hedge and took a proper look. Two little girls in matching red tartan skirts were playing badminton on a large, well-kept lawn. The older of the two shouted toward him.

"Hello," she said. She had a mop of curly hair and a rather serious expression on her face. "We've lost our shuttlecock. Did you see it come over your way?"

"No," said James, "but I'll have a look for you."

He glanced around and saw the shuttlecock nestling in the branches of a tangled old tree.

"Would you get it down for us?" the girl shouted, in a manner that told James she was used to getting her way.

He quickly scrambled up and tossed the shuttlecock over to the girls.

"Thank you ever so much," said the older girl. She couldn't have been much more than eight years old, but seemed terribly grown-up for her age. "You are a very kind boy."

"Lilibet always hits it too hard," said her younger sister, who was a pretty little thing and lacked her big sister's seriousness.

"It was no problem," James called down from his perch in the tree.

"You are frightfully good at climbing trees," said the little sister.

James shrugged.

"I should like to climb trees," said Lilibet. "But Crawfie won't let us."

"Who's Crawfie?"

"Our governess."

"Well, you shouldn't always do exactly what Crawfie says."

The girls laughed and ran off back to their game as James swung down from the tree and found Dandy waiting at the bottom with Roan.

Dandy had put his knife away.

"Come along," said Roan. "We should be getting back. I don't want you to get into any trouble, James."

Dandy had a small open-backed lorry with the Eton crest on the side. He stowed the picnic things in the rear and offered Roan and James a lift back to the school. The three of them crammed into the cabin, James squashed between Dandy and Roan.

"Well, you certainly made a very useful friend there, bucko," said Dandy, once they were under way.

"Do you think so?" said James. "She was only a little girl."

"Only a little girl, he says. If things had been just a tiny bit different, she'd be our next queen."

"What do you mean?" said James.

"You really don't have any idea who you were just chatting to, friendly as you please?" said Roan.

"No, they looked vaguely familiar, but . . ."

"They were the royal princesses, Elizabeth and Margaret. Their father is the Duke of York and their uncle is Edward Albert Christian George Andrew Patrick David Windsor—the Prince of Wales—your future King."

"You mean that was Windsor Lodge?"

"The very same." Dandy laughed and elbowed James in the side. "James Bond, by royal command."

"They seemed quite ordinary," said James.

"Don't you believe it," said Dandy.

"Now that you're pals with the royal family," said Roan, "I suppose you'll be too high-and-mighty for the likes of us."

"Come off it," said James. "I don't expect I'll ever meet a single one of them ever again."

"But who on earth would want to kill you?"

"If I could answer that question I'd be a step closer to knowing what was going on."

James was sitting in his room with Pritpal and Tommy. They were eating toast with anchovies and listening to a program of popular songs on Tommy's radio; Al Bowlly was singing "The Very Thought of You." James had had to prepare tea for Theo Bentinck earlier, and there had been the end of a loaf of fresh, crusty bread left over. Bentinck had told James to throw it out, but instead he had brought it up here, and they had toasted it for themselves.

"If I didn't know you better, James," said Tommy, "I'd think you were making it up."

"If only," said James. "I thought at first I might be imagining it. But not anymore."

"At the risk of repeating myself," said Pritpal, "why would anyone want to kill you?"

"And at the risk of repeating *myself*," said James, "I have no idea."

"It was not a rhetorical question," said Pritpal. "We need to analyze the situation. Let us think clearly and try to work it out; what possible reason could anyone have for murdering you?"

"I see what you're driving at," said James. "Okay . . . it could be someone I've upset in the past; there are plenty of them knocking about. It could be something I've done, something I know, something . . . dammit, Pritpal, it could be anything!"

"Did anything happen to you in Austria?"

"Apart from falling down a mountain, not a lot."

"Did you meet anyone odd?"

"No . . . unless you count Graf von Schlick."

"He sounds pretty bloody odd," snorted Tommy. "Who is he?"

"He was a patient in the clinic I ended up at," said James. "I only mention him because he sticks in my mind."

"Why does he stick in your mind?"

"It was late at night. He was in pain, raving. Shouting about how someone wanted to kill his cousin."

"Ah—so you are not the only one in danger," said Pritpal, with mock seriousness. "Graf von Schlick's cousin is also at risk."

"I wouldn't have thought much of it," said James, "except his manservant came in. A creep and a thug. There was a real air of menace about him. Afterward, when I went back to say good-bye to Miles Langton-Herring, I saw the *Graf* again.

Only this time his bandages were off, and he looked at me like . . ."

"Like what?" Tommy interrupted.

"Like he knew me."

"Well, he did," said Pritpal. "He had met you that previous night."

"Oh, I can't explain it," said James. "The whole thing was just not quite right somehow."

"And it was after that you started seeing the Invisible Man?"

"No," said James. "I'm pretty sure I first spotted him on the way to Kitzbühel."

"So the two things cannot possibly be connected," said Pritpal.

"I don't suppose so," said James. "If I hadn't had my misadventure with Miles, I would never have ended up in the hospital. I would never have heard the *Graf* raving about his cousin."

"Who is his cousin?" said Tommy.

"He's called Jürgen," said James. "That's all I know."

"Ach, my poor cousin Jürgen," said Tommy with a dreadful German accent. "Zey are going to blow him to smizzereens!"

The other two laughed at Tommy's half-Chinese, half-German pronunciation, and they were still laughing when the door opened and Theo Bentinck walked in.

"What are you laughing at?" he said.

"Oh, it's a crime to laugh now, is it?" said James.

"It depends on what you were laughing at," said Bentinck.

"Well, you can rest assured we weren't laughing at you," said James.

Bentinck looked around James's room with some distaste, his small mouth pulled tight. His eyes widened as he spotted the remains of his loaf.

"That is my bread," he said.

"You were going to throw it out, if you remember," said James.

"That's not the point," said Bentinck. "It's been stolen."

"No it hasn't."

"Who took it?"

"You know perfectly well who took it," said James. "I was tidying up, and—"

"Be quiet," said Bentinck. "I wasn't talking to you." He shifted his gaze to Tommy. "Did you take it?" he said.

"No," said Tommy sheepishly, and Bentinck turned his attention to Pritpal. "What about you?"

Pritpal wasn't sure what to say. He glanced at James.

"Leave them out of this," said James. "I took it."

But Bentinck still had his eyes fixed on Pritpal. "Have you been eating it?" he said.

Pritpal still had a corner of toast in his hand, so he could hardly deny it. He nodded his head.

"You have been eating my stolen bread."

"It's not stolen," said James. "You were going to throw it away. I didn't like to see it go to waste."

"It strikes me that all three of you are guilty," said Bentinck, ignoring James.

James flushed with anger and jumped to his feet.

"If you have your heart set on punishing someone, then punish me," he said hotly.

"No," said Bentinck, clearly enjoying himself. "I don't

think I will. You three are messmates. From now on I will hold you all equally responsible if any one of you steps out of line. Have you got that, James Bond? If *you* do anything wrong, then I will beat one of these two."

"But that's not fair," said James.

"Isn't it?" Bentinck grinned. "Here at Codrose House we are trying to build team spirit and responsibility toward each other. From now on you are responsible for these two. You may think you're tough enough not to be bothered by another beating, but let's see how this pair of saps like it. You, Nandra, come up to Library for your punishment."

James was so angry he didn't know what to say, and when Bentinck crooked his finger at the petrified Pritpal, he exploded. He pushed his way between the two boys and shoved Bentinck hard into the corridor.

"You keep your hands off Pritpal," he said.

"Just for that," said Bentinck, "I'm going to thrash both of them."

James raised his fist, but Tommy stopped him.

"Don't," he said, walking out of the room. "You're only making things worse."

James stood there quivering with rage. All he could do was watch as Tommy and Pritpal followed Bentinck toward Library.

CHAPTER 15—GUEST OF HONOR

"Quite a pile," said the taxi driver as he steered around a bend in the long gravel driveway and saw Miles Langton-Herring's family home for the first time.

It was indeed quite a pile. A recently built mansion in the popular Tudor style, it was extensive and rambling, with two long wings, a steep red-tiled roof, countless elaborate chimney stacks, all sorts of outbuildings, and a garage big enough to fit four motorcars. Light spilled out through its diamond-leaded windows, and there came a hubbub of music and voices from inside.

A line of Rolls-Royces, Daimlers, and Bentleys were waiting to drop guests off at the front steps, and more cars were arriving every minute.

"I'll get out here," said James.

The house stood in its own grounds on the south side of the Great Park. James could have ridden over on a bus, but he had gone to the extravagance of taking a cab because he was running late. Since the incident with the bread, Bentinck had been making his life hell. James had been dashing around for him like an obedient dog so as not to get Pritpal and Tommy into any more trouble. This evening Bentinck had deliberately kept him busy for over an hour, as he knew that James was going out.

It looked like the party was already in full swing.

James paid his driver and walked along the row of cars to the front of the house, where two uniformed lackeys were greeting guests at the door. James filed in behind a man in a gleaming top hat and a woman weighed down with furs and diamonds.

He hadn't known what to expect, and had assumed from the way that Miles had described it that the party would involve just his immediate family and a few friends, with maybe a cold buffet and drinks and some music playing on a gramophone.

It was becoming obvious by the second that he couldn't have been more wrong. This was no intimate reception; it was a society ball. At least James was wearing his school uniform, complete with top hat, so he didn't look too out of place among the men in evening dress and the women in their best gowns.

He walked into the hallway and stopped to look around. The largest floral display he had ever seen was standing in the center, next to a string quartet that was struggling to be heard above the noise of the party. Oil paintings hung on the wood-paneled walls, and twin staircases fanned up to the next floor.

James handed his hat to a girl and followed a small group toward the next room. He gave his name to the butler on the door, who was obviously expecting him, and found himself in a large, packed ballroom.

A jazz orchestra was playing at the far end, and some of the more adventurous guests were dancing. Most people, however, were simply standing and chatting at great volume. James made his way slowly into the adjoining room, which turned out to be a dining room. There was indeed a cold buffet, but it went far beyond anything he had imagined.

The long table was near to collapsing beneath the weight of huge sides of meat, whole salmon, lobsters, game birds, bowls of seasoned rice, potatoes, every type of salad you could imagine, as well as cheese and fruit and trifles and huge glistening cream cakes and chocolate gateaux.

James carried on exploring. The next room he came to was a library, where older men with wide bellies and bald heads sat smoking cigars and drinking brandy. Then there was a billiards room, and after that a formal sitting room, then a conservatory, then a smaller sitting room. Finally, James found himself back in the hallway.

He wondered, not for the first time, what he was doing here and looked longingly at the open front door. He appeared to be the youngest person at the party and felt completely out of place among the dukes and duchesses and millionaires. He wouldn't be missed if he went home now. With all these people here, Mr. Langton-Herring would never even know if he had arrived or not.

He was just thinking about doing one final circuit before departure when he heard a familiar voice call out to him, and he spotted Miles coming awkwardly down one of the staircases on his crutches.

"James," he said, hobbling down the last few steps and coming over to shake him warmly by the hand. "I'm so glad you made it. Father will be so pleased."

"Are you sure? It looks like he has some far more important guests than me here."

"He loves to throw a party," said Miles. "The house was

only recently finished and he'll snatch any opportunity to show it off. Now then, have you had something to eat?"

"Not yet."

"Oh, but you must. There's some rather superior beef from our farm in Hereford—so tender you can cut it with a fork."

James smiled. How strange that he should be pleased to see this boy who before had been nothing but an irritation. Ah well, any old port in a storm. He let Miles prattle on about the food as they went into the dining room and filled their plates. The food at Codrose's was the worst in Eton, and although the boys could make up for it by buying extra things for their tea, he was never really satisfied. He had to admit that this spread was a welcome change.

He and Miles went and sat on the stairs to eat their food, and they chatted about this and that and not very much. James began to think that maybe the party wouldn't be such a bore after all.

Afterward they went into the ballroom to watch the band.

"How's the leg, by the way?" James asked.

"Not so bad. The cast will be off in a couple of weeks. No dancing for me tonight, though."

"Me neither," said James, backing out of the way as a young man in baggy trousers swung a startled girl across the dance floor. Another group of guests parted to give the dancers room, and James caught sight of Miles's father, who, at almost the same moment, spotted James.

James was struck once again by how much the man resembled some wild furry animal, with his bushy mustache and sideburns and mane of unruly hair.

"Aha, the man of the hour," said Mr. Langton-Herring, and he clapped his big hands together. "I was just looking for you, young Bond. They told me you had arrived in one piece, but I could find neither hide nor hair of you. Follow me!"

So saying, Mr. Langton-Herring cleared a path to the stage, barking good-natured commands to his guests to get out of the way. James and Miles fell in behind him, and they made their way across the dance floor in a small procession.

As Mr. Langton-Herring approached the band, he bellowed at them to stop playing. The bandleader hastily brought the song to an end and Mr. Langton-Herring took the stage. He raised his hands for quiet, and a hush slowly descended on the room.

James looked around. More guests were filtering in from the other rooms, and all eyes were on the stage.

"It's time for the speeches, I'm afraid." Langton-Herring's voice boomed out, and there were theatrical groans from his audience. "It's a good lesson to learn," he said. "We must pay for our pleasures. And your payment tonight is to listen to old windbag Langton-Herring give one of his infamous orations!"

Now James knew where Miles got his talkative habits. Though he hadn't quite the charm of his father.

"Tonight is a very special night for me," Langton-Herring went on, "because I have not one but *two* guests of honor, and I should like to say a few short words about each of them. Actually I should like to say a great many long words about them, but I fear I might be shot."

A ripple of laughter passed through the guests.

"My first guest of honor is a man whom you all know,

and whom you will one day know even better. He is my neighbor, and it is my great privilege to call him my friend, but to you lot, you unruly rabble, he is your Royal Highness, the Prince of Wales, our future King, Edward."

A roar of approval filled the room. There were shouts of "Hurrah" and "God save the King," and a scattering of applause.

"As I say, it is my very great honor to have him here tonight. So would you all raise your glasses . . . To the Prince!"

"To the Prince!" went up a great shout, and two hundred glasses of champagne were upended.

"My second guest of honor tonight is someone you won't know," Langton-Herring continued once he had everyone's attention again. "Although I am quite sure that he *too* is destined for great things. He is a boy. A boy at my son's school. A boy called James Bond. Where are you, James? Come up here, lad."

Miles shoved James forward, and he stumbled onto the stage, wishing more than ever that he had not come tonight. He hated being the center of attention.

He stood there looking out over the ranks of grinning faces.

Mr. Langton-Herring put an arm around his shoulders. "Some of you may have heard the story," he said, "and most of you will have seen poor Miles hopping about the place on his crutches. He had a nasty accident on a mountainside in Austria, and his friend James Bond saved his life. He brought him down the mountain at great risk to himself, and it is entirely due to his efforts that Miles is here with us tonight. So please raise your glasses in a second toast . . . to James Bond. . . ."

James hoped he wasn't blushing to his roots. He felt desperately uncomfortable as everyone lifted their glasses toward him and shouted "James Bond!" before emptying them.

Everyone, that is, apart from one man who stood out from the crowd by remaining completely still. He simply stared at James with empty, lifeless eyes, and James stared back.

It was Graf von Schlick.

What the devil was he *doing here?*

James realized that Langton-Herring was still speaking, and he tore his eyes away from the blank-faced man in the crowd and turned to his host.

"Miles tells me you have no watch, James," he was saying. "So I'd like you to have this as a small token of our gratitude, for saving our son's life."

Langton-Herring passed James a velvet pouch, inside which was a beautiful watch.

"It's a diving watch. The very latest thing," said Langton-Herring as James studied it. "A Mido Multifort, the first automatic, waterproof, and shock-resistant watch on the market. I guarantee you'll be the only boy at Eton with one of these on his wrist."

"It's really quite something," said James, turning the watch in his hand. It was simple and tough-looking, with a brown leather strap.

"It's waterproof to a depth of one hundred feet," said Langton-Herring. "Should be sufficient for you, eh?"

"You really shouldn't have," said James.

"Oh, but I should," said Langton-Herring with a grin. "It's the very least I can do. Miles tells me you're quite a sporting lad and a keen swimmer. Go ahead, try it on."

James strapped the watch on. It could have been made for him. For a moment he forgot all about the other guests, and when he raised his head he realized that they were no longer looking his way and had gone back to enjoying the party. There was no sign of Graf von Schlick.

He stayed on the stage talking to Miles and his father for a few more minutes, and when he finally went down the steps to the dance floor, he found his path blocked by two pretty girls.

"This is Tillie and Maya," said Miles. "They are friends of a cousin, or cousins of a friend—I can never remember which. They came with Mrs. Dudley Ward. I think they'd like to meet you."

James shook their hands. They were staring at him with awe.

"Are you famous?" said Tillie, the older of the two.

"Not really," said James.

"You're a hero," said Maya.

"No, I'm not," said James, and he tried to walk away. When he turned around he saw that they were following him.

"It seems you have some fans," said Miles.

"Tell me," said James. "I thought I spotted the Graf von Schlick earlier. Was I seeing things?"

"No, he's here all right," said Miles. "As you know, he was in the clinic with me, and it turns out he knows the Prince of Wales. I suppose they're probably related—the von Schlicks were originally from Germany, like our own royal family."

"What do you mean?" said Maya, who had popped up at Miles's elbow. "Our royal family aren't German, they're English."

"Queen Victoria was a Hanover," Miles explained. "And the Hanovers were a German royal dynasty who came over here in 1714. Then, when Victoria married Prince Albert, she became a Saxe-Coburg-Gotha. But during the Great War it didn't look good for the British royal family to have a German surname, so Victoria's grandson, George, changed the family name to Windsor, after the town. The royals are all Windsors now, and I don't suppose that they will ever change back again."

"I didn't know that," said Maya.

"I did," said Tillie.

"You're just showing off," said Maya.

As the two girls began to argue, James saw his chance to escape. He slipped away and went off to find a lavatory.

There were so many rooms in the house, however, that it was difficult to know where to start. One likely-looking door led to a servants' stairway, another opened into a closet full of hunting equipment. As he came out he found his way blocked by a young man with a big grin and a small notebook.

"Hi," he said, "I'm Parker Liautaud, European correspondent for *Time* magazine. I wonder if I could ask you a few questions about your recent adventures in Austria."

"I'd rather you didn't," said James. "I don't want any attention."

"I'm sure our readers would be greatly interested in what you had to say; it's quite an exciting story."

James looked around for some way of escape and caught sight of the thuggish-looking man with the swollen eyelids, von Schlick's manservant. He was making his way slowly along the corridor.

James turned back to the young reporter. "It's all been exaggerated," he said. "I've nothing to say."

The thug was getting nearer.

"Just a short quote?"

"Talk to Miles," said James hotly, and he barged through the nearest door and slammed it loudly behind him. He waited there for a few seconds, watching the doorknob, until he was sure that neither the reporter nor the thug were going to follow him.

The room was in half darkness and James had assumed it was empty, but when he turned around, he saw two people sitting next to each other on a sofa, lit by a dim table lamp. They were both staring at him.

He recognized one of them immediately: it was the Prince of Wales. How strange to meet three members of the royal family in one week. His partner was an older woman with dark hair and a thin, clever face. They stood up politely, and there was a slightly awkward moment.

"I'm sorry," said James. "I didn't think there was anyone in here." The room appeared to be a gentleman's study.

"Are you lost?" said the woman, who was evidently an American. "Easy in a large house like this."

"I was looking . . ." James was suddenly overcome with embarrassment about saying exactly what he had been looking for. Was it proper to talk about these things in front of the heir to the throne?

"I was looking for someone," he mumbled.

"You're that young chap Langton-Herring was talking about, aren't you?" said the Prince.

"Yes, that's right, sir."

"How do you do?"

James went over and shook Edward's hand; the Prince then introduced the woman as Mrs. Wallis Simpson.

"It seems we're both guests of honor here," said Edward. "I gather you helped Miles out in some way, did you?"

"Yes, sir."

"Jolly good, yes. Well done. And you're at Eton, as well, are you?"

"That's right, sir, I am."

"Yes, jolly good. Tremendous stuff."

Edward was friendly enough, and genuinely seemed to enjoy chatting to James, but Mrs. Simpson had sat down again and appeared to have no interest in him at all. James thought she was probably one of those adults who didn't like children.

"Jolly good school, Eton," Edward said, patting his pockets and then thrusting his hands deep into them as if not sure what to do with them.

"Yes, sir, I like it enough."

"Between you and me"—Edward leaned toward James and gave him a wink—"and I shouldn't really be telling you this, but my father, the King, is going to be visiting the college for the Fourth of June celebrations."

"Really, sir? I didn't know."

"No, no. It's, ah, not yet common knowledge. A bit of inside gen for you. I'm sure you can keep it under your hat. Us royals have always had very close ties with Eton."

"Yes. The Fourth of June is a celebration of George the Third's birthday," said James. "He was a great benefactor of the school."

"Yes."

James realized he was babbling like an idiot, but he couldn't stop himself.

"So, King George is going to be visiting?" he went on. "I mean our present King George, of course."

"Of course," said Edward. "It would be difficult for the old King to visit, as he's . . . as he's dead."

"Yes," said James, and he looked at Edward, not sure if he'd made a joke or not. Edward kept a straight face for a few seconds and then broke into a smile. James laughed.

"They're giving a lunch in his honor," Edward added.

"Ah, I see."

"One has to beware of all these lunches in one's honor," said Edward, staring out the window. "They can be rather heavy. One needs to guard against putting on any weight. Difficult business."

"I can imagine it is, sir, yes."

"My father is always telling me to eat more," said Edward.

Mrs. Simpson gave a snort of laughter from the sofa, where she was reading a magazine. Edward was reminded of her presence.

"Can I get you anything, dear?" he asked.

Mrs. Simpson threw down the magazine and stood up.

"I was just leaving, actually," she said. "This party's an awful bore, but I suppose one must show one's face." She smiled forcedly and went out of the room.

James felt very aware that it was just the two of them in the room now, and he didn't know what to say. He took a deep breath and was just about to try to find a way to leave politely when there was a knock on the door and three men entered.

Two of them he had never seen before, but the third was Graf von Schlick.

He turned his awful, bland, unreadable face toward James, and James felt a chill pass through him.

CHAPTER 16—A BLUNT OBJECT

Powerful urges were battling each other inside James. On the one hand, he wanted to get well away from the *Graf*, and on the other, he wanted to stay and find out more about him. In the end the decision was made for him by the Prince, who started to introduce James to the new arrivals.

The first two, Viscount Lymington and "Chips" Channon, had heard Langton-Herring's speech, so they at least knew who James was and made a token effort to say something positive about him. Finally, Edward introduced the *Graf*.

"Von Schlick is from Austria," he explained unnecessarily as they shook hands. "Do you know the country?"

"Only from my recent trip," said James. "With Miles, for the skiing," he added when the Prince looked blank.

"Ah, yes, of course."

"I know Germany better," James continued. "We went there often when I was younger."

"A tremendous country, Germany. Such a pity that we fell out with them," said the Prince.

"Indeed," added Chips Channon. "The Great War was in so many ways unnecessary."

"Yes," said James. "It was a shame."

A shame? *What was he saying? The war was a hell of a lot worse than just a* shame. *It was a tragedy. A disaster. Millions of young men had died, and for what?*

"We must make sure it doesn't happen again," said Viscount Lymington, a balding man with reptilian features.

"Yes," said Edward. "It did terrible damage. But I am so glad that Germany is at last getting back onto its feet. This man Hitler is doing great work, I gather."

"I wouldn't really know about that, sir," said James.

"You're too young," said Channon. "But take it from me, I have seen what he is about. He has industry working again, the people filled with hope for the future."

"It's all rather exciting, really," said Edward. "England is falling apart around our ears and Germany is rising from the ashes with great vigor. I think we might want a dictator in England before long, if only to sort out the Communists."

The Prince gave a little chuckle then looked slightly self-conscious.

"Now, you'd better run along, James," he mumbled. "I need to talk to these gentlemen."

James said good-bye to Viscount Lymington and Chips Channon, and finally shook hands once again with the *Graf*, who still wore a pair of thin white leather gloves.

The *Graf* whispered, "Good night," holding his throat, which had evidently been affected by the fire. "It was nice to meet you."

"Actually," said James, "we have met before."

James saw a flicker of emotion in the man's eyes. But it was impossible to read what it meant.

"In the clinic," James explained. "In Austria."

"Ah," said von Schlick, the light dying in his eyes and the bland look returning.

"I was there with Miles."

"Of course you were," hissed von Schlick.

James decided to press things further. He felt desperately uncomfortable in the man's presence, but he needed some questions answered.

"On the night before your operation, sir," he went on, "you were crying out in your room. You were obviously in some distress. I woke up and came in to see what the matter was."

"I do not remember," said the *Graf* bluntly.

But James was not going to be put off so easily. "You were shouting about how somebody wanted to kill your cousin Jürgen," he said. "It stuck in my mind. Is he all right? Your cousin, I mean? You seemed very worried."

"I must have been dreaming," the *Graf* whispered. "It is nonsense. I was heavily sedated."

"So, he is all right?"

"I can assure you," said the *Graf,* more forcefully, "I do not have a cousin George."

"I'm sorry to have brought it up," said James. "At any rate, I'm glad the operation went so well."

The ugly scarring and bruising on the back of the man's head had settled down, but it was still a marked contrast to the smooth, almost too perfect face.

The *Graf* thanked James, who muttered some more hasty good-byes and backed out of the room with some relief.

Later, sitting in the back of the taxi on his way back to Eton, James ran through the episode again in his head. Something had struck him as odd, and he wanted to remember what it was while the conversation was still fresh in his mind. It was something the *Graf* had said. Something not quite right, but James had been so flustered at the time that he hadn't picked up on it. What was it?

Something about his cousin Jürgen?

Yes, that was it.

The *Graf* had said that he didn't have a cousin *George*.

Why had he used the English version of Jürgen, when James had used the German?

Maybe he was just humoring James by using the language of his hosts.

No matter how often James went over it in his head, he couldn't make sense of it. He was finding it hard to think straight and concentrate on one thing. So much had happened tonight it was hard to take it all in. It had been a distinctly unreal experience.

There was solid proof that he hadn't dreamed it all, however.

He pulled his sleeve back and looked at his new watch.

He didn't feel that he deserved it, but it was very handsome nevertheless.

A few days later, James was trudging back over Fifteen Arch Bridge after a particularly dull cricket match on Upper Club when Dandy pulled up alongside in his works lorry.

"Are you busy, bucko?" he said, winding down the window.

"Not particularly," said James. "I have a Latin construe to write, but it can wait."

"I could be doing with some company, if you fancy a little trip."

James didn't know what to make of Dandy. Behind his

friendliness, there was an unpredictability and a wildness about him, but he had readily helped James when he had spotted the Invisible Man in the woods at Windsor Park, so he might be a useful ally.

"Why not?" James climbed into the cab and settled down on the old worn seat. The smell of the countryside mingled with oil and petrol fumes.

"Where are we going?" he asked as Dandy wrestled the lorry into gear and they rattled off up the road toward Slough.

"I've to get some supplies," said Dandy. "I can do it meself, but it'll be easier with two pairs of hands."

"What sort of supplies?" James asked, watching the patterns the sunlight made filtering through the passing trees.

"Oh, just stuff for the grounds," said Dandy. "Weed killer, fertilizer, nothing very exciting, I'm afraid. It takes a lot of work and a lot of chemicals to get those cricket pitches looking as beautiful as they do. And I've to deliver a ton of cut flowers to the chapel for the Fourth of June. It's a specially big event this year. So what have you been up to, then, since our adventures in the park? Seen any more spies?"

"No." James laughed. "Do you not believe me?"

"Oh, I believe you. Same as I believe in leprechauns and pots of gold at the end of every rainbow."

James laughed again. "It does seem a little far-fetched, I suppose."

He decided to change the subject.

"Life has been all too normal lately," he said. "Though I did go to a big party on Saturday night."

"Lucky you."

James told Dandy all about his night at the Langton-Herrings' house, and Dandy listened with amused interest.

"Well, now," he said after a while. "You've certainly been seeing how the other half lives."

"I think you're right."

"But does it seem fair to you, Jimmy, that your man Langton-Herring should have all that money, should have rooms full of fine food and champagne, when everyone else in the country is trying to scrape a living together right now?"

"I don't know," said James. "What's the alternative? To just give it all away?"

"That's never going to happen," said Dandy. "Nobody's ever going to give away their wealth off their own bat; sometimes you just have to take it."

"You sound dangerously like a Communist," said James with a smile.

"Maybe I am at that, bucko," said Dandy. "But this country could do with a mighty kick up the backside."

"You think so?"

"Ah, the French had it right. *Vive la révolution!*"

"So what do you think we should do?" said James. "Chop King George's head off, or put him up against a wall and shoot him like the czar?"

Dandy smiled and nodded his head. "Maybe. Do you think anything's ever going to change in this bloody country as long as you have a King?"

"Does anything need to change?" said James.

"God, yes," said Dandy.

"What about the little princesses we saw the other day?" said James. "Would you behead them, too?"

"You can't think about the individual, bucko. In the great scheme of things, the great sweep of history, two little girls don't account for a great deal. You have to think about the bigger picture."

"I still don't think it could ever be right," said James.

"Sometimes you have to do the right thing for the wrong reasons," said Dandy. "Or do the wrong thing for the right reasons, if you catch my meaning."

"I'm not sure that I do," said James. He was intrigued and wanted to carry on the conversation, but Dandy fell quiet and didn't say anything else until they arrived at their destination: a group of barns and ugly concrete sheds on the outskirts of Slough.

Dandy pulled in through the gates, parked the lorry in a yard, and handed James a sheet of paper.

"Here's the order," he said. "I'll go into the shed and pick up the supplies; you take that in and get it signed off. We don't need to pay; the college deals with them direct. We just need to get the truck loaded up."

James crossed the muddy yard to the office and went inside.

A man with a drinker's red nose and watery eyes sat behind a counter reading the *Racing Post* and smoking a cigarette. James handed him the list, and he gave it a once-over.

"Fertilizer, weed killer, silver paint. It's all there waiting to be picked up." He licked his lips, signed the list and stamped it, then he handed a receipt to James to sign.

"So Eton's getting the boys to do all the work now, I see?"

"I'm just helping out a friend," said James.

"Well, don't go too near some of them sacks, son. It's nasty stuff, a lot of it. That's the thing with plants and flowers: if you want them to look lovely and fresh and colorful, it seems you've got to cover them with all sorts of poisons and chemicals these days. Potassium chlorate, potassium permanganate, saltpeter, sulphur powder, I don't know—'spect you know all about that from your science classes, but it's not my idea of gardening. Still, it pays my keep, so I'm not complaining."

James went out just as Dandy and another man were loading up the last of the sacks. He scrambled up into the cab and waited for Dandy, who appeared a minute later and started up the lorry.

"There's a lot of it," said James as they set off back to Eton.

"There's a lot of grounds at the school," said Dandy. "It owns half the land around here."

"I suppose once you've shot the King you'll burn the school down," said James.

"Maybe I will," said Dandy.

"Well, I'm sure you'll find plenty of boys willing to help."

The two of them laughed, then Dandy turned to James with a serious look on his face.

"You're keen on our Roan, aren't you, James?"

"What do you mean?"

"Ah, don't think I didn't notice, bucko."

"Notice what?"

"I saw the way you were looking at her in the park, like a lovesick mooncalf."

"I wasn't," James protested.

"Weren't you, now? Well, let me tell you something, James. You can't be too careful around that one. She's probably told you she's a witch? You'd better believe it. Watch out for her. Keep away from her. A girl can cause you a great deal more pain than a bullet."

James bumped into Pritpal when he got back to Codrose's. He had hardly seen anything of his two messmates since Bentinck had punished them over the bread incident. They seemed to be avoiding him, and James took the opportunity to ask Pritpal about it.

"We were looking forward to you coming back," said Pritpal sadly. "We thought you were going to be our savior, our knight in shining armor, but instead you have only made things worse."

"That's not fair," said James. "It isn't my fault that Bentinck's a damned sadist."

"You like trouble, James," said Pritpal. "You need excitement in your life, and danger, but we don't. And now your love of danger is going to make life impossible for us."

"So you're going to have nothing to do with me?"

Pritpal couldn't look at him. He scratched his nose and stared at the floor.

"I have never been so miserable in my life," he said. "I used to enjoy school. Life was fun, but not anymore. I dread waking up in the mornings and having to face another day, another day of creeping around in fear, another day pretending to like games, another day of trying to join in, to please Bentinck."

"If there was anything I could do," James protested, "I would do it. But what *can* I do?"

"I don't know," said Pritpal. "I wish I did. I think it's best, though, if in the meantime you do nothing. Nothing at all."

He walked away, his head bowed. At that moment Bentinck appeared, marching down the corridor with two other boys from Library in tow. Pritpal cringed out of his way and flattened himself against the wall.

When Bentinck came to James, James found himself standing stiff and straight, as if to attention.

As soon as he realized that he was doing it, he hated himself. And he hated Bentinck for making him feel this way. But he let the boys pass without doing or saying anything.

He walked wearily toward his room. On the way he passed the corridor where Roan's room was, and he made a quick decision. He checked to see that there was nobody around and then knocked on her door.

"Who is it?"

"James Bond."

In a moment Roan's face was in the open doorway, her dark eyes shining.

"And just what do you think you're doing, young man?" she said, the ghost of a smile playing around her full lips. "Knocking on a girl's door like this."

"I need someone to talk to," said James.

"And you want to talk to me?"

James shrugged.

"Come in, then, you daft beggar."

James went in and sat down on a hard wooden chair by the window. The room was very similar to his, but Roan had tried to make it her own with a few personal items: a picture of Ireland on one wall, a patchwork quilt on the bed, a little woven rug on the floor.

"So what's the matter with you, then?" she asked, sitting down on the bed.

"I'm confused and I don't have anyone else to talk to."

"What about your friends?"

"They're avoiding me like the plague. They think I'll get them into trouble."

"And will you?"

"It's Bentinck. He's got the whole house terrified."

"Ah, you mustn't worry about him. He thinks you're a threat to his power, and he's scared of you."

"He's taking it out on my friends. They can't stand up to him."

"And is it them you're feeling sorry for, or yourself?"

"Well . . ." James sighed. "Both."

"It's a mean old world sometimes, darling. And we none of us know the best way to cope with it. And you, you're just a boy; you can't be expected to always know what to do."

"I used to think I did."

"You're growing up, James. You're finding out that things aren't as simple as you thought. You've been running hard, James, I can see that in you, and when you're running, things are simple. It's when you stop running they get complicated. Why do you think men throw themselves into their work, or go happily off to war, or try to walk to the North Pole or climb the highest mountain? They're escaping real life, James, with all its problems. Problems that can't be sorted by running or fighting."

"It's the only way I know," said James.

"You're a blunt object, aren't you, darling? Oh, I'm not saying you haven't got any hidden depths. Because I know there's a lot going on beyond that cool surface of yours. You're a lot more grown-up and interesting than most boys your age. But you'd still rather take on the world with your fists than with your brain, or with your heart. You've got to learn to use your heart, because if you don't, it'll become weak. And a weak heart is easily broken. If someone wants to hurt you badly, they'll aim their arrows at that heart of yours."

James was very aware of the nearness of Roan in the small room. He had a powerful urge to lean forward and kiss her, but he remembered what Dandy had said. But why had he said it? Was he trying to keep James away so that he could have Roan to himself? And what did Roan feel for the Irishman?

"I saw Dandy today," he said casually.

"Oh, yes?"

"Did you know him before?" James asked. "I mean before you came to Eton?"

Roan jumped up off the bed.

"Come along, you need to go to your room, James. It's too risky you staying here. If Bentinck knew you were *consorting with a common maid* again, he'd probably beat you and every other boy in the house. He'd probably try to beat me as well, but if he did it'd be the last thing he ever did on this earth."

James went to the door. Just as he was about to leave, Roan stopped him.

"Be careful around Dandy," she said.

"That's exactly what he said about you," James replied as he went out of the room, more confused than when he'd come in.

CHAPTER 17—SCIENCE IS NOT A BORING SUBJECT

James was standing with a boisterous gang of Eton boys, waiting to buy a flower from the old woman on Barnespool Bridge who set up her stall there every year. This was another ritual of the Fourth of June celebrations.

James remembered how last year the day had been ruined by his friend Mark Goodenough trying to kill himself when he found out that his father had been murdered. He prayed that today would be different.

As he paid for his flower and slotted it into the buttonhole in his lapel, he thought about how easily he was slipping into the unchanging routine of Eton, how quickly he was accepting its strange traditions. Already he felt an old hand at this. This was his world now, his life for the next four years.

He watched three boys in Pop strut past in their gaudy waistcoats, lording it up over the lesser boys. He looked ahead to the time when he would be one of them, having been witness to countless other Eton rituals along the way.

And then what? He had no father's footsteps to follow in, no expectations from his parents. His future was a blank book, and he could write in it whatever he wanted.

There was his Aunt Charmian, of course, who had looked after him ever since his parents had died, but she led an unconventional life herself and had never tried to steer James in any particular direction or map out his future for him. It wasn't that she didn't care; it was rather that she had always encouraged James to be his own man.

He would be seeing his aunt later. She was coming to Eton just as she had last year. James checked his brand-new watch. She would be here soon. He was going to meet her by the Burning Bush, the elaborately decorated streetlamp that was a handy local landmark.

As he was heading back up the High Street, he met Pritpal and Tommy coming the other way. They both looked rather shifty.

They said hello and James assured them that he wasn't angry with them for avoiding him.

"I know how hard it must be for you," he said. "And I'm sorry if I've made things worse. I promise I'm going to do something about it, and in the meantime I'm going to try my damnedest to stay out of trouble. You're going to see a new James Bond. Your friendship means a lot to me, and I'd hate to foul things up."

Pritpal smiled sheepishly. "It's all right, James," he said. "I was feeling particularly low when I saw you yesterday. It is not fair of us to blame you."

"All the same," said James, "I'm going to be considerably more levelheaded in the future. I shall be the model schoolboy. No more adventures."

Tommy laughed. "I find that hard to believe."

"Just you wait and see," said James, and he carried on up the High Street. He had not gone more than ten paces, however, when he was stopped in his tracks, as solidly as if he'd just walked into a brick wall.

Suddenly all the promises he had made to his friends seemed very hollow.

Standing outside Spottiswoode's, staring at the display in the shop window, was a familiar figure. A woman. She had her back to him, but it was a back he would never forget.

No, it couldn't be her. He must be imagining it.

He moved into the shade of a building and waited for the woman to turn around so that he could be sure.

He studied her carefully, taking in all the details. The stout black shoes, the gray stockings and skirt, the matching jacket that was too small for the stocky, muscular peasant frame, its seams straining as if about to burst apart. The chunky head sitting like a boulder on the broad shoulders. The hair, gray like the rest of her, and cut short . . .

Colonel Sedova. Known within the Russian secret service as Babushka, the Grandmother.

It couldn't be anyone else.

The only thing different was the hat. A ridiculous, shapeless object decorated with flowers that looked utterly out of place on that solid gray foundation.

Come on . . . turn around. Let me get a good look at you.

A noisy group of parents and sightseers in festive mood came along the pavement and swept past Spottiswoode's. When they had gone, so had the figure in gray.

James cursed and knocked his fist against his forehead. It couldn't have been Sedova. What would she be doing here at Eton? He had last seen her disappearing down a tunnel beneath London after a day of bloodshed and carnage. James had destroyed her plans to build a massive decoding machine and could have shot her. In the end he had decided that there had been enough killing for one day, and he had let her go.

Had that been a terrible mistake?

What was going on?

A tangle of confused thoughts swam up from the murkier depths of his brain, where he had kept them pushed down out of the way. If only he could make sense of them. It was as if there were something important going on in a room, but he was trapped on the other side of the door, and no matter how hard he battered on it, he couldn't get in.

There was an odd assortment of people inside the room. The Invisible Man, Theo Bentinck, Dandy O'Keefe, Roan Power, Graf von Schlick, Prince Edward, and now Sedova.

It was quite a party.

He was so wrapped up in his thoughts that he didn't notice someone waving at him until he had virtually walked into them.

"James. You've got your head in a cloud!"

It was Charmian, standing outside School Library, shaking her head.

James grinned and said hello, kissing her on the cheek, all dark thoughts instantly forgotten. Charmian was wearing a simple, narrow-waisted, cream-colored suit and a man's hat tilted down over one eye. She couldn't have looked more different from the other mothers and aunts, who had taken the opportunity to show off their most expensive summer dresses and jewelry.

"And look who's here," said Charmian.

There was such a crowd that James hadn't noticed a girl standing patiently at Charmian's side.

She was about sixteen, pretty, and self-assured, but with a rather sad, faraway look about her.

With a shock James realized it was Mark Goodenough's sister, Amy. They had shared many adventures together last summer in Sardinia, when James had rescued her from the hands of a crazed Italian count.

"Amy," he said, and her face brightened into a smile as he gave her a quick kiss.

She looked different, older, more of a woman and less of a girl.

James felt slightly awkward. He hadn't really kept in touch after the summer; there had been too much going on in his life. They had exchanged a couple of letters at first, but perhaps because their time together had been so intense, so filled with danger and fear, it had made it harder for them to keep up any kind of proper relationship back in the real world.

"So, what are you doing here?" James asked.

"I have a cousin," said Amy, making a face. Even her voice was different—lower, more grown-up sounding. "A horrid little boy called Philip. Well, I call him a cousin; he's actually more of a third cousin twice removed or something; it just seems easier to call him a cousin. His parents are out in India and couldn't make it today. That's him over there with my aunt and uncle."

She nodded to where a skinny little fourth-former stood chatting to a well-dressed man and woman.

"Actually, he was just an excuse," Amy went on. "I really wanted to see you. I called Charmian, and she told me where you were meeting."

"It's lovely to see you," said James, hoping it didn't sound forced or false. "Are those the relatives you live with now?"

"Yes," she said. "You and I are in the same boat." Amy smiled, but the sad, distant look returned to her eyes.

"I've not been back here since Mark left," she said quietly. "It all seems like another life now."

"How is Mark?" said James, feeling guilty that he hadn't written to his friend at all.

"He's much better now," said Amy. "We both went through some very bad times. We both still do have some wobbly moments, but the hurt is fading slowly." She turned to James. "I suppose you know how it feels."

"Yes," said James. He still sometimes dreamed of his mother and father, and when he was feeling low he would wonder how differently his life might have turned out had they not died in the climbing accident.

Amy's relatives came over and there were introductions all around. It was decided that they would tour the school together, and Philip took charge.

The Fourth of June was an open day for Eton, a chance for the boys to show their families what they got up to, and a chance for outsiders to get a good look at the boys up close.

"So what do you want to see?" said Philip, leading the party off down Common Lane.

"Everything," said Amy's uncle, Peter, a cheerful northerner who was slightly overweight. "I've heard so much about the place but have never been here before. I want to see it all. It's quite an eye-opener, to see all these well-behaved boys going about the place all got up like miniature undertakers."

"There are some areas I can't show you until later, I'm afraid," said Philip. "The King is visiting the school today and there's a service starting in the chapel at eleven."

"Oh, I've seen my fill of churches," said Uncle Peter. "I want to see where you study."

So Philip started his grand tour. James and Amy hung back. James gradually began to feel more relaxed with her, and they soon forgot about everyone else and were chatting away without a care.

Philip was being very thorough. They visited the Warre schools, the gymnasium, the fives courts, the drawing schools, and then tramped all the way over to the music school and the new science buildings.

As they entered one of the science classrooms, they found a group of older boys presenting a demonstration with a slightly anxious teacher overseeing them.

"Some boys think science is boring," one of the boys was saying. "But we say science is *not* boring. You can do some very interesting experiments and learn all sorts of interesting things, like how to make explosions, for instance!"

He nodded to one of his pals, who dropped a lump of something white into a flask with some tongs.

There was a pop and a flash, and a couple of shrieks from mothers, then a small round of applause. Philip came over to grab Amy.

"Come along," he said. "Let's go and take a closer look."

Amy tried to protest, but Philip was insistent. She gave a despairing look to James, and he was just about to follow her when he heard a mocking voice at his side.

"Who's your girlfriend?"

It was Roan. She was wearing a bright summer frock and a smart white hat.

"She's not my girlfriend," said James. "She's just a friend."

"She's very pretty."

"I suppose so."

"Do you think she's as pretty as me?"

"That's a trick question," said James. "And I'm not going to answer it."

"Suit yourself," said Roan. "Are you having a nice day?"

"I suppose so."

"It's grand to see so many people enjoying themselves," said Roan.

"Are you changing your attitude to the school?" James asked.

"Not the school," said Roan. "The people. I thought everyone here would be stuck-up and snooty. Some are, but not all. You're not."

James had never seen her like this before. She seemed somber, lacking her usual liveliness and sense of fun.

"Have you seen Dandy today at all?" she asked.

"No. Why?"

"Oh, no reason."

"Have you?" said James.

"He's helping with the King's visit. He has to get the chapel ready." Roan paused, looking away toward the boys as another small explosion went off. She seemed to be struggling to make a decision about something. In the end she spoke without turning back to face James.

"Dandy told me to tell you he could be doing with some company. An extra pair of hands . . . I think he was joking."

"Probably," said James. "I helped him the other afternoon. I'm busy today, though."

"So I noticed," said Roan. "With your pretty girlfriend."

"I told you," said James. "She's not my girlfriend."

Roan suddenly gripped him by the elbow and turned the full power of her gaze upon him.

"Stay with her, James. Enjoy the day. Take her to the river. Don't think you have to save the world all by yourself."

"As far as I can see, the world doesn't really need saving," said James.

"No." Roan laughed, but the laugh quickly died away. "God, but it's a lovely day," she said, and then snapped her eyes away from him and hurried off.

James shook his head. He wanted more than anything to follow her, to be with her. But he knew he couldn't. He had to stay with Charmian and Amy.

Amy . . .

He had always liked her, but she had never made him feel the way Roan did: happy, miserable, excited, and scared, all at the same time. When Roan looked at him with her big black witch's eyes, his insides turned to jelly.

He was shocked back to reality by a sudden bang, much louder than all the others. The boys doing the demonstration looked around happily at the shocked reactions of the people in the room.

The master in charge obviously felt that he should say something to show that this wasn't just boys messing about and blowing things up.

"You would be surprised how easy it is to make an explosion," he said, in that way that teachers have of making fun things slightly dull. "Many elements react violently to air or to water, and, of course, heat. If you mix together the right elements, you can make a considerably more spectacular explosion than the ones we have been making here today. I shan't give you the exact recipe, but if you wanted to make a really big bomb, all you would need would be some potassium permanganate and potassium chlorate, which can both be found in commonly available products, such as weed killer and fertilizer—"

James shoved through the crowd to the workbench where the master stood.

"What did you just say?"

"Erm, I was talking about bombs. Why? Are you keen on science?"

"What did you say about weed killer?"

"Just that if you knew how to go about it, you could make a rather nasty bomb out of potassium permanganate and—"

"Sulphur powder?" said James.

"Yes, you would need that."

"Saltpeter?"

"Yes."

"Silver paint?"

"Silver paint? I'm not sure that—oh no, wait a minute, yes, there is aluminium powder in silver paint.... You're quite an expert, I see. I hope you're not planning to blow anyone up."

"I'm not," said James, pushing back through the crush of people. "But I know somebody who is!"

CHAPTER 18—THE INFERNAL DEVICE

It was as if a rusty cog had freed itself in James's mind. It turned and everything fell into place. Dandy was planning to assassinate the King. He'd practically spelled it out for James. He'd been taunting him from the start.

What an idiot James had been. Why hadn't he seen it? He felt like someone who had been wandering around Egypt unable to find the pyramids, when all along they'd been right in front of him.

Miles had told him that Graf von Schlick was related to the British royal family. Then Amy had told him that a cousin need not necessarily be a first cousin.

"*Sie werden meinen Vetter Jürgen töten . . .*"

They are going to kill my cousin Jürgen . . .

The Graf's *cousin Jürgen was King George.*

Somehow the *Graf* must have known about the plot. Maybe he had been trying to warn the Prince of the danger? That would explain why von Schlick had been so shifty when James had asked him about it.

But if they had known about the danger, why was the King still here today?

There was no time to work it all out now. James looked at his watch in a blind panic. The hands made no sense to him. He took a breath and tried to calm his racing heart.

He looked again.

It was a quarter to eleven. He had fifteen minutes before the service was due to start in the chapel.

Where were Charmian and the others?

There. At the far end of the room, looking at some newts and frogs in a fish tank. He was about to go over to them when he saw a flash of gray.

This time there was no mistaking her. It *was* Babushka. She was walking slowly down the length of the room, evidently looking for something—or someone. A few paces behind her was the Invisible Man, his distinctive trilby hat covering his face.

They were all in it together. It was a massive Communist plot.

James had to think fast and act fast.

He couldn't get to Charmian without Sedova seeing him.

He turned and ran out of the building the way he had come in. He tore past Lower Chapel, and as he emerged onto South Meadow Lane, he turned right and carried on running. He pounded along Keate's Lane, barging people roughly out of his way, and onto the High Street.

There must be a policeman here somewhere. The only problem was that even if he found one, would he have time to persuade him to do something? Would the policeman even believe him? *Would anyone believe him?*

He kept moving. If Dandy had built a bomb powerful enough to blow up the chapel, it would need to be pretty big. The only place to hide it would be underneath in the crypt.

Dammit. There must be a policeman somewhere. He was nearly at School Hall and the seconds were ticking away.

He crashed into a group of people coming around the corner from the library, stumbled through them and straight into a circle of boys chatting on the pavement.

He ignored their angry shouts and was just about to head for the Burning Bush in the middle of the road when someone grabbed his sleeve and spun him around.

"Bond! What the bloody hell do you think you're doing?"

"Get off me, Bentinck!"

"You're behaving like a hooligan."

"I don't have time for this," James yelled, and shoved Bentinck away, knocking his spectacles off. Bentinck staggered back into another boy, who supported him.

"You're going to pay for that!" snarled Bentinck, and he advanced on James with an outstretched finger.

"Save it!" James snapped, but Bentinck took hold of his lapels and wouldn't let go.

Without thinking, James brought his knee up sharply between Bentinck's legs. Bentinck gasped and instantly let go.

James turned and ran slap-bang into a policeman.

Thank God.

"All right, then, what's all this about?" the policeman asked. "You boys know better than to fight in public."

"It's an emergency," said James.

"What is?"

"Someone's planning to kill the King. You have to come with me."

The policeman stared at James for a moment and then started to laugh.

"Very good," he said. "Had me going for a moment. One day you boys are going to go too far with one of your pranks."

"It's not a prank," said James. "It's a Communist plot. They're going to assassinate King George."

"Yes, and I'm going to fly to the moon," said the policeman.

James looked around in desperation. The policeman wasn't the only one laughing. James was in the middle of a ring of howling, jeering boys.

"It's true," he said. "You have to believe me." But the policeman was already wandering off, and Bentinck had got his breath back. In another moment he would be coming back at James even angrier than before.

James cursed, broke through the circle of boys, and sprinted across the street toward School Yard.

He ran through the arch and turned right, nearly knocking over two parents who were studying the plaques on the wall.

He apologized and slowed down. There was a throng of dignitaries in the yard waiting to go into chapel. At the center James could just make out the small bearded figure of the King. He couldn't risk drawing attention to himself. If anyone saw him, he would be thrown out.

He walked purposefully along the colonnade beneath Upper School, for all the world as if he was meant to be there, and went through the old door at the far end.

A colleger was standing guard on the wide, wooden stairs that led up to the antechapel.

"You can't go up there," he said as James approached.

"The Head Master wants you," said James firmly.

"The Head? What for?"

"How the devil do I know?" said James. "But he sent me to get you; he said it was urgent. I'll take over here for you."

The colleger dithered, but when James barked at him

to hurry, he dashed off in a state of some confusion.

James carried on up the stairs into the antechapel, where a group of ladies were busy putting the finishing touches to some large floral arrangements.

James strode over to one of them.

"How do I get to the crypt?" he asked, and she nodded to the small vergers' vestry where a circular staircase wound downward.

James was on the move again. Across the antechapel and down the stairs. At the bottom was the crypt, which was long and narrow and dark. Part of it had been closed off by a brick wall, but James saw that someone had recently dismantled some of this wall to create an opening.

James looked through. This part of the crypt, which ran the length of the chapel, was filled with ancient coffins. He could see no signs of movement, but lying on the floor near the opening was a verger. He was completely still. James climbed through to get a better look. He just had time to take in that there was a dark pool of blood spreading around the man's body when there was a terrific crack as he was hit from behind, and he was sent flying backward.

He hit the wall hard. His head whipped back onto the stonework, and he blacked out.

"Any sign of James?"

"No. He's not out here."

Charmian and Amy were waiting on South Meadow Lane.

"He must have wandered off somewhere," said Charmian. "You know what boys are like."

"I saw him talking to a girl," said Amy. "I didn't like to interrupt. Then I was with you looking in that tank, and when I looked again he had gone."

"The same thing happened last year," said Charmian. "He just disappeared. He was gone for ages."

Amy looked disappointed. Charmian put a hand on her arm.

"Don't worry. He'll turn up," she said. "He always does."

James's head hurt like hell.

That was good.

It meant that he wasn't dead.

His eyes were closed. It would be too much of an effort to open them. If he just stayed like this, he knew he would never have to face whatever was waiting for him.

He was in a chair, his head slumped forward, and if he hadn't been tied to it, he knew he would have fallen onto the floor.

There were ropes around his chest, and his wrists were secured behind his back. There was a chain around his ankles.

He couldn't have moved even if he'd wanted to.

"I know you're awake."

Dandy's voice.

James's head whipped to the side, and there was a harsh burn on one cheek. Dandy must have slapped him.

James opened his eyes at last. The light was dim, but it made his head hurt worse than ever.

Dandy was standing in front of him, smiling.

"That's better," he said, then he tutted. "Jesus, you took

your time getting here, didn't you, bucko? I was beginning to think you weren't going to make it to the party."

James looked around the crypt. There was a big steel drum tucked in between two of the coffins. A long fuse led away from it and snaked down the crypt and back again.

So that was the bomb. It looked so dull, so ordinary. But he could tell from its size that it was designed to bring the whole building down.

"Yes," said Dandy, "there she is, my Brenda. You know what they call a bomb? *An infernal device.* Well, Brenda is all set to blast them upstairs to hell. I picked up most of the stuff with you the other day. I already had some mothballs, some flour, some sugar, and the other bits and pieces I needed. It's going to be quite a bang."

"What's it going to achieve?" said James.

"It's going to get rid of a King, for a start. He'll be sitting right above here, at the west end. As long as old Georgie-boy is in power, the ordinary working people of this country will never rise up and take control. Revolution, James, it's the only way to change things. A short sharp shock."

"And me?" said James. "How do I fit in with all this?"

"You're an enemy of the people."

"What?" It was so ridiculous, James almost laughed.

"I had orders from the start to do you in, James," said Dandy, checking the fuse. "Orders from the top."

From Sedova?

She had obviously never forgiven James for ruining her plans in London. He was wishing with all his heart that he had never let her escape. She must have been plotting all this time to strike back at him.

"It was me that pushed you in front of that lorry," said Dandy. "You've the luck of the devil."

"And in the park?" said James. "You were going to stab me, weren't you?"

"The thought did cross my mind, but you were saved by the Princesses. And then I had a better idea. To bring you here and blow the lot of you up together. Say your prayers, bucko, because the Princesses won't save you this time, and *you* won't save their grandpapa."

Dandy straightened up from his work, wiped his hands on his trousers, and tested the ropes around James.

"They're going to be pleased with how well it's worked out, bucko," he said. "True, there won't be anything much left of you, but once this has all gone off, I'll be posting some letters to the newspapers. They explain all about how Communism is going to spread throughout Europe, and they explain how you helped by putting this bomb in here."

"Don't be an idiot," James scoffed. "Nobody will believe that."

"Won't they? Why do you think I made sure your face was seen picking up the chemicals? You're going to be the villain of the piece, a clumsy villain who went and died in his own blast! A martyr for the cause. How does that make you feel? Keeping the red flag flying?"

"Everyone knows I'm not a Communist," said James. "I'm not the type."

"I'll tell you what type you are, bucko," said Dandy harshly. "You're a dissatisfied type who's had a difficult life, parents dead, no father figure, being bullied at school, looking for revenge."

"No," said James. "It's not like that."

"Come on. A boy like that could be easily influenced by the wrong *types*. Everyone knows you've been moping around after Roan. It was plain for all to see that you were sweet on her. People will do crazy things for love."

"So she's in this with you, is she?"

"Afraid so, bucko."

"Why did you warn me to stay away from her the other day?" said James.

"She's not as hard-hearted as me," said Dandy, taking out his knife. "I was worried she might be getting too fond of you. But she's proved how she feels by sending you here today. Well, we live and learn, we love and learn. Except in your case, you're not going to live. So the lesson's come too late to save you. Never mind. You always wanted to be a hero, didn't you? This way you will be. Not in Britain, though. You're going to be a hero in the Soviet Union. They'll probably put up a statue of you." He pinched James's cheek.

"Poor James Bond. He died for the wrong cause."

"How could you be so sure I'd come?"

"It was too easy. A little nudge from Roan was all it took. We know all about you, James: you're a loner, thinking you can sort everything out all by yourself. Well, this is a man's game, bucko, and you're just a boy. Sure, and it's the same with Roan. Did you really think you had a chance with her when there was a real man like me around?"

"You're so sure of yourself, aren't you?" said James. "But what if I'd brought a policeman with me? What then?"

"Then he'd be as dead as your man over there," said Dandy,

throwing his knife across the crypt, where James heard it stick into a coffin.

"It's very civilized that the coppers in this country don't carry guns," said Dandy, "but it sure does make life easier for the likes of me. Now, I've talked too long."

Dandy looked at his watch.

"Five past eleven," he said. "They should all have settled down nicely upstairs. I'm going to light the fuse now and leave you to it, if you don't mind. I need to get into a good position to watch the fireworks. It's a ten-minute fuse. At quarter past, by my calculation, the band of the Grenadier Guards will be marching past here like so many tin soldiers. They'll be wearing their red uniforms and their bearskin caps and carrying Union Jacks, and the crowds will be cheering, and then—*BOOM!*—the remains of this chapel, the symbol of the greatest school in England, will rain down on their heads. This day will be remembered for centuries, James. *You'll* be remembered; *I'll* be remembered. We're going to write our names into the history books with blood. So long, and thanks for all your help, bucko."

Dandy winked at James and tied a gag around his mouth. Then he took out some matches, struck one on the rough stone of the wall, and set light to the end of the fuse. James heard him go to the coffin and retrieve his knife, and a second later Dandy gave a short chuckle before climbing out through the hole in the wall.

James was moving instantly.

He hadn't been idle while Dandy was talking. He had been working on a plan. He knew he had to remain clearheaded and to act carefully and methodically.

Fear wouldn't help him now.

He had less than ten minutes to get free and cut the fuse.

Was it enough time?

It had to be. There wasn't any choice.

He checked his situation. His legs were chained and padlocked to the chair legs. His hands were fastened behind his back with cord. Thicker rope was wound around his upper body and a stone pillar behind him. The knots were tight and expert, but James could still move his fingers. He reached down and pinched the back of his coat. He closed his eyes, concentrating hard, pulling the heavy cloth upward between his fingers.

Inch by agonizing inch.

He was terrified he would drop the coattail and have to start again, but at last he felt something hard between his fingers. It was one of the razor blades. He gingerly eased it out of its little pocket, and then, by curling his fingers up, he was able to start working on the ropes.

Ssssssssssssssssssss . . .

All the while he had been aware of the steady hiss of the fuse as it made its leisurely way across the floor of the crypt, sparking and smoking.

He worked quickly, sliding the blade backward and forward, wishing he could see what damage, if any, it was doing to the cord. Then he felt something give as a strand came loose. It was working, but, God, it was slow progress.

Ssssssssssssssssssss . . .

He glanced over at the fuse, trying to work out how much time he had left.

Not long by the look of it.

Another strand came loose, then another, and then at last his wrists snapped apart. Now he had to work his hands around to the front. The ropes around his chest and upper arms made it difficult.

Difficult, but not impossible.

He wriggled and squirmed, keeping a firm hold on the precious razor blade.

There!

He could see his hands. They were cut and bleeding where he must have nicked them with the razor without knowing.

Never mind that. Get on with it, James.

Sssssssssssssssssss . . .

He slashed at the ropes around his chest, slicing through the outer layers. The woven hemp strands frayed and curled back as he cut through them.

Faster . . . Go faster . . .

A sudden flare from the fuse made him look up for a second. There were only a few feet left before it reached the bomb.

Then—horror—in his panic to speed up, the blade slipped in his bloody fingers and dropped.

His breath stuck in his throat.

He hardly dared look down.

It was all right. The razor was sitting safely in his lap. He snatched it up and went back to work.

Sssssssssssssssssss . . .

One of the ropes dropped away, cut clean through. It was all James needed. He felt the tightness loosen around his chest. He twisted his torso, punching with his shoulders, and was able, finally, to shrug the rest of the ropes off. They slithered down to his waist and he pulled his arms free.

Now there were only his ankles left.

But they were held fast by a padlock.

He looked at the fuse. It was almost at the bomb.

He made a quick calculation of the distance . . .

If he was quick . . .

But what if he was wrong?

If he was wrong there was very little he would know about it, because he would be instantly blown sky-high.

Ssssssssssssssssssss . . .

With a furious yell he threw himself forward, taking the chair with him, flinging his arms out in front.

He crashed face-first onto the floor, his hands landing directly on the bright, dancing flame. He ignored the pain, gripped the still smoldering end of the fuse in one hand, and tugged with all his might.

It came away from the steel drum. The danger was snuffed out.

James lay there, breathing heavily, his face pressed against the cold stone, hardly daring to believe he had done it.

It wasn't over yet, though.

Dandy was still out there.

CHAPTER 19—ONE MOVE AND I'LL TEAR YOUR THROAT OUT

James retrieved his set of lock picks from their hiding place in his coattails. In less than a minute the padlock was open. Red Kelly had taught him well. He freed his ankles, stood up, and checked his injuries. There was a lump on the back of his head, and his chin was sore and grazed where Dandy had hit him. He had bruised his knees and ankles when he had crashed to the floor, and both hands were cut and bleeding. His left hand was also scorched and blackened from where he had grabbed the burning fuse. He wrapped his handkerchief around it. It wasn't perfect, but it would do for now.

He didn't have time to be playing Florence Nightingale. He had to stop Dandy from getting away.

He put the picks and the razor blade in his pocket. The razor would be useless in a fight, but he did have the metal skewer. He fished it out of his coattail and slid it up his left sleeve, holding the blunt end tightly in his bandaged fist. It would be out of sight, but if he needed it he could simply draw it out with his right hand like a sword from its scabbard.

He was ready. He ran up the steps toward daylight.

There was music and singing coming from the chapel. The antechapel was empty. James hurried through to the stair, where the colleger was back at his station.

"Another message from the Head Man," James shouted

as he sped past. "Nobody, but *absolutely nobody*, is to go down into the crypt without his permission. Have you got that?"

"Yes, but—"

James didn't wait to hear any more. He was outside and heading for the archway at full speed. He took a quick look at his watch; the bomb should have gone off a minute ago. He had no idea how accurate the fuse timing had been, but he guessed that Dandy wouldn't want to go back and check, and risk blowing himself up.

He burst out onto the High Street and found himself in the heart of a huge crowd.

How was he ever going to find Dandy in all this?

Think, James, think . . .

Dandy had said he was going to "watch the fireworks," which meant that he would have to stay close enough to see the chapel. It was the largest building around, so it was visible from almost anywhere, but if Dandy really wanted to see the effect his bomb was going to have, he would want to stay close to School Yard.

James wished he hadn't blundered out onto the street. If Dandy was watching the archway he would have spotted him.

Or would he?

James looked around; the pavement was packed with boys, all identically dressed.

Sometimes there was something to be said for wearing a school uniform.

He tucked in behind a group crossing the road. There was no traffic, and in the distance he could hear the thump of drums.

Of course, the parade. He saw the tail end of the first

marching band as they moved away up the Slough Road. A second band was approaching from the direction of Windsor. That was why the streets were busier than normal, even for the Fourth of June. People were jostling for the best view. If the bomb had gone off, they would have all been caught up in the carnage.

Masonry and rubble would have tumbled out of the sky and into the street.

That meant that Dandy would be taking shelter and not standing out in the open.

Where was the best spot?

James thought back all those weeks ago to when he had glimpsed the Invisible Man hiding in the narrow space between Durnford and Hawtrey.

That was the most obvious place. That was where James would have chosen. If he worked his way behind the buildings, he could come up on the alley from the rear.

But he would have to hurry. By now Dandy must have realized that something had gone wrong.

James skirted around School Library and dodged between buildings until he found the back of School Hall, then slowed down. He was at the rear entrance to the alleyway. It seemed very dark after the bright sunlight of the High Street.

He peered around the corner. A man was standing at the far end, smoking a cigarette and looking the other way, with his back to the alley.

James grinned.

Got you!

Now what, though?

He could hardly catch Dandy single-handed. Especially

as Dandy was armed with his knife, and all James had was the thin skewer up his sleeve.

Idiot! He had nearly charged into another dangerous situation without thinking it through beforehand.

He was wondering what to do when the man dropped his cigarette to the ground and stubbed it out with his shoe. As he turned to leave, his face caught the light.

It wasn't Dandy.

So where was he?

His question was answered immediately as a strong hand was clasped over his mouth, and a second hand brought a long, cold blade up to his neck.

Dandy must have spotted James and followed him around to here.

"One move and I'll tear your throat out."

James stayed still, hardly even daring to breathe. Though he could feel Dandy's breath, hot on the back of his neck, he could also sense that Dandy was shaking, and his body felt slightly damp.

For all his coolness in the crypt, the man was scared.

"How did you get away?" Dandy's voice hissed in his ear. "Tell me—but I warn you, if you cry out or make a sound, I'll cut the tongue from your head."

Dandy released his grip on James's mouth.

"Someone came," James lied. "Another verger. I was spotted going down into the crypt. He defused the bomb. They know all about you."

"Yeah? I don't believe you, bucko, but it makes no damned difference. I may have missed the King this time, but you're next on the list, and I'll not miss you."

Dandy put his free hand back up to hold James's head steady, and in so doing he lowered the hand holding the knife just for a moment.

It was all James needed. He didn't think twice. Dandy had offered him this tiny window of opportunity, and it might be his last.

He thrust his left elbow back hard, forcing the skewer along his sleeve, so that the end was sticking out behind him.

How far it was sticking out he had no idea—he just prayed it was enough to do some damage.

Dandy grunted and swore at James, but as he raised his arm to bring his knife up, he grunted again and coughed. James felt his whole body shudder.

Dandy had obviously discovered that James had done more than just elbow him. He was more badly injured than he had imagined.

Again James seized his opportunity. He bit hard into Dandy's wrist, forcing him to drop the knife. Then he shook himself loose and bolted.

Dandy made a grab for him and took hold of his flying coattails, but he screamed as the second hidden razor blade cut deep into his fingers.

James was free.

He didn't stop to look back, but ran faster than he had ever run in his life. He knew the way to go—and followed exactly the same route he had taken when he was following the Invisible Man.

He sprinted behind Keate's and out onto Eton Wick Road, skidding to a halt as a car went past, its horn blaring. He then looked quickly back. There was no sign of Dandy.

He would be safer where there were crowds.

He carried on running until he reached the High Street, where the second marching band was passing by, cymbals crashing, brass blaring, drums thundering. The cheers from the bystanders added to the general deafening din.

James edged between the people on the pavement, moving in the direction of Windsor. He passed Spottiswoode's, and as he came to Hodgson House, something hard jabbed him in his side.

He whirled around, ready to defend himself, but it was only a small boy waving a flag.

As he turned back, though, he found his path blocked.

By a man in a trilby hat.

His right hand was jammed into his jacket pocket and he was staring straight at James.

It was James's first chance to see what he looked like.

There was nothing particularly memorable about him. He had a hard, lean face with thick black eyebrows and thin lips. Stubble showed blue-gray against his pale skin. He had a slight rash around his shirt collar.

"Stop," he said bluntly.

But James was in no mood to follow orders. He gave the man a mighty shove and sent him sprawling into the path of the band.

There was instant chaos, and it was all James needed to get away. He realized that this was the very spot where Dandy had tried to kill him before. That meant that the entrance to Jourdelay's Passage was nearby.

Yes. There it was. He ducked off the street and started to run.

He was halfway down the passage when he realized there was someone coming the other way.

It was Dandy. He had his knife in his left hand; his right hand was hidden inside his jacket, where there was a dark stain across his stomach. He was dripping blood onto the flagstones and looked pale and feverish.

He grinned when he saw James. A horrible sick grin. Like a death's head.

He raised his knife. James knew that with his right hand Dandy was an excellent shot.

How good was he with his left?

James wasn't going to stick around to find out.

He turned on his heels.

And that was when he discovered he was trapped.

The Invisible Man was coming the other way, slowly advancing down the passage, moving lightly like a cat. His hat jammed down on his head. His expressionless eyes fixed on James. This was a man doing a job. There was no enjoyment in it, nor was there hatred or anger.

He pulled a stubby black revolver from his pocket.

James spun around and hurled himself to the ground just as Dandy let fly with the knife. A single shot rang out, barely audible above the racket from the marching band.

James lay on the ground, tensed and shaking. It wasn't possible that the knife and the bullet had both missed him, and yet he had felt nothing. He knew that when a body was scared, it flooded with adrenaline, which sometimes masked all pain. But surely he would have felt something?

Well, if they had missed him, it would surely only be a matter of moments before they tried again. He curled up, waiting for the second shot, his hands wrapped around his head, his eyes clamped shut.

The shot never came.

Instead he heard the sound of running footsteps. Slowly he uncurled and opened his eyes.

Dandy was lying motionless on the ground, his arms flung wide. There was a neat bullet hole in his forehead and a rapidly spreading pool of blood around him.

Before James could react, before he could even properly take in what he was seeing, he felt himself gripped by two strong arms and hauled to his feet.

"Move it," a voice barked, and he was frog-marched down the alley. Two more men laid a blanket over the dead body. One of them was the man with the cigarette he had mistaken for Dandy earlier.

James was being pulled rapidly to the back end of the passage, his heels dragging over the flagstones. He tried to struggle but was gripped firmly and expertly. As they left the passage, James caught a glimpse of the two men rolling Dandy up in the blanket.

A black car screeched to a halt by Queen's Schools, the doors flew open, and James was bundled into the back. In a moment they were off, racing down the Eton Wick Road, away from town. The driver maneuvered through the narrow streets at a dangerous speed, at one point scraping against an old brick wall. He swore but didn't slow down.

The Invisible Man was sitting next to the driver while James was alone in the back with the man who had hauled him out of the passageway. He was big and square jawed with a guardsman's build. He kept his eyes fixed straight ahead and showed all the animation of a shop-window dummy.

James considered opening the door and trying to jump out, but knew it would be futile. These men were too well organized.

For now, he was alive. If they'd wanted to kill him, he had no doubt that they would have done it already. Instead the Invisible Man had shot Dandy, and James was more curious than scared.

Who were these men and what did they want from him?

The Invisible Man lit a cigarette and opened his window to let the fumes out. Then he turned around in his seat to face James, his eyes pale under the thick brows. "We need to talk," he said. James wasn't sure exactly what he had been expecting—a foreign accent of some sort, probably Russian, certainly not the soft Scottish brogue that issued from the man's lips.

"Back there in Jourdelay's Passage?" the man went on. "With the gardener O'Keefe? Was it how it looked?"

"How did it look?" said James.

"It looked like he was trying to kill you."

"He was," said James.

"Why?"

"You mean you don't know?"

"Just answer the question."

James thought about it for a moment then decided to tell the truth, and he sketched out the rough details of what had happened that morning.

As he spoke, nobody else said anything. The mood in the car was tense.

When James finished, the Invisible Man said something

quietly to the driver, who nodded. After that, nothing more was said, and a few miles out of town they turned off the main road and onto a short, tree-lined drive. At the end of the drive was an old redbrick house with ivy growing up the walls. It had a slightly neglected air; the windows were dark, the flower beds and lawn overgrown. The car drove around to the back and parked by the kitchen door, where the Invisible Man jumped out. The driver sounded the horn three times, and a heavyset man in shirtsleeves emerged from the house. He glanced briefly into the car, gave James a once-over, then opened his door and nodded for him to get out.

No sooner had James put both feet down on the ground, than the car roared off back out of the drive at full pelt.

James followed the two men into the house. They were deep in hurried conversation.

The kitchen they came into was bare. There was a kettle on the range, some tea-making things, and a half-eaten packet of biscuits, but nothing more.

They went through to a dark and gloomy hallway that had a polished parquet floor. The man in shirtsleeves knocked twice at a door and went in without waiting for an answer. The Invisible Man hurried to the other end of the hallway, snatched up a telephone, and started barking terse commands. James could only make out the odd few words.

". . . the crypt . . . no, it was the Irishman . . . for God's sake keep a lid on it . . . no, make sure everyone is out of the chapel before you go anywhere near the thing . . ."

The man in shirtsleeves reappeared.

"Come in," he said, and James went through into a living room. An older man was sitting in the bay window, looking out at the garden. The smell of pipe smoke filled the room.

James could see a few overgrown apple trees standing among the long grass, a rusty abandoned bike leaning against one of them. A fly buzzed at the window, trying to get out.

There was a dreary, unlived-in feel to this room. The few bits of furniture didn't match: a couple of wooden dining chairs, an uncomfortable-looking armchair, and a moth-eaten old sofa. A card table stood against one wall with a mess of papers splayed out on it.

The man at the window stood up. James recognized him instantly. His first thought was that Mr. Merriot didn't usually light his pipe.

"Sorry about all the cloak-and-dagger stuff, James," he said, rubbing his beaky nose. "But we can't be too sure."

He offered James a small, reassuring smile, but his eyes looked worried.

"I expect you want some answers," he added.

CHAPTER 20—THE SHADOW WAR

James sat down on one of the hard wooden dining chairs, his mind racing, trying to take this all in. He could make neither head nor tail of it, though, so he gave up trying. Too much had happened today. He would let Mr. Merriot explain just what the hell was going on.

"I'm afraid I don't really know where to start," said Merriot, sitting down opposite James in the armchair. He nodded to the man in shirtsleeves, who then left the room. Merriot was evidently in charge here.

"I hope they didn't hurt you."

James shrugged.

"It was for your own safety. We had no way of knowing who else might be around."

"The man who brought me here?" said James. "The man in the trilby? Who is he?"

"His name's Dan Nevin," said Merriot. "Captain Dan Nevin. He's been watching you."

"Why?"

"To make sure you didn't come to any harm. Good thing, too, as it turned out. He's been covering your back ever since you returned from Mexico."

"But why, sir?"

"Because I asked him to," said Merriot, puffing hard

on his pipe. He seemed nervous, fidgety, embarrassed to be talking to James like this.

"Is he a policeman?"

"Not exactly. Have you heard of the Special Intelligence Service, I wonder?"

"The SIS?" said James. "Yes. They're sort of spies, aren't they?"

"*Sort of spies.* That's the simplest way to describe what they do, yes."

"Are you saying those men work for the SIS, sir?"

"Yes."

"Maybe you should start at the beginning," said James. "I'm finding this all rather confusing."

"Not surprised." Merriot took his pipe out of his mouth and looked at it. It had gone out.

"Never could keep the beastly thing lit," he said, knocking out the tobacco and setting it down on the arm of his chair. "But I thought it was what a schoolmaster would do. Smoke a pipe."

"Are you saying that *you* are a spy, as well, sir?" said James.

"*Was* a spy. Pretty much retired from that side of things now, but I do still work for the SIS after a fashion."

"I thought you worked for Eton College, sir," said James.

"That I do. That I do. I work for both."

"Is that allowed?"

"'*Is that allowed?*' he asks. I am governed by a higher authority than the Head Master," said Merriot. "For me it started before the war. The British didn't have a terrifically organized spy network back then, but any fool could see that there was trouble brewing in Europe, and the powers that be wanted to keep an eye on the Germans, in particular on their navy. Our secret service grew rapidly and went through a few changes before it was split into two parts. The army were in charge of catching foreign spies on British soil, and the navy were given the job of spying overseas. These two divisions are known as The Directorate of Military Intelligence Sections five and six. More commonly—MI5 and MI6. I was recruited by MI6—naval intelligence, overseas work—while I was at university, as I speak good German and was quite an athletic type. The man in charge, 'C,' sent me to study in Hamburg."

"'C,'" sir?"

"That was the code name of Captain Sir George Mansfield Smith-Cumming, the director of MI6."

"And why did he send you to Hamburg?"

"It is Germany's major seaport, and the idea was for me to keep my ear to the ground and make note of shipping movements. When war broke out I stayed on until it got too hot, then I pulled out. By then there was a great need for spies, but we had very few experienced men. It became my job to recruit and train our chaps, brief them on their missions and suchlike." Merriot paused, mulling something over in his mind. "I knew your uncle, as it happens."

"Uncle Max?" said James.

"Uncle Max. Yes. I'm glad he lived long enough to become an uncle. Most didn't. The failure rate was horrendous. We were all still learning, you see? Making it up as we went along. But we learned fast. He was one of the best, your uncle Max. Of course, neither of us could talk about it. He took his secrets to the grave, for the most part."

"He told me a little of what happened to him," said James.

"A brave man," said Merriot. "After the war our operations were obviously scaled down," he continued, "but it was all too clear that we needed a permanent and organized secret service. The efforts of the SIS have been largely directed at Russia since then. The threat of Bolshevism is very real."

"And you are still involved, sir?"

"The most important thing we learned in the war," said Merriot, "was that there will always be a need for intelligence, and intelligence officers. There are men like me all over the country now, in the schools, the universities, the armed forces, in business and government, who are constantly looking out for young men and women who we think would serve the country well."

"As spies?" said James.

"Call them what you will," said Merriot. "Spies, secret agents, intelligence officers. I pulled a few strings to get you sent to Eton, you know? I wanted you here so I could keep an eye on you. Your uncle was a good man, one of the best. I felt that perhaps his nephew might be made of the same stuff."

"What about my father?"

"I knew him, too. He was never formally a part of the service. But his job as an armaments salesman after the war made him very well placed to gather certain intelligence for us."

"So you've been watching me from the start?" said James.

"I've been watching you, yes, James, following your progress. You are a remarkable boy. What you have been through has been quite extraordinary. Most grown men would have cracked before now, let alone a young boy. Your adventures have been . . . well, I don't need to tell you all that. I have had some long hard talks with the Head Master about you since you arrived, first with Dr. Alington and lately with Claude Elliot. There have been times when they thought it would have been better if you had quietly left the school, but I have insisted you stay."

"Do they know all about you?"

"They know enough."

"And did you know about Dandy's plot?"

"Ah, now . . ." Merriot got up, unfolding his long limbs from the armchair, and began to pace the room. The walls were bare, marked here and there where paintings had once hung. There was a bookshelf with a few forgotten volumes on it; Merriot stared at the titles without really seeing them.

"We intercepted some intelligence in Lisbon," he said, without looking at James. "Rather, we stumbled across it. We have many informants there. It's a lawless place and a hub of several international spy networks. There was some trouble in one of the Soviet cells. Some agents were killed. We don't know the exact nature of what happened, but in the confusion we managed to intercept a coded message that was being sent to Moscow. We weren't able to decipher it all, but we cracked enough of it to know that it concerned a major plot. We could tell it was something big, but we couldn't be one hundred percent sure of just what exactly the plan was. Today we found out."

"I still don't understand, sir," said James, "why Captain Nevin has been following me."

"One of the parts of the message that we decoded," said Merriot, "was a name. Your name. James Bond."

"Me?"

"Yes. We didn't know what it could mean. We still don't.

Do you have any idea why they wanted to implicate you in this assassination?"

"No, sir," said James. "Except that perhaps it might be about what happened with Colonel Sedova last year."

"Mm."

"When did you know about Dandy?" asked James.

"About twenty minutes ago when Nevin told me he had shot him," said Merriot.

"You had no idea he was involved in this plot?"

Merriot's face clouded. "Unfortunately not. He was not a known Soviet agent. We're looking into his background now."

"But if you were watching me . . ." said James.

"There have been bigger fish than O'Keefe swimming around here lately, James," said Merriot. "Some pretty dangerous sharks."

"Colonel Sedova," said James.

"Indeed. Babushka. We were so intent on watching her and her OGPU thugs that we took our eyes off the ball. It was pretty unforgivable, but Dandy O'Keefe was clever. He never once made contact with any of Sedova's people. In all the confusion this morning, Nevin lost you and decided to stay with Sedova."

James nodded his head. That explained why he had seen the two of them together in the science school.

"Quite frankly, it was a mess," said Merriot, "and it nearly ended in tragedy. It is of the utmost importance that nobody knows what happened today. And we must make sure that nothing like this ever happens again."

"How?" said James.

"We need to hunt down the other members of the cell

that Dandy O'Keefe was operating in. We need to follow the chain of command to the top and flush them all out. It's clear they were not working directly with Sedova, which means that there is a very dangerous group of people out there that we know nothing about. And that's where you come in."

"Me, sir? What do you want me to do?"

"Tell me about the boys' maid, Roan Power."

"What do you want to know?"

"She was working with Dandy? Yes?"

James sighed and looked at his feet. "Yes," he said flatly.

"She is our only point of contact now that Dandy is dead," said Merriot. "And it is most important that she doesn't find out what happened. She will of course know that something has gone wrong, that the bomb didn't go off, but she won't know about Dandy's death. We need to keep it that way."

"Are you going to arrest her?" said James.

"Not yet," said Merriot. "We need to find out what she's going to do next. If she cuts and runs, she may well lead us to the senior members of her cell, but if we can glean any information from her before then, it would be most useful. Our hope is that she will wait until she hears from Dandy before making her move. You can help us there. We need to supply her with some false information."

"You mean lies?" said James. "You want me to lie to her?"

"Yes. We can use her, James. Through her we can weed out the whole nest of them."

"I'm not sure I want any part of this," said James.

"I understand your feelings," said Merriot, "but you must understand who we are dealing with. The Communists executed their own royal family, and countless thousands of their own citizens. They are hell-bent on rolling out their brand of state-run thuggery throughout Europe. They constantly plot to undermine our democracies. They are fanatical and ruthless, and all we can do is guard against them. Everyone tells us that the Germans are our enemies, that sooner or later there will be another terrible war against them. There is a belief that Hitler has ambitions to rebuild the German empire and take over Europe, but there are others among us who believe that the real enemy is Russia, and that if there is a war it will be against them. It will go either way, James—either we will side with the Soviets against the Germans, or we will side with the Germans against the Soviets. The truth is that we are already fighting a war, a secret war, a shadow war. And it's a dirty war that is fought by its own rules. You can never win it because it will be going on forever; an ally today might be our enemy tomorrow. We spy on the Germans, the Soviets, the Americans, the French . . . and they spy on us. No, we can never win this war, but we can win the odd battle. We have the chance here to make a difference. If we use the girl."

"What do you want me to do, exactly?"

Merriot looked at his watch.

"For now, nothing. Everything has happened very fast and they have caught us on the hop. We are still putting together a plan. It is now a quarter past twelve. When did you last see your aunt?"

"About an hour and a half ago."

"Good. We have created a cover story for you. One of my men has already told your aunt that you got into a fight with another boy and that I have been hauling you over the coals in my rooms. That will explain your absence and your generally disheveled state. We'll patch up those cuts before you go, by the way. You will join your aunt for lunch. She is waiting for you in the Shippe Inn on the river. If by any chance you see Roan, and she may well come looking for you, then you will tell her that you have a message for her from Dandy but can't speak until later when there are fewer people around. At half past five you will meet me on Agar's Plough and I'll tell you what to do next. By then we will have made up a story for you to give her."

"But, sir, I'm not sure I—"

"Go now," said Merriot. "Think over what I've said. We'll talk later. And be careful. Dandy and Roan are cut from the same cloth. They're tricky, the Irish; they're a dangerous mix of sentimentality and violence."

"But what on earth were you fighting about, James? You look like you've been dragged through a hedge backward."

James was sitting in the inn, having lunch with Charmian and Amy, who seemed highly amused by his story. James, though, was taking no pleasure in it. He had lost his grip on reality and was still trying to make sense of everything.

"And who was this boy?" said Amy, taking a spoonful of chicken soup.

"His name is . . . Spooner," said James. "He said something rude about you," he added, looking at Amy.

"Oh, so you were fighting over my honor?" said Amy with a laugh. "How romantic."

"I suppose so," said James, who hated lying to them. "I'm sorry to desert you both for so long."

"Well, you're back in one piece, at least," said Charmian. "And we can enjoy the rest of the day now."

James tried. He tried to pretend that he was a normal schoolboy going about a normal Fourth of June. They watched the Parade of Boats. They watched some cricket. They had tea on the lawn. They chatted. But James drifted through it all as if he were in a waking dream. Half the time he wasn't even aware of what he was talking about. Only a few hours earlier he had defused a bomb and fought for his life. If it wasn't for his painful wounds, he might believe none of it had really happened.

He had saved the King's life, and there was nobody he could tell about it.

Five o'clock came around and it was time for Charmian to go home. James kissed her good-bye and waved as she headed for the station.

Then it was Amy's turn to say farewell. He could tell that she knew something was wrong, but she didn't say anything.

They promised to keep in touch, but their parting was stiff and formal.

He watched her walk over to where her own aunt and uncle were waiting, but halfway there she stopped and suddenly ran back to him.

She kissed him and gripped his hands tightly.

"It was lovely to see you again," she said. "I think about you all the time."

And then she was off, and James was left standing by himself on the pavement.

He thought, not for the first time, how lonely it was to have secrets.

CHAPTER 21—THE MEN IN GRAY HATS

Eton was still busy—it would be until after the fireworks—but the cricket matches had finished and the playing fields were quiet, apart from a small group of boys playing a makeshift game in a corner of the Triangle. James and Mr. Merriot were walking beneath the row of huge elm trees on Upper Club, deep in conversation.

"I knew Nevin was following me," said James. "I spotted him a couple of times."

Merriot smiled. "Yes. I wasn't wrong about you. You do have your uncle's blood running in your veins. You're very observant—you don't miss a thing, do you?"

"Did he follow me all the way to Austria?"

"All the way. It was not entirely coincidence that I took you boys to Kitzbühel, James. I was there on business, looking into something. . . ."

"Business?" said James. "You mean secret business? To do with the bomb plot?"

"No, no, no. A low-level threat from elsewhere. I don't suppose it will amount to much, but I'm keeping an eye on it. I didn't mean to give you the impression that it's only the Russians we have to watch out for. Hitler could become very troublesome. We know the Nazis will try anything to overrun Austria; they believe in uniting all the German-speaking peoples. There was trouble in Austria back in February, and we can't trust the Nazis not to try something again. Kitzbühel is close to the German border, and we have a few people in the area. They had reported increased German activity. You don't need to know about all that, though; it doesn't concern you."

"Doesn't concern me?" said James angrily.

"Not at all," said Merriot, taken aback. "It has nothing to do with what the Communists are up to."

"You took us all to an area where you were carrying out spying work and you say it doesn't concern me?"

"I knew it wasn't dangerous, James," said Merriot. "It was just intelligence gathering."

"And how many times have you done it before?" said James.

"What do you mean?"

"How many times have you used us boys as a cover, or worse?" said James, trying to control his anger. "Did you know about Lord Hellebore, for instance? The Millenaria? Fairburn and his Nemesis machine . . . ?"

Merriot stuck his pipe in his mouth and looked away.

"I had my suspicions," he said quietly. "My fears about all of them."

"You were using me?"

"You were useful, James, I'll admit it. More than useful. I would never knowingly have put you into a dangerous situation, though . . . until now."

"You want me to spy on Roan?"

"Yes. She has no one else to turn to. Get her to open up to you. We need names, contacts, dates. . . ."

"I don't know if I can do it."

"She's not your friend," said Merriot, a hint of steel in his voice. "She handed you over to that butcher O'Keefe."

"Maybe she was just fighting for something she believed in," said James.

"And how, pray, was murdering you going to make the world a better place? Hm?"

James fell silent. The sun was still bright on the grass and turning the leaves of the elms an intense green. Behind them the ancient buildings of the school were glowing honey-colored against a soft blue sky. There was the scent of flowers and freshly mowed grass on the breeze, and in the distance the towers and turrets of Windsor Castle rose up over the whole scene, the royal standard fluttering in the breeze.

"This is what *we* are fighting for," said Merriot with an expansive sweep of his arm. "This is what *we* believe in. Cricket, and soccer, and cream teas, the royal family, the Houses of Parliament, schools like this one, rowing on the river, the music halls, beer and pies and laughter and common decency. Look at these elm trees; someone planted them a long time ago, with the belief that his children's children might sit in their shade. They have grown and spread and been cared for by generations of gardeners. And they will stand here for long after we have gone. In a hundred years, boys like you will enjoy their shade in the summer, and the trees will gladden their hearts in the springtime when they burst into leaf. But there are some people who would cut these elm trees down. They would say, 'If we can't all enjoy their shade then nobody should be allowed to sit under them.' There are some people who would light a big fire and destroy everything. But that is not our way—we English like to muddle through in our haphazard manner."

"It's not quite as simple as that, though, is it, sir?" said James.

"Isn't it?"

"Nevin shot Dandy O'Keefe in the forehead. How does that fit in with cream teas and rowing on the river? Just so that we can enjoy all this, somebody is fighting dirty somewhere and behaving just as badly as Dandy O'Keefe."

"Let's not forget, James," said Merriot with a distinctly hard edge, "that the only reason Nevin shot Dandy is because he was trying to kill you."

"I know, sir," said James. "And I'm glad that he did. Dandy was a killer, but even so, some of what he said made sense."

"If Communism made sense," said Merriot, "then surely the Soviets wouldn't have to murder so many people and cause so much pain and human misery to get their way."

"But if we lie and cheat and kill, sir," said James, "are we not just as bad as them?"

"It is not so simple as that," Merriot snapped, and there was real anger in his voice for a moment. Then he relaxed and went on in a gentler tone. "I understand your concern, James. There *is* unfairness in the country. Some people are very rich and some are very poor. Things will change. But change slowly. We do not want a bloody revolution, with people lined up against the wall and shot. How many people would have died if Dandy's bomb had gone off? Hmm? Not just the King. But all those other men and women and children. The Communists don't care about individuals, about you or me, or anyone. For them there is just the mass, the proletariat, the people as one."

"But don't you operate in exactly the same way, sir?"

Merriot stopped walking, taken aback.

"No, absolutely not," he said.

"You work for the good of all as well, don't you?" said James. "The good of the country, the British Empire. Which must sometimes mean that individuals get hurt. You make the same excuses as Dandy, that in order to do good you must sometimes do bad things. And you want me to be a part of it. You want me to lie to Roan, to trap her. You want me to forget that she is a human being. Is that the British way?"

James was getting heated and emotional. He knew deep down it had nothing to do with believing anything that Dandy had said, but everything to do with his feelings for Roan, despite what she'd done.

"When you are young," said Merriot, "the world seems so simple and straightforward. There is right and there is wrong. In the cowboy films, the goodies wear white hats and the baddies wear black. As you get older you realize the world is not so simple. There are men in gray hats."

"And what color hat do you want *me* to wear, sir?"

"James, just answer me one thing."

"Yes, sir?"

"Would you rather that bomb had gone off?"

"No," said James quietly.

"That is the only question you have to ask yourself. Leave the rest to the grown-ups. This is not a game. We could have a fanciful political discussion, but the reality is a whole chapel full of innocent people blown to atoms."

James looked over at the ornate roof of the chapel and tried to imagine what the skyline would look like without it.

"What do you want me to do?"

James found Roan as soon as he got back to Codrose's. She was hanging around in the hallway near the slab, pretending to be busy, and he got the feeling that she had been waiting for him. She seemed agitated but was trying to disguise it with breezy cheerfulness.

Almost the first thing she asked him, in a casual way that he could tell was not casual at all, was whether he'd seen Dandy.

James waited before replying, weighing in his mind whether or not he could go through with the deception.

"I saw him, yes," he said as he had been instructed, trying to keep his voice neutral. "At the chapel."

"The chapel?"

"In the crypt."

Roan put her hand to her mouth, waiting for more.

"We can't talk here," said James. "Meet me at the fives courts—I'll go now; you leave in five minutes."

Roan gripped his arm.

"James, you have to tell me what happened. Is he all right?"

"I'll tell you in a minute. We can't talk here."

He pulled away from her and walked quickly out into Judy's Passage before she could say anything else.

His heart was pounding; he felt a layer of cold sweat under his sticky clothing. He had delayed talking to Roan because all the confusion had returned. When he had left Merriot, he had been certain of what he wanted to do, but now, seeing her again, he had been thrown back into turmoil. When he was with her he could no longer think straight.

The streets were deserted; everyone else was making their way to the banks of the river for the fireworks. The fives courts were on the northern edge of the school next to School Field, and James had counted on them being empty.

The courts were modeled after a section of the chapel wall, between two buttresses, where generations of boys wearing heavy gloves had hit balls to each other against the stonework. In the end the game had become so popular that the school had built more than seventy replicas of this court for the boys to play on.

There was nobody playing when James got there, and the low sun was throwing the courts into deep shadow. It was very quiet. Other boys might have found the peacefulness calming, but not James. He wished that he were smashing a ball as hard as he could against one of those brick walls.

He waited for a long time, the shadows lengthening, half of him hoping that Roan wouldn't show up, that she would run and never come back, the other half of him desperate to see her again.

Then he heard the *clack-clack-clack* of her shoes approaching, and there she was, looking small and even more anxious than before. James hated feeling that he had this power over her.

"I came as quick as I could," she said. "I had to run an errand for the Dame."

"Were you followed?" said James.

"Followed? I don't think so," said Roan. "I wasn't really looking. How much do you know, James?"

"Dandy told me everything."

"Oh, God. But what happened? I have to know. I've been going crazy."

"I went to the chapel," said James, "to the crypt, and I found him there. I knew what he was planning to do."

"But he didn't do it."

"No," said James. "I think he was looking for an excuse not to. I talked him out of it. The idea of killing all those people . . ."

"But where is he?"

"He made me promise, Roan, if he didn't do it, he made me promise that I wouldn't say a word to anyone, and that I'd look after you, help you, not get you into trouble." James could almost believe it himself, and he wished with all his heart that it was the truth.

"But I don't understand," said Roan. "Where is he now? Where's he gone?"

James looked at her; there was fear in her big black eyes.

"He wouldn't tell me," he said. "I suppose he thought it would be safer that way. All he said was—"

"What? What did he say?" Roan interrupted desperately.

"Be quiet and I'll tell you," said James angrily.

"Sorry. But I've been so scared. When he first explained what we were going to do, I thought it was terrible. Terrible but necessary."

"To kill all those people?" said James.

"That wasn't the original plan," said Roan. "Originally it was just one man. Just the King. When I found out we were to blow up the chapel . . ."

"Well, Dandy obviously feels the same way," said

James, remembering how different it had really been when he had faced the cold-blooded killer in the crypt. "Because he had a change of heart. He said he was going to go into hiding, and once he was sure that it was safe he would come back for you."

"Come back for me?" Roan scoffed. "Who does he think he is? Does he expect me to sit around here like a dope waiting for him?"

"Yes," said James. "He was very insistent."

"That man, he's only ever thought about himself." A thought suddenly struck her, and the fear returned to her face. "What about the bomb?" she said, her voice almost a whisper.

"He got it in there without anyone seeing," said James. "He must have got it out all right as well. I've seen no police. Everything at the school is completely normal."

"I know," said Roan. "I've thought I was dreaming."

James licked his lips and took a deep breath. It was time for the next step.

"If I'm going to help you, Roan," he said, "you have to tell me everything. How did you end up here? Who are you working for? What was your escape plan? What did you plan to do next?"

"I can't tell you anything, James."

"You must."

"It would put you in too much danger."

James gave a harsh cold laugh.

"Put me in danger?" he said bitterly. "Only this morning you were plotting to kill me. Dandy sent you to make sure I went to the chapel, didn't he? So he could blow me up along with the King and everyone else."

"But I tried to warn you, James, didn't I?" said Roan. "I didn't want you to go, really I didn't. Don't you remember? Why do you think I said those things if I truly wanted you to go there?"

"But you didn't stop me."

"I couldn't. I like you, James, I like you a lot, but I'm scared. Scared of Dandy. I didn't want to cross him. He can be very violent, James. And I'm scared of the people who hired us to do this job. They're very powerful and very dangerous. I don't want you mixed up in this anymore."

"Yes, but I *am* mixed up in it, aren't I?" said James. "And I don't know why. And I need you to tell me."

"I don't know, honest I don't," said Roan. "You have to believe me. We were just following orders. And now that we've failed, they'll probably come after us. They don't like failure."

"That's why you have to tell me who they are so I can help," said James.

Roan put her fingertips to James's face and gave him a sad smile.

"You're very sweet, darling, but you're just a lad. What can you do?"

"I may be just a boy, but I'm all you've got now that Dandy has gone," said James. "And *you're* all that I've got. They want me dead, and maybe, just maybe, you're the only person who can stop that. Unless . . ."

"Unless what?" said Roan warily.

"Unless I just go to the police and tell them everything."

"No." Roan took hold of James with both hands now and stared deep into his eyes. "You have to promise me you won't do that, darling. It'd be the end for me."

Then she put her arms around him and kissed him on the mouth. Her skin was cool but her breath was hot. James could smell oranges and something spicy.

She put her lips to his ear.

"The code name of the operation is Snow-blind," she said. "My code name is Diamond, Dandy's is Emerald, the man we report to is Amethyst. Amethyst works for Ruby. Ruby runs the cell in Portugal. His real name is Ferreira, Martinho Ferreira."

"And who does Ferreira report to?" said James. "Who is the next in command?"

"I only know his code name—Obsidian," said Roan. "He's not based in Portugal. I'll tell you more later, darling. I've already said too much."

"Will you tell me one more thing?" said James.

"What?"

"Did you know from the start, when you first met me? Did you know I was part of the plot?"

"They've been planning this for a long time," said Roan. "When Katey, the old boys' maid, left Codrose's, they managed to get me in there. We had to be close to Windsor and the King. When we found out he was going to be coming to the school today, the date was decided."

"You haven't answered my question."

"They told me to make friends with you, that's all."

"So you've been pretending all along to like me?"

"No. I liked you as soon as I first set eyes on you, darling. There's something about you. There'll always be a special place in my heart for you."

James looked away. He understood all about the shadow war now. He pictured two people standing, talking politely to each other, while their shadows fought like demons on the wall. He was in a world of half-truths and half-lies. He didn't know who he could trust anymore, who he could believe in. Nobody was who they had seemed to be, and nobody was telling the whole truth. Not even him. He hated Merriot for putting him in this position, but no matter how hard he tried, he couldn't bring himself to hate Roan.

That night James lay in bed unable to sleep. In the morning he would report to Merriot all that Roan had told him, but his mind was racing. Too much had happened today, and not all of it made sense to him.

Snow-blind.

That's what Roan had said the operation was called, and that was what Graf von Schlick had shouted out that night in the clinic.

Schneeblind.

How did the *Graf* fit in to all this? He had seemed genuinely fearful before, so why hadn't he warned the Prince about the plot against his father? And how had he known about Snow-blind in the first place? It was a dangling loose end that made no sense to James.

Maybe Merriot would be able to explain, although James was sure that he wasn't telling him everything.

It was too much for James to try and understand. For now, he couldn't concentrate; his mind flitted madly, and one thought kept coming back to him and knocking all other thoughts out of his mind.

He had saved the King's life that morning.

In a normal world he would have been carried down the street on the shoulders of a rejoicing crowd, but instead he could tell no one. It must forever remain a secret. Merriot had placed too heavy a burden on him.

Ironically, apart from Merriot, the only other person who had even an inkling of what he had been through was Roan, and he couldn't tell her what had really happened, because he was having to lie to her and lead her into a trap.

She was just a scared girl, barely older than he was.

He wanted to run away and hide. He wanted to lash out at someone. He wanted to scream from the rooftops. He wanted to be with Roan. He wanted her to like him and trust him.

He didn't know what he wanted.

He wished that his mother and father were there to put their arms around him and tell him that everything was going to be all right.

But they couldn't save him from this mess.

No one could.

He pulled back the curtains and looked at his new watch by the light of the moon.

It was nearly eleven o'clock.

He would do what he always did in times like this.

The time for thinking was over.

It was time to act.

He got out of bed and started to dress.

CHAPTER 22—A COLD-BLOODED KILLER

James didn't knock. He didn't want to make a sound. Instead he opened the door as silently as possible and slipped inside. Roan was there, sitting at her dressing table in her nightgown, brushing her hair. She looked like she had been crying. Her eyes went wide and she drew her breath in sharply when she saw James, but then she relaxed. She opened her mouth to say something, and James shushed her.

"Get dressed," he whispered, closing the door behind him.

"Why, what is it?" said Roan. "What's the matter?"

"I lied to you," said James.

"What do you mean?" A look of wariness hardened her dark eyes, which glittered like jewels in the half-light of her room.

"Dandy's dead," James said quietly.

"No."

"I can't say that I'm sorry," said James, "but I won't let it happen to you."

Roan got up and came over to him. She looked like a different person, wild and animal-like.

"What are you talking about?" she hissed.

"I defused the bomb and Dandy came after me," said James, keeping his voice level. "A man called Dan Nevin shot him. Nevin works for the SIS. They're onto you. They know everything."

"You're lying."

"I wish I was. They wanted me to spy on you, to find out everything you know, but I can't do it."

"Dandy's dead?" Tears came into Roan's eyes. "He can't be dead. He was so full of life."

"For God's sake," said James. "Save your crying for later. For now you have to get away from here. Get dressed, bring your purse and anything you'll need for traveling, but don't bring a suitcase—they might be watching you."

"You expect me to just wander off into the night all by myself with just the clothes on my back?"

"No," said James. "I'm coming with you. I've a plan."

"You? What can you do?"

"Stop asking questions and do as you're told," James snapped. "The longer you delay the more likely I am to get cold feet. I don't like any of this. But I won't see you hang. If you don't want my help, then I'll leave you to it."

"No. I'm coming."

"Do you have your own key?"

"I've one for the back door."

"Good. When you go, leave it unlocked. I'll follow when I'm sure it's safe. Go to Beggar's Bridge. I'll meet you there as soon as I can. You need to be very careful. Make sure no one follows you. Don't go by a direct route. Keep out of sight until you're sure it's me. If I'm not there in half an hour it means that something's gone wrong; come back here and we'll try again tomorrow night."

"James, why are you doing this?"

"If you really need to ask, then I'm making a big mistake."

* * *

Ten minutes later James slipped out of the back door at Codrose's. He waited a few moments, making sure there was nobody around, and then hurried off. It was possible, of course, that Nevin, or one of his men, was watching from a darkened window, but he thought it unlikely. As far as they knew, James was safely tucked up in his bed for the night. He nevertheless decided to take a roundabout route to Windsor.

It wasn't just Nevin's team he needed to look out for, though. If any beak caught him up and about at this time of night he'd be in trouble. He had dressed in ordinary clothes, but he might still be recognized if he was stopped and challenged.

He set off through the back alleys and gardens between Common Lane and the Eton Wick Road. He knew this area all too well now and felt like he could navigate it with his eyes shut. He was filled with a mixture of fear and excitement. He was about to betray Merriot, he was about to betray his country, and he was about to help a girl who had plotted to kill him. His life would never be the same after this.

He was leaving behind everything. All the friends he had made at Eton: Pritpal and Tommy, Andrew Carlton and the boys from the Danger Society. He would never be able to come back here. He would never again see the Fourth of June Parade of Boats or take late absence, or play the Field Game—there would be no more saying lessons, no more white tickets, yellow tickets, report cards . . .

The rituals he had struggled so hard to learn, the slang, the traditions, all meant nothing now.

It was wasted time.

He stopped.

It was not too late to turn back.

He didn't have to do this. He could just let Roan fend for herself. He owed her nothing. Was she really worth throwing his life away for?

"Bond?"

James spun around. Someone had come up on him without him seeing.

It was Theo Bentinck.

"What are you doing out of house at this time of night?"

"I might ask the same of you," said James. He really couldn't be bothered with Bentinck now. He was from another world. James wanted nothing to do with the strutting little nonentity.

"I make my own rules," said Bentinck haughtily.

"I know," said James.

"Codrose allows me to do as I please," said Bentinck. "As long as I keep order in the house."

James could smell beer on the boy's breath.

"You've been in the pub," he said.

"What of it?"

"Go back to Codrose's," said James, his voice cold and hard, "and forget you ever saw me."

Bentinck grabbed James by the collar.

"I'll take you back with me, you insubordinate wretch."

James was angry. He recognized that. He was angry and confused. Maybe that was what Bentinck felt? Maybe that was what had turned him into a bully. Maybe Bentinck had some terrible problem in his life that he didn't know how to deal with and he took it out on other boys?

Right now James didn't give a fig about that. He had too much pent-up rage inside him. He wanted to hurt someone. If that someone was Bentinck, then all well and good.

James looked at his unexceptional face with its small mouth and pointed chin.

Then again, maybe Bentinck didn't have an excuse. Maybe he was just a sadist, pure and simple; someone who got pleasure out of causing pain to others. James had never understood that. He had hurt people in his time, but only ever in self-defense, and he had never enjoyed it.

This was different. Even though there was anger boiling up inside him, there was something cold-blooded about what he was about to do.

"I'm going to enjoy thrashing you," said Bentinck.

"No you're not," said James.

"Oh, yes I am," said Bentinck. "I'm going to enjoy it more than anything else in my life. I'm going to break you."

"No," said James. "What I meant was—you're not going to thrash me. I'm sure you would enjoy it, but it's not going to happen."

"Oh, isn't it?" said Bentinck.

"Not tonight," said James.

Bentinck still had a hold of James's collar; he twisted it, tightening it about James's throat. James didn't mind the pain.

"And when I've finished with you, Bond," said Bentinck, "I'll start on those two little wogs who hide behind your skirts."

"No," said James. "It's all over." And then, before Bentinck had any idea what was happening, James gave him a tight-armed jab to the gut that hammered into him with tremendous force. Bentinck groaned and doubled up in agony, still hanging on to James's collar. James stood there and waited calmly for Bentinck to regain his breath.

"You're going to regret that for the rest of your miserable little life," Bentinck said at last.

"Am I really?" said James, and he chopped Bentinck in the neck with the side of his hand. Bentinck let go and fell to his knees with a small cry, his spectacles falling to the ground. But James hadn't hurt him as much as he had hoped, because Bentinck was up in a flash and coming at him with both fists. He grabbed James in a messy hold, one hand on his jacket, the other around the back of his head, and threw him against a wall. He slammed him back a couple of times and then aimed a wild punch at his head. James ducked, and Bentinck's fist connected with the bony top of his skull. James was hit hard enough to be rocked on his feet, and there was a white flash, but Bentinck had got the worst of it. He gave a shout of pain, and James straightened up to see him clutching his right hand in his left. He had probably broken some fingers.

James's counterattack was merciless, vicious, and unrelenting. He rained a series of blows on Bentinck. To his belly and kidneys mainly, then, when he was too dazed to defend himself, James started on his face. He was careful not to risk using his fists and end up breaking some bones, as Bentinck had done. Instead he used the back and sides of his hands. And even slapped him open palmed.

James stood outside himself and coldly watched what he was doing. There was something horribly professional and methodical about it as he slowly beat Bentinck into the dirt. The older boy was sobbing and begging James to stop. But

James carried on until he could see Bentinck's face dark with blood.

He pushed him over with his foot and stepped on his throat, then pulled his foot back, ready to kick him.

"Stop, dear God, please, stop," Bentinck sobbed through broken teeth and bloody lips. "You'll kill me."

One thought flashed through James's mind.

Yes. Kill him.

And then he returned to his body, shocked and scared. Looking down at the whimpering boy at his feet. He felt sick.

"I *should* kill you," he spat angrily. "For all the misery you've inflicted on others. For all the hurt you've given. Well, no more. You hear me? No more. You're going to promise me here and now that you will never beat another boy as long as you live."

"I swear," said Bentinck. "On my mother's life. Just leave me alone."

"If I hear that you've broken your word, Bentinck," said James, "then I surely will kill you. Do you believe me?"

He knelt down and lifted Bentinck's face up, looking hard into his swollen eyes, one of which was nearly closed.

"I believe you," said Bentinck, and James could see the raw fear in his eyes.

"Go back to your room," said James, passing him his unharmed spectacles. "And don't ever tell anyone you saw me tonight. You will never breathe a word about who did this to you. Say it was a local boy, if you like, say you fell under a bus—I don't much care what story you make up. But you will never speak to anyone of this again. Is that understood?"

"Perfectly," said Bentinck.

"And just remember," said James, "Pritpal Nandra and Tommy Chong are my friends. Nobody hurts my friends."

Bentinck said nothing, and James watched him limp away.

James stood there, his chest heaving, his breath coming shallow and fast. Slowly he was engulfed by sadness, and soon there were tears rolling down his cheeks. All the fear and tension and uncertainty of the day were coming out of him. He felt terrible for what he had done to Bentinck. He knew that it wasn't right to take it all out on the boy. He was no better than a bully himself. He could have scared Bentinck without hurting him so badly. And he was unnerved by how it had felt, how in the moment of hitting the boy he had felt so calm, almost happy.

He was no better than Dandy.

He was no better than any man of violence who thought he could make the world a better place with a bomb.

In the end, Bentinck had been right: James would regret what he had done for the rest of his life.

Roan was waiting at Beggar's Bridge, which carried the Slough Road over Chalvey Brook near Upper Club. She was ducked down out of sight below on the muddy grass. Half an hour was nearly up, and she was wondering if James was still going to come.

James Bond. What a surprising boy he was. Whenever she thought she had the measure of him, he pulled something new out of the hat.

She heard the growl of a powerful engine, and a car drove up and stopped. She tensed. Ready to run if needed. She was a fast runner and had yet to meet the man who could best her.

She also had the advantage of darkness, and if necessary she would fight.

There was a gun in her purse. A Russian-made TT-33.

Then she heard a voice.

"Roan?" It was James; he was leaning over the edge of the bridge.

She smiled at him.

"Hurry up," he said. "The coast's clear at the moment."

Roan scrambled swiftly up the bank and saw a big, slightly battered-looking Bentley Blower parked in the road, its engine ticking. James was already back behind the wheel.

"You *are* joking, aren't you, darling?" she said.

"Get in," said James. "We've no time."

James Bond. Full of surprises.

"Where are we going?" she asked, climbing in beside him.

"London," said James. "I've made arrangements."

"And then what?"

"That's up to you, Roan."

PART 3—FUGITIVES

CHAPTER 23—BLOND BOMBSHELL

"James Bond. Thought I'd never see you again. I m-might have known you'd tip up on my doorstep in the m-middle of some m-mad adventure, you pirate!"

James smiled at his old friend Perry Mandeville and introduced Roan to him. Perry whistled.

"So you're the famous Roan Power," he said, giving her an appreciative look. "I heard a lot about you at Eton before they booted m-me out."

"You were at Eton?"

"Afraid so. Hasn't James told you all about m-me?"

"Not a thing."

James butted in. "Perry, the less she knows about you, the better, and the less you know about her, too."

"Ah, very m-mysterious. All par for the course with the great James Bond. You're a terror, James, an absolute m-monster! I dread to think what you're up to now. But come in off the doorstep. I've sent all the servants off to bed for the night, so we should have a bit of privacy."

The Mandevilles lived in a grand house with a classical white facade on the edge of Regent's Park in London. James let Perry go on ahead, while he held Roan back by the elbow and spoke quietly to her. "Perry's family are at their country place," he explained. "He's taking a big risk, hiding us, so don't do anything that might put him in any danger."

The drive up had been tense but uneventful. James had driven fast and had only begun to relax when they'd reached the busier and more anonymous streets of London. They had come in on the Great West Road, through Shepherd's Bush, along the Bayswater Road, past Hyde Park and Marble Arch, then up Baker Street to the Park.

All James had told Roan was that he had telephoned a friend on the off chance that he might be at home and able to help.

Inside, the house was equally grand. It was Roan's turn to whistle now as she looked around the huge marble-floored hallway.

"You live in some style, Mr. Mandeville," she said, and James hoped she wasn't going to make some comment about the unfairness of wealth and privilege.

Luckily, she said no more.

"Yes, well. I'm not here a great deal these days. I've been packed off to bonny Scotland. I think m-my folks thought that a strict Scottish regime would knock some sense into m-me and rid m-me of m-my wild ways."

"And has it?" said James.

"Not a bit of it," said Perry. "I wouldn't be here if I wasn't skiving off this week."

Five minutes later they were all three sitting laughing together in the kitchen while Perry cooked scrambled eggs. The kitchen was warm and inviting with rows of gleaming copper pots and pans hanging from the ceiling next to a gigantic iron stove.

"You've done a terrific job getting the m-motor on the road," said Perry.

"I can't take any of the credit for that," said James. "Andrew Carlton and the others fixed her up."

"So, what are you going to do with her now?"

"I'm going to give her to you," said James. "I want you to keep her out of the way for a while until you're sure the police aren't going to show up asking awkward questions. Then you're free to use her until I get back. It's the least I can do, especially as you paid for most of the work."

"It's m-my birthday in a couple of weeks," said Perry. "I'll be legally old enough to drive."

"There you are, then."

"I'll look after her with m-my life," said Perry, scraping the scrambled eggs onto slices of toast. "But when you say, 'until I get back,' get back from *where*, exactly?"

"I have to get Roan out of the country as quickly as possible," said James. "I have no idea when our disappearance from Eton will be discovered and how quickly they'll realize that Roan and I are together, but there's every possibility that the police will be alerted tonight."

Perry glanced at the kitchen clock.

"There's a boat train that leaves Charing Cross at four o'clock for Dover," he said.

James looked at Roan. She nodded.

Perry crossed the room to the door leading back upstairs.

"I've got something for you," he said as he went out.

Roan put her hand on James's.

"Thank you," she said.

"I assume you have a passport?" said James.

"I've three," said Roan. "One in the name of Roan Power, one I had forged in Dublin in the name of Violet Mackintosh, and one I was given by Amethyst in Lisbon. It's an English passport in the name of Isabel Downing. But the photograph in it is pretty grim. I look like a hag."

"Use that one," said James. "I'll have to get used to calling you Isabel for the time being, until we're safely away."

"And what shall I call you?"

"I'm traveling on the only passport I own. I feel inadequate only having the one. You'll just have to call me Bond. James Bond."

Perry returned a few minutes later and sat back down at the table with them.

"I've packed a bag with some of m-my old clothes," he said, "and another one for you, Roan. Just some ancient bits of m-my m-mother's that I don't think she'll m-miss. They're going to look pretty ghastly on you, I'm afraid. You'll want to bury them in a large hole at the earliest opportunity. M-maybe you can buy yourself something in France? The latest Parisian fashions!"

"Maybe I'll do that," said Roan.

"And I don't suppose either of you have any m-money."

"I've a few pounds," said James, while Roan shrugged.

"It's shillings with me," she said. "They don't exactly pay their maids a fortune at Eton, I can tell you for nothing."

"I thought that m-might be the case," said Perry, dropping a brown envelope on the table. "There's some traveling funds for you in there."

"Perry, I can't," said James. "You've done more than enough already."

"You won't get far on a few pounds, James," said Perry. "There's fifty in there. Think of it as a loan. I'll take the Bentley as security. If I never see m-my m-money again, I'll keep the m-motor. Which will be a pretty decent bargain."

"It's a deal," said James. "But where on earth did you get your hands on fifty pounds in cash?"

"Why do you think I'm down here, James? I wouldn't m-miss Ascot for anything. I had a surefire tip on the gee-gees that came good. There's no racing in Scotland. They're a m-miserable bunch. I'd rather you had the m-money, as a m-matter of fact—I'd only gamble it away again."

They were too excited to sleep, and the three of them stayed in the kitchen, drinking coffee, laughing, and chatting as if the world outside the room had ceased to exist and time had stopped.

For this one brief magical moment, as Perry told a string of funny stories about his exploits over the past six months, James could forget about his troubles. He recalled evenings spent with Perry in the past, lounging on the rooftops of Eton, talking about . . . ?

What had they talked about?

Not anything serious or important, that was for sure. They had just been boys enjoying each other's company. Could James ever go back to such an uncomplicated time?

He wondered if this was what grown-up life was like— brief moments of simple pleasure, idle chatter, and good company, separated by long periods of stress and fear and tangled emotions.

Eventually Roan stood up and stretched.

"I think I should go and get ready," she said. "I'll change into some of your ma's rags and fix myself up."

Perry went to show her where everything was, and James laid his head in his arms on the table.

He closed his eyes and in seconds was asleep.

He had no idea how long he slept before Perry shook him awake.

"Are you bearing up, old thing?" his friend asked.

"I'll do," said James, rubbing his temples.

Perry leaned against the warm stove.

"You quite sure you know what you're doing?" he said.

"Of course I'm not," said James. "I know this is madness, Perry. One day I'll tell you all about it. But for now it's safest if I keep my mouth shut."

"She's very pretty," said Perry. "A lot of m-men have been driven m-mad by pretty women. I sense she's leading you into something."

"I don't know who's leading whom," said James.

"Looks like you and I are both in the same boat now," said Perry. "There'll be no going back to Eton for you, after this."

"No," said James. "How is Fettes?"

"Cold and Scottish."

"Am I a fool, Perry?" said James.

"You?" Perry thought about it. "Not a fool, James, a m-madman."

They laughed, and then Perry gave James a concerned look. "Be careful," he said.

"I've never been careful in my life," said James. "And I'm not about to start now."

* * *

James wrote a short letter to his Aunt Charmian, telling her that he was all right and not to worry about him, but not telling her where he was going or who he was with. He finished by saying he would write to her again as soon as he could. He sealed the letter and gave it to Perry to post when they had gone. He hated doing this to her, but there was no other way.

He went upstairs and changed into an old suit of Perry's and a hat of his father's. At a distance he might just pass for a young man about town, but close up he was all too clearly just a schoolboy. Then he picked up the suitcase and went downstairs to the hallway, where Roan was already waiting for him.

For a second James didn't recognize her and thought she might be one of Mrs. Mandeville's friends. When he realized it was her, he laughed. She was wearing a smart navy blue dress with a traveling coat and hat, a pair of severe glasses, and her hair was blond.

"Is that a wig?" he said.

"Do you like it?" said Roan. "It was given me by Amethyst. In case I ever needed a disguise."

"You look strange," said James. "It'll take some getting used to. The spectacles as well."

"They're just plain glass," she said, "but they do make me look plain. I'd hate to be plain, James. I want to stay young and pretty all my life."

Perry came in the front door.

"There's a taxi waiting around the corner," he said. "I thought it best if the cabbie didn't know which house you came out from."

"Well done," said James, and he embraced his friend quickly. As he broke away, Perry slipped something into his pocket.

"What's that?" said James.

"M-my passport."

"What do you mean?"

"It's pretty obvious that something serious is going on, James. We've shared some scrapes together; I only wish I could come along with you on this one. But I think if I get into any m-more trouble, m-my old m-man will disown m-me and cut m-me off, and I should end up begging on the streets."

"I can't take your passport, Perry."

"Why ever not? I won't be needing it until the holidays. You can post it back to m-me from France. No one will ever know."

"But, Perry . . ."

"They m-might be watching the ports, James. Checking names. Looking out for runaway boys. Even if they aren't, you don't want it on record that you, James Bond, went through Dover this m-morning. Cover your tracks, old thing."

"But I look nothing like you," said James. "They'll see the picture."

"The fellow in the photograph looks nothing like m-me," said Perry. "I've had it since I was twelve, when I was sent away to stay with an aunt in Kenya one summer. I dare say you've changed a bit since you were twelve. The only thing you'll have to re-m-member is to act like you're sixteen, going on seventeen, which shouldn't be too m-much of a stretch for you. Now go, before I change m-my m-mind and call the police."

* * *

They got to Charing Cross in no time and sat apart on the train to Dover. Everything had appeared quite normal at the station, but they wanted to take no chances and arranged not to speak again until they were safely on the ferry.

As the train rattled through the dreary gray suburbs of south London and out into the open Kent countryside, James pretended to read a newspaper, but it might have been written in Greek for all it meant to him. For her part, Roan stared out the window, lost in thought.

When they were nearing Dover, James took out Perry's passport and grinned at how daft Perry had looked at twelve. He soon sobered up, however, as he remembered that this picture was now supposed to be him. He tried to adopt the foolish expression of the young Perry Mandeville and decided in the end not to bother, as it might just attract more attention to him.

As it was, having checked the name, the officer on duty at Dover barely glanced at the passport before waving James through to the ferry. He waited anxiously at the top of the gangplank until he was sure that Roan was safely on board, and went to get himself some breakfast.

They had made it this far without a problem, which meant that nobody knew yet that they had left Eton.

By the time they arrived in France, though, their disappearance would surely have been discovered. They would have to plan their next move carefully.

After a gloomy start, the day turned fine and sunny. The Channel, which could be unpleasantly choppy, was flat as a millpond, and the ferry steamed smoothly ahead. James strolled around the deck to stretch his legs, and once he had spotted Roan, who was sitting reading a book in the fresh air at the stern, he did one more circuit to check that there was no possibility of anyone watching them.

When he returned, Roan was at the rail, as they had arranged.

He strolled casually over to the spot next to her and stood watching the wake as it foamed and frothed behind them.

Roan had put on a pair of sunglasses and held her blond wig in place with a scarf.

"So far, so good," she said without looking at James.

"It might be harder in France," said James.

"We'll be all right," said Roan. "Our luck's held this far, but let's not tempt it. After we've talked we'd better split up again and meet at the railway station in Calais."

"And then what?" said James.

"Maybe Paris," said Roan. "But you don't need to come with me, James. Once I'm away."

"I want to come with you."

"What would you do in Paris, darling? That fifty pounds won't last forever."

"What are *you* going to do?" said James.

"I haven't thought much beyond getting away," said Roan, "but I can find work anywhere."

"You mustn't try and contact your people," said James. "I don't want you going back to your old ways. Forget about going to them for help. I'd hate to have to stop you from blowing anyone else up."

"Don't worry, darling, I've learned my lesson," said Roan. "Besides, my useful days as an agent are over. After what's happened, their only thought will be to get hold of me and keep me quiet, for good. They'll kill me sooner than have me falling into the hands of your government."

"That's just great," said James. "We're on the run not only from the British authorities but also the Soviet secret service. I'd rate our chances of survival at just about zero."

"The saints are watching over us, darling, don't you worry. Now, are you sure there's nobody in Europe you know who could help us? You don't have any more useful pals like Perry M-Mandeville tucked away anywhere?"

"There is someone," said James. "It's a long shot, but it's the best I can come up with."

"Who is this someone?"

"A man I met in Austria. He said that if I ever needed help I could go to him."

"Does he have a name?"

"Hannes Oberhauser. He's a mountain guide. We could stay with him for a while. We'd be well off the beaten track."

"The mountains, you say?"

"Yes, in the Tyrol, about as far away from all this as you can get."

"Whereabouts in the Tyrol?"

"Near a little town called Kitzbühel."

Roan thought about this for a while, watching a flock of noisy seagulls as they wheeled and dived behind the ferry. Finally she touched his hand on the rail, just for a second.

"Let's do it," she said, and walked away.

James spent a few tense minutes at the French passport control, where the *douanier* went through an elaborate rigmarole of checking pieces of paper and copying down details from James's passport, all the while looking from his notes to James with watery eyes. He didn't spot that the photograph was of someone completely different, though, and at last he stubbed out the cigarette that had been hanging from his lower lip and went into a wild flurry of stamping before passing the passport back to James. James was ahead of Roan, and once he had gone through he couldn't resist waiting for her, even though their arrangement was not to meet until they got to the station. He sat on a bench in a small porch at the end of the customs shed and tried to look like a relaxed young man of the world enjoying a little peace and quiet, rather than an anxious boy waiting to help an enemy spy on the run.

At last, there she was. She walked toward him swinging her handbag, and there was a skip in her step. She was smiling broadly, and as she passed James she gave a little wink before slipping on her sunglasses. She was humming a jolly tune, and James realized it was "La Marseillaise."

He watched her as she went outside and was swallowed up by the brightness of the sun.

Perry's voice sounded in the back of his mind with words

of warning, but he shut it out. He had chosen this adventure and was going to go through with it whatever happened.

He stood up and carried his suitcase out into the warm French air.

When he arrived at the railway station he saw Roan waiting in a queue at the ticket office. He had given her some of the money, and the plan was to separately buy two through tickets to Kitzbühel.

James held back and scanned the station, keeping one eye on Roan. Although they had come this far safely, it was always possible that someone might be watching them.

He had become quite skillful at looking out for suspicious activity in the past few weeks. He was reasonably confident that if anyone *was* hanging around who shouldn't be there, he would be able to spot them.

He did two or three sweeps of the area, then strolled over to the newsstand and bought a map of Europe and a French newspaper, which he pretended to read. Then he moved to the toilets and looked inside. When he came out he walked slowly around the edge of the concourse and looked carefully at the men and women in the cafe and at the flower stall.

He could see nothing out of the ordinary and was just going to join the queue for tickets, when he caught sight of someone he hadn't noticed before.

He couldn't put his finger on it, but there was something wrong about this person. There was an alertness, a watchfulness. He was standing in the gloom beneath the station clock, keeping close to the wall. Like James he had a newspaper, and like James he wasn't really reading it.

James edged closer, keeping among the other travelers.

He was to the man's side and out of his line of sight unless he turned his head, so he was able to get close enough to properly study his face. He had the tough, confident look of a policeman or a soldier about him. He was definitely on the lookout for something; his eyes were darting around the station concourse.

As James watched, the man nodded. A tiny, almost invisible jerk of his head. James followed his line of sight, and there stood a familiar figure in gray.

Colonel Sedova. Babushka.

She was here. Skulking over by the newsstand.

James was already on the move, back around the way he had come, away from the man under the clock and on the opposite side of the concourse to Sedova. He saw a noisy and excited group of young priests crossing toward the ticket counters, and he joined them, keeping his head down.

An old woman in a floppy hat walked away from the queue, clutching her ticket, and Roan stepped up to the counter.

As she opened her mouth to speak, James grabbed her by the elbow.

"Don't say anything," he hissed, and dragged her away. He could feel her tense, but she made no sound and didn't resist. James rushed her quickly toward the platforms.

"Just keep moving," he said, and he glanced across at the destination board. The train waiting on platform three was heading for Paris and was leaving in five minutes.

"This way," he said, pulling Roan again toward the platforms.

"I don't have a ticket," she protested. "Are you sure that's our train?"

"Don't worry about tickets," said James, pulling her faster.

"What's going on, James?"

"There's someone on our tail."

"Who?" Roan struggled in his grip.

"Don't look around," he said as they hurried along the platform. The last few passengers were climbing aboard, and the train was shrouded in clouds of steam as the engine boiled up, ready to be off. There were shouts from the porters.

"*En voiture!*"

James wrenched a door open and shoved Roan up the steps.

He glanced back down the platform. Babushka and the man with the newspaper were barging their way past people at the far end. A whistle blew. The train gave a metallic groan, as if straining to be under way.

James hesitated for a moment then swung up onto the train after Roan. He pulled the window down and leaned out. Their pursuers were clambering up the steps about four carriages behind them. If they had left it a moment longer they would have missed the train.

Good.

"James, are you sure this is our train?" asked Roan, who was looking angry and confused.

"It doesn't matter," said James. "Follow me."

He crossed the compartment to the corridor at the other side. A fat man was struggling along with a bulging suitcase. James opened the window in the door and looked down at the tracks.

"As soon as the train starts to move, we're getting off," he said. "Can you do that?"

"Sure I can," said Roan, and she gave him a wry smile. "Full of tricks, aren't you, Mr. Bond?"

There was a jolt and the train shunted forward, the carriage shaking, the wheels squealing. James looked at Roan.

"Ready?"

"After you?"

James swung the door open, threw down his suitcase, and dropped after it onto the tracks. He looked back at the train. It was picking up speed. For one chilly moment he thought Roan might not follow him, but then her suitcase tumbled out, and a moment later there she was, jumping lightly down. He ran to her and caught her as she stumbled, then they retrieved their luggage and hurried across the tracks to where a second train stood waiting at the opposite platform. They opened a door and chucked their bags on board before hauling themselves up and scrambling to their feet. They crossed the carriage and got out the other side.

"Keep walking," said James. "We're not going to risk taking a train. Let's just get well away from here. Once we know we're safe we'll plan our next step."

They walked briskly down the length of the platform and went back through the station and out onto the streets.

"That was too close," said James. "We mustn't forget that we'll have to be careful every step of the way."

They made their way to the bus station and hopped on a bus that seemed to be going in roughly the right direction. Once they were clear of Calais and in open countryside, they got off at a deserted stop.

They stood there and watched the bus trundle away down

the road. Soon they were all alone. Skylarks darted in the blue sky. Flat green fields of potato and turnips spread out all around them.

"Now what?" said Roan.

"We walk," said James, and he looped his arm in hers. He glanced at Roan. She looked glum.

"Cheer up," he said. "We made it. We got away."

"But now what?"

"We've the whole of France spread out before us," said James. "The whole of Europe, the world. We needn't stop in Kitzbühel; we can just keep on traveling forever if we want. We're free, Roan. No more school. No more adults telling us what to do. No more report cards or Latin construes, no more Pop, no more Library, no more beatings. Just you and I together on the road."

Roan laughed. James struck up "La Marseillaise," which she had been humming earlier, and she joined in. Arm in arm they marched down the road, singing at the top of their voices.

They bought some bread and cheese in a village and ate lunch on top of a small hill looking out across the countryside.

"I could almost be back home," said Roan. "Reminds me of Ireland."

"Where did you grow up?" James asked.

"I was born in Holycross, in County Tipperary, in the west. It's the sort of tiny place that if you sneeze, the whole town knows about it the next day. All I ever thought about was getting out of there. My dad was a drayman, delivering beer to all the pubs in the area with his big old horse and cart. There were five brothers and six sisters. Two of me sisters died young, and one of me brothers. The rest of us, we never got on that well with one another, if you want to know the truth. We were always fighting for attention. But I did love me eldest brother, Johnnie. He was like a grown man to me. He always seemed so tall and handsome, and he sheltered me from being bullied by the other kids. When he was old enough he went off to Limerick to look for work, though. He joined a printer's, but when the civil war broke out he was caught up in the siege of 1922. The government troops thought he was an anti-treaty IRA man and shot him. He wasn't fighting for anyone; he just happened to be in the wrong place at the wrong time. God, I still miss him. I was only six years old. I was so miserable at home after that."

"So what happened?" said James. "How did you end up at Eton?"

"That was all down to Dandy," said Roan. "My life changed when he turned up in Holycross one day, on the run from the police. He hid out in an old barn and I used to take him food. I was just sixteen and he was twenty-five. Sure and he reminded me powerful of my dead brother, Johnnie."

"Why was he on the run?" James asked.

"He was a rebel," said Roan, "and he was wild. He was a red, more of an anarchist than a Communist. He'd already blown up a rich man's house in Belfast. He reckoned the IRA had it all wrong, reckoned they should be fighting for the poor against the rich. That was the real struggle. He filled my head with ideas and my heart with passion. In the end I ran away with him. We wound up in Dublin, and we met all sorts there. Communists, playwrights, criminals, IRA men—what a time we had. We planned to blow up the parliament, but someone ratted on us and we had to leave Ireland in a hurry. We went to Spain, and then to Portugal. Once we were there we fell in completely with a group of Reds. We went to secret meetings, we studied books and pamphlets, we learned how the world really turns. Then one day Amethyst appeared on the scene. He'd heard all about us. He worked for a top-secret Communist cell and told us how they were planning something spectacular, something that would really make a difference."

"Operation Snow-blind?" said James.

"Yes. It was so hush-hush we weren't allowed to discuss it with anyone. Amethyst and Ruby trained us, and then I was sent over to Eton in January."

James was silent for a long while. He wondered, not for the first time, what he had got himself into.

"I presume you changed your names," he said at last. "You and Dandy."

"We might have done."

"The SIS knew nothing about you. What was Dandy really called?"

"Well, it can't harm him now he's dead, I suppose. His real name was Sean Cullinan."

"And yours?"

"Ah, now. That's for me to know and you to find out."

"Don't you think, Roan," said James, trying not to lose his temper, "that after all I've done for you, you owe me a little something in return."

Roan kissed him.

"I'm like a character in a fairy story, aren't I, darling?" she said. "Only when you know my real name will you be able to defeat me."

"I don't want to defeat you," James snapped angrily. "I only want to know who you really are, Roan . . . or whatever you're called."

"Don't be cross, darling," said Roan. "I told you I was a witch."

Before James could say anything else, Roan had picked up her bag and was marching down the hill toward the road.

CHAPTER 25—FALLEN AMONG FRIENDS

James was rattling along the Inn valley on the same train that he had arrived in Kitzbühel aboard all those weeks ago. Only this time he had Roan with him and he was on the run. They had been traveling for days, southeast to Amiens from Calais, then on through Picardy to Reims, then down to Nancy. They had crossed into Switzerland near Basel, and from there it was a straight run to Kitzbühel. They had traveled by train and bus and foot. Sometimes they had hitched rides with farmers, riding in battered old lorries or on the back of horse-drawn carts. They had even bought bicycles and cycled part of the way. Some nights they had slept in fields under the stars; other nights they had spent in farmhouses. Occasionally they had stayed in cheap hotels, and one special night, in Reims, on Roan's nineteenth birthday, they had stayed in a smart hotel and had an expensive meal. They had bought knapsacks and French clothes and felt at home on the road. It had been like the most glorious holiday James had ever spent, because there was no end to it.

Except that every day there was a little less money in the brown envelope, and they knew that sooner or later the real world would catch up with them.

The scenery was very different compared to James's last sight of it. There was still snow on the very highest peaks, but down in the valleys the grass was bright green, there were flowers everywhere, and the trees were in full leaf. The countryside was bursting with fresh life, taking advantage of the warm sunny conditions before the cold returned. Longhaired cows stood in the meadows, birds sang from the rooftops, and everywhere men and women in Tyrolean dress went cheerfully about their business.

James's skin was tanned a deep nut brown from being in the sun all day. He was lean and fit and felt comfortable in his worn and dusty clothing. All the belongings he had in the world were fitted into his knapsack, but that was fine. What more did he need?

He was no longer a schoolboy; he had grown into a young man. He sat next to Roan, who was gazing out the window at the passing scenery. Whenever they traveled on a train or bus they were especially careful and rarely spoke to each other, in case anyone heard their foreign voices and wondered who exactly this young couple was.

As they got closer to their destination, James became more and more nervous. He had been at his most carefree in the country lanes of France, striding along in the sunshine, chatting to Roan. Now there was a full stop approaching. They had always had their sights set on Kitzbühel but had never really discussed what would happen once they got there.

There was something else worrying him, too. A niggling doubt that he had pushed to the back of his mind. Now that he was getting closer to where it had all begun, though, he couldn't help but brood over it.

He kept coming back to that strange night in the clinic

when he had been woken by Graf von Schlick's shouts from his private room.

"*They are going to kill cousin Jürgen . . .*"

It was one of the things that had alerted James to Dandy's plan.

But the more he thought about it, the less sense it made.

Von Schlick had been at the Langton-Herrings' party in Windsor. He had spoken to the Prince of Wales. Yet when James had asked him about that night in the clinic, he had denied all knowledge of it. That was perhaps understandable—the man had been delirious and he might have forgotten all about it. But why, then, had he claimed that he didn't have a cousin George? It was entirely possible, of course, that he didn't want a nosy schoolboy talking about it. But if he *had* known about a plot to kill King George, then why had he not said anything to the Prince?

Why had the King not been warned?

One possibility was that, although they knew about a plot, they didn't know the details.

But surely the SIS would have been informed, wouldn't they?

James knew all too well that on the morning of the Fourth of June he seemed to be the only person who was aware of what was going on. Merriot, Nevin, and the others had had no idea about the plot, even though it was being carried out right under their noses.

Another possibility was that the *Graf* had been simply rambling under the influence of morphine that night. He really knew nothing about any plot, and James had made a false link.

No. He had definitely shouted out "*Schneeblind*"—"Snow-blind," the name of Roan and Dandy's plot.

James had quizzed Roan about this, but she had been vague. She knew nothing about the *Graf*. Her contacts had all been in Lisbon. She had no idea how this minor member of the Austrian aristocracy could have heard about the plot. But then Roan had been vague about a lot of things. Despite his gentle probing, she had not really told him anything more of import about the plot and the characters involved, beyond giving a name to Amethyst—Vladimir Wrangel.

In the end, James had given up asking. In truth he didn't really want to know any more. He wanted to put all that behind him. He had saved the King and that was enough. Snow-blind, Amethyst, the *Graf*, they were all part of his old life.

He was just telling himself to stop worrying when they pulled out of Jenbach station and a man entered their compartment hefting a bulky rucksack with a climbing rope wrapped around it. He looked to be in his twenties, with the firm build of a soldier. He was dressed for hiking in the mountains with long socks, stout boots, a hunting jacket, and a soft felt hat. There was something unmistakably English about him, and James watched him out of the corner of his eye.

James had bought an English newspaper in Switzerland and had found nothing about either him or Roan in it, but that did not mean that his disappearance hadn't been noted. He glanced at Roan, a practiced look that told her to be wary.

As the man reached up to put his backpack in the luggage rack, his jacket flapped open and James caught sight of something that caused the breath to catch in his lungs.

"*Kommen Sie mit, lassen Sie uns erhalten Frischluft schnuppern*," he said to Roan. She couldn't understand any German, but as he stood up and smiled at her, she quickly got the message and obediently followed him out of the compartment into the corridor.

"What did you say?" she said once they were out of earshot.

"I said let's take some air."

"You could pass for a real German, you know."

"That was the point," said James. "I don't know who that man is that just got on, but he has an Enfield Number Two Mark One British service revolver in a shoulder holster."

Roan blanched. "Are you joking?"

"I wish I was."

"Do you think he's on to us?" Roan looked nervously back toward their compartment.

"I don't know," said James. "It's a pretty clumsy approach if he is, but I don't aim to stick around and find out. We'll have to get off at the next station and make our own way from there."

"And we were so close," said Roan wearily. "I was just beginning to let myself think we might make it in one piece."

"We'll get there," said James, and he put a reassuring hand on her arm. "Now let's not draw any attention to ourselves."

They sat back in their seats until the train stopped in Wörgl, then took their bags and got off.

James was relieved to see that the man didn't follow them.

They were still about twenty miles from Kitzbühel, so they decided in the end to take a taxi the rest of the way. It was an extravagance, but they had been careful with their money and they were bone tired from traveling. All they wanted to do now was reach journey's end.

As they drove, Roan looked out the window.

"I thought we were going to see some snow," she said. "I love the snow when it's fresh on the ground, so clean and pure and white. What use is a mountain without snow? It's just a big ugly lump of rock."

"There's no snow here," said James. "Not in the summer. These mountains aren't high enough."

"Well, the least you could have done was to arrange some for me."

James asked the driver to drop them off on the outskirts of town, below the Oberhausers' chalet. He wanted to walk the last part of the way and arrive on foot. He told himself that he didn't want the driver to know exactly where they were going, but he also needed a little time to think.

He had always assumed that Hannes Oberhauser would welcome them with open arms. But what if he was wrong? What if he had read too much into Oberhauser's offer? What if Hannes was merely being polite? Mouthing the words that everyone used to a guest as a matter of course? "Oh, yes, come back any time you like—you'll always be welcome here. . . ."

Well, there was no turning back now.

The light was fading from the sky, and an indigo glow had descended on the valley. They could hear the *clonk-clonk* of cowbells and a stream chattering nearby. There were two tents pitched in the apple orchard, and up behind them the dark wood of the chalet looked almost black. James felt a nervous cramp grip his stomach.

He hesitated and looked back across the valley toward Kitzbühel.

"Do you want me to wait here?" said Roan. "Just in case you've made a mistake. If you don't call me in ten minutes, I'll make myself scarce."

"Will you be all right?"

"Don't you go worrying your pretty little head about me, James Bond. I can look after myself."

"Thank you," said James.

"Don't be daft," said Roan. "It's me that should be thanking you. Whatever happens, I'm glad I spent this time with you. I can tell you, it's far better to be free than stuck in some godforsaken British prison."

She hugged him quickly then pushed him away. "Go on with you," she said. "Go and see your man."

James walked up to the chalet, his throat dry, and pulled the twist of rope hanging by the door.

Inside, the bell rattled, and a moment later the door opened.

As soon as James saw Hannes Oberhauser he knew that everything was going to be all right. All his doubts and fears and worries drained away. He felt like a boy again. A boy coming home.

"James?" said Hannes, a frown creasing his tanned friendly face. "What are you doing here? You look troubled. Is everything all right?"

James bowed his head and fought to keep tears away.

"It is now," he said.

Half an hour later, James was helping Hannes put the cows into the barn for the night. The big shaggy animals moved slowly, grunting and belching as they jostled for space.

James had told Hannes a version of the truth. A version that left out some of the major details, but that wasn't a lie in itself. He had told a story of falling in love and running away from school.

Hannes had been gentle and understanding, not pushing James, letting him explain himself at his own speed, but he was also firm.

"I know some of what you have been through in the last year," he said. "I understand how hard it must have been for you. It was much for a boy to carry on his shoulders. I understand how you would want to escape. But you are still young, James. The girl is old enough to do whatever she pleases. You are just a boy."

"When the time is right I shall go back," James said. "But for now I need to hide away from the world."

Hannes smiled.

"I like you a great deal, James," he said. "I will be happy to look after you, but I must tell your aunt."

"Not yet," said James. "In time."

"She will be very worried."

"I sent her a letter from France," said James. "I'll write to her again and let her know I'm safe and well and in good hands."

James had indeed sent Charmian a letter, but he had put it inside an envelope addressed to Perry for him to post in London or Scotland so that nobody would know where James really was. He would do the same again now that he was in Kitzbühel.

"I just need a little time to get some things straightened out in my mind," he said. "I'd rather nobody knew where I was just now."

"You have done nothing wrong, James?"

"No."

"And the girl?"

It was then that James told the only real lie. He told Hannes that Roan was on the run, not from the Special Intelligence Service but from the police.

"She was caught stealing something," he said. "I don't want her to get into trouble."

Hannes chuckled quietly.

"It is an old story often told," he said. "About a boy who throws his life to the wind over a girl."

"I'm sure I'm being a damned fool," said James.

"It is best to make your mistakes when you are young," said Hannes. "And you can still learn. We should all be damned fools before we grow too old. That is what youth is for. But you have made your life difficult, James."

"I know," James said. "But now that I am here, I'm hoping to make it a good deal less complicated."

Hannes smiled sadly at him. "You can run away from school, James, you can run away from the police, but you cannot run away from yourself. Sooner or later the world will catch up with you."

"I know," said James, "and when it does I want to be ready for it."

* * *

As it turned out, James and Roan were not the only guests staying at the chalet. The Oberhausers made a little extra money looking after campers who stayed on their land. Helga had cooked a big pot of spicy goulash, with potatoes and fresh greens, and the pot was being swiftly emptied by the hungry guests around the dining table, who were mopping the juices up with thick chunks of bread.

James looked around the table. Roan was gabbling away and charming everyone. When she turned on the full power of her personality she was like a bright burning star, and like a moth to a flame, you couldn't help but be attracted to her. Next to her sat a middle-aged Englishman called Mike Nicholson. He was an artist who was walking in the Alps, sketching the mountains and the flowers and plants that grew on them. James didn't worry about him knowing anything, as he had been traveling abroad since the springtime and seemed to have had little contact with anyone back home. He was a short, round fellow with a neat black beard and spectacles. At first James had thought he was a little dour and miserable, but he soon discovered that he had a wry sense of humor and was good company. The two other campers, Luca and Bernard, were enjoying a climbing holiday together before starting at the University of Geneva in the autumn. They were keen mountaineers, and when James had told them that he had done a little climbing when he was younger, they had offered to take him out with them one day.

The room was full of laughter and warmth and good cheer. The food was plentiful, the beer was flowing, and the conversation was jolly. James had a strong sense that he had fallen among friends.

Roan looked at him and smiled.

He felt at last that he should be able to relax . . . but he couldn't. What if there were hidden dangers here and he just couldn't see them?

What if he were blind?

Snow-blind.

CHAPTER 26—THE STINK OF DEATH

"I'm bored, darling. Let's go for a walk." Roan was sitting out on the veranda in a hanging chair, swinging herself backward and forward with one foot, while keeping the other curled up underneath her.

"That suits me fine," said James. He couldn't remember a time like this since starting at Eton. A time when there had been nothing to worry about. He couldn't remember ever being so untroubled, but he could also never remember feeling so empty. They had been here for three weeks, but it felt like three years.

This afternoon the emptiness had seemed more complete than ever, and he had drifted into a dark and gloomy mood. He had to admit that he, too, was bored. The difficulty, the fear and tension and exhilaration of getting here hadn't prepared him for this easy life. He felt a sudden bitter pang of regret that flared up into anger. He directed the anger at Roan.

It was her fault.

She had brought him here.

No. Don't think those thoughts, James. They won't lead anywhere useful.

Face facts. It was all his own doing. He had chosen this path. As usual he had blundered into something without fully thinking through the consequences, and now he was stuck here. In the meantime, going for a walk seemed as good an idea as any. Physical exercise had always been his way of shaking off the dark and inward-looking thoughts that attacked him when his defenses were lowered.

He got up, stretched, and stepped off the deck into the sunlight. The view across the valley was clear, and all the sounds of the countryside traveled for miles on the still air.

Cowbells.

In the right mood he found them charming; in his present mood he found them ridiculous and irritating.

"Come along, then, if you're coming," he said to Roan, who was still lounging lazily in the chair.

"I was sort of hoping you'd talk me out of it," she said with a sly smile, "or suggest something more exciting to do."

What else was there to do? Since arriving they had been busy, swimming in the Schwarzsee or cycling along the valleys, getting to know all the little farms and villages. Twice they went to visit the ancient white-walled fortress in the center of Kufstein, near the German border, where every day at twelve a great organ in one of its towers played a short concert as a memorial to those who had died in the Great War; the sound echoed for miles down the valleys. There always seemed to be something happening somewhere—a festival, or a wedding, or a party, with music and dancing. Sometimes James would help out around the farm, chopping wood or digging in the vegetable patches. The children had shown him how to milk a cow, and he'd watched Helga making cheese in the dairy. Then of course there were the mountains. They had walked the lower slopes, they had ridden up in the cable car and hiked across the peaks, admiring the spectacular views.

A few times James had been climbing on the Wilder Kaiser with Hannes and the students while Roan went shopping or sketching with Mike Nicholson, who seemed to have taken quite a shine to her. But James was living in a bubble. When he had first met Roan she had accused him of not living in the real world. Well, this was surely more unreal than his life at Eton. He only had to look at the mountains and hear the cowbells to know that he wasn't at home. It was as if he had stepped into another boy's body. Now he had everything he had always dreamed of. He had safety, a family, a girl on his arm. . . .

No matter how he looked at it, though, there was no getting around the fact that he was bored.

Had he really been fooled by the cozy dream of spending the rest of his life here with Hannes and his family? Perhaps working as a farm boy, or a guide, or even a ski instructor?

"Come on, then," he said, shrugging off his gloominess. "I'll race you to the gate."

He set off at a sprint, and a moment later heard Roan hurrying along behind him. She soon caught up, and they ran side by side to the orchard gate. James vaulted over it with one spring, but Roan stuck her tongue out, opened the gate, and simply walked through.

"James Bond," she said. "You exhaust me. You've always got to be on the move, haven't you?"

"You're just lazy, Roan."

They followed the path down the mountain toward Kitzbühel.

"So, where do you want to go, then?" James asked, picking up a stick.

"You know," said Roan, "we really don't have to do this, if you'd rather do something else?"

"We're out now," said James. "It'll be a few hours till supper. We might as well make the most of it."

A cloud passed over the sun, plunging them suddenly into cool shade. Roan took James's arm and squeezed it almost in fear.

"I hate it when the sun goes in," she said. "It's like someone's died."

"Don't be so silly," said James. "It's just a cloud."

Roan grew thoughtful. She stopped walking and let go of James's arm.

"Let's go back," she said. "I've changed my mind."

"You change your mind every five minutes," said James.

Roan looked down the valley. "I wish Dandy were here," she said after a while. "He always loved the mountains."

James felt a stab of guilt. Roan never talked about Dandy. It was a subject they carefully avoided.

"He always knew what to do," she went on. "He always made his mind up fast, and once he'd made it up, he stuck to his guns. Of course, he wasn't always right. Sometimes his pigheadedness got him into trouble. But he'd know the right thing to do now."

"It's not such a big deal," said James. "Whether or not we go for a walk. But standing here talking about it is even more boring than sitting doing nothing."

"They never gave him the last rites," said Roan.

"What?"

"When they killed him. They wouldn't have had a priest. He died in sin."

"I expect God made up his mind about Dandy a long time ago," said James.

Roan gave James a fierce, angry look, and he realized he had said the wrong thing. Roan's smile had faded. Her dark eyes looked smoky and troubled.

"Do you not care anything for him?" she said.

"It's not like that," said James. "I don't know what I think about him. He tried to kill me, remember?"

Roan was silent for a while, her chest rising and falling with her breathing. At last her smile returned, or something like a smile.

"Come on," she said. "Let's get moving."

She stalked off, not bothering to look back to check whether James was following. He shook his head and then ran to catch up with her.

"So, where are we going?" he said.

"Let's walk to that little chapel above St. Johann."

"That's miles," said James.

"Is it too far for your little legs?" said Roan scornfully.

"No," said James. "I was thinking of you."

"Well, don't bother, James Bond. I can look after myself, thank you very much."

So saying, she ran ahead of him with a laugh, and he chased after her.

They joined the road out of Kitzbühel and crossed over the Kitzbühler Ache by a bridge on the edge of town. On the other side of the river there was a path leading around the lower slopes of the Kitzbühler Horn that was more pleasant than walking along the road. They walked briskly and purposefully. At first Roan seemed to have got all her old fire back, and she chatted away nineteen to the dozen, jumping from one subject to the next as quick as thought. She barely left any spaces for James to add anything of his own to the conversation, and he got the impression that she was gabbling away to avoid any silences. The subjects she chose were of no importance. She talked about the flowers—Mike Nicholson had taught her many of the names. She talked about Mike, and did a funny impersonation of him. She talked about the cows, and about her shoes, about fashion, the clothes the local girls wore. She talked about her childhood in Ireland, about films she had enjoyed, about the music she liked to dance to, but slowly, as they walked on, her chatter slowed. She was running out of things to say.

By the time they finally spotted the chapel, they had been walking for nearly two hours, and it was another half an hour before they got there. By then Roan had fallen into an edgy silence. James wondered if she was still thinking about Dandy. He tried to talk to her and lift her mood, but she had become sullen and was chewing her ragged nails. Maybe she was just tired out by the long walk. Whatever was on her mind, though, she wasn't telling.

The little chapel stood alone next to a small patch of woodland on the northern slopes of the Kitzbühler Horn. Like most other buildings it was wooden and had a steep sloping roof.

"Race you to the door?" said James, in a last effort to snap her out of her funk, but Roan stopped walking and put a hand on his arm. Then she kissed him.

"What was that for?" said James.

"For nothing," said Roan. "For everything."

"Why do girls never make sense?" said James.

"We make perfect sense," said Roan. "It's just that boys don't always understand us."

"If you say so," said James.

Roan kissed him again and held him tightly in her arms. "James," she said quietly into his ear.

"What?"

"I know you helped me because you feel something for me."

"Yes."

"But did you also help me because maybe you believe a little bit of what I believe in?"

James didn't know what to say, and hesitated too long before replying.

Roan sighed and walked briskly away toward the church. James ran after her.

"I'm sorry," he said, when he caught up.

"No," said Roan. "It's me who should be sorry." And James saw that there were tears in her eyes.

"Well, now we're here, what do we do?" said James, trying to change the subject. "I must confess I've never been that interested in nosing around old churches."

"It doesn't matter," said Roan sadly. "Nothing matters anymore."

"I really don't understand what you're talking about," said James, and a moment later two men came out of the church.

He knew instantly that something was wrong. These were not hikers or sightseers, and they certainly weren't here for a church service. They wore sunglasses, somber dark suits and hats, and one was wrapped in a long black leather coat. They stood for a moment looking at James, then one of them nodded and they walked quickly over.

James looked questioningly at Roan, but she wouldn't return his gaze. As they got nearer, the man in the leather coat produced a Luger and pointed it at James's belly. James was too stunned and shocked to think of running, and to fight would be pointless. Instead he felt a terrible heaviness and despair settle on him, and he felt dreadfully tired.

The men took his arms and frog-marched him around to the back of the church, where two matching black Mercedes-Benz limousines were hidden among the trees.

James was pushed into the back of one, and the man in the leather coat settled beside him. Roan got into the second car with the other man.

There was a driver already behind the wheel with a passenger by his side. The passenger said something in Russian, and the driver started the engine.

As they moved off, James craned his head around to see if Roan's car was following, and the man in the leather coat slapped his face.

"Face front," he said.

James was reminded of his drive to the safe house with Nevin and the surprises that had been in store for him then. Well, it was happening all over again. He had no doubt that in a little while his world was going to shift on its axis again, and he would have to deal with a whole new set of realities. One thing was for sure, though. Roan had betrayed him. She had lied to him and deliberately led him here to this trap and handed him over to . . .

Who exactly were these people?

As they trundled slowly and carefully down the steep mountain track to the proper road below the church, the man in the coat drew curtains across the side windows. James could still see out of the front, but the scenery that had earlier seemed quaint and pretty now looked hateful to him. The few farmers they passed stared at the car with blank uninterested faces.

He hated them. He hated the whole rotten country.

The man in the leather coat lit a harsh Turkish cigarette. With the curtains drawn, the smoke had nowhere to go, and it filled the car with thick, choking fumes. James soon began to feel sick.

The man in the front passenger seat opened his window a crack and said something to the driver, who laughed. He then turned around and James got his second surprise of the day.

He recognized him.

The man's bloated puffy eyes were unmistakable. James had last seen him at the Langton-Herrings' house with Graf von Schlick.

But that didn't make any sense at all. Von Schlick was Austrian, not Russian. Of course that didn't mean he couldn't be a Communist, but there was something going on here that James couldn't fathom.

At least he was still alive. If they had wanted to kill him, James supposed that they would have done so by now.

Once they were down the mountain, they headed back to Kitzbühel and then south toward the high Alps. Soon after Jochberg, they left the main road and slowed down. The road began to slope upward and they had to negotiate a series of tight hairpin curves to the left and right, which meant that they were climbing higher.

It was another twenty minutes before they arrived at their destination, and it was growing dark. James could just make out walls built out of massive blocks of gray stone and a pair of huge black wooden gates. He heard shouts and heavy iron locks being opened. The gates swung back and the car drove in over cobbles, the sound of the engine bouncing back from the high surrounding buildings. They had entered a courtyard of some sort. The car stopped and he heard the gates being closed behind them.

Then he was shoved out of the car without a word.

The first thing that struck James was the smell. There was a horrible blocked-drain, rotting-food stink about the place that forced him to clamp a hand over his mouth and nose.

He was standing in the courtyard of an ancient Alpine *Schloss* high on the mountainside. There was a cold, cheerless feel about the place even though it was early July. The buildings were tall and angular with tiny windows. The walls were running with damp and covered in moss and lichen. Dominating all was the peak of the mountain that towered overhead.

The second car drove up and parked nearby. James caught a glimpse of Roan scurrying into a side building between two men, her hair a bright flash of silver in the murk.

The man in the coat had been smoking for almost the whole journey, lighting a fresh cigarette from the stub of the one he was finishing. He now dropped his last cigarette half-smoked and stamped it out on the cobbles. James had hated the smoke at the time, but he much preferred it to the bad drain smell filling the courtyard. It was the stink of death.

There came a rattle of locks, and then a large door at the top of a flight of steps creaked open. A man walked out and stood looking at James.

It was the Graf von Schlick.

He was dressed in the long black fur-trimmed coat and astrakhan hat, and still wore a cravat around his neck and leather gloves on his hands. As usual, the smooth skin stretched like a mask across his bland features showed no emotion.

"James Bond," he said, his voice as flat and featureless as his face. "Welcome to Schloss Donnerspitze. I trust you will not have a pleasant stay."

"Thank you," said James, whose calm exterior was belying the fact that his brain was working away like mad. The *Graf* was no longer speaking in a whisper, and James was sure he knew that droning voice from somewhere, but it went with a different face.

"I apologize about the smell," said the *Graf.* "My men are looking into it. A pipe is blocked somewhere, or some unfortunate creature has crawled into the walls to die."

The man walked toward James and only stopped when he was a few inches away from him.

"You really don't recognize me, do you?" he said. "I did not believe it at first. The surgery was more effective than I could ever have imagined. *Your* face, however, I will never forget. It is burned into my memory."

That voice. So familiar. Flat and monotonous, with no ups and downs.

Where had he heard it before?

"Throughout all my long and painful operations, one thing kept me going," the man went on. "The thought that one day we might meet again and I could finish what was started at Loch Silverfin."

"Silverfin?" said James. "But then . . ."

"Perhaps you assumed that I had died in the fire. I very nearly did, but I managed to escape. Not without terrible injuries, though."

It was like talking to a doll—the voice was mechanical and the features barely moved; the mouth only opened a tiny slit and the unblinking eyes showed nothing.

"Dr. Perseus Friend," said James.

"Yes. Now, we have a lot to catch up on. Perhaps you would like to come inside and we can talk a little before you die."

CHAPTER 27—KEEPING UP APPEARANCES

The great hall was long and very tall, as if it hadn't been built for human use at all, but rather for some fairy-tale giant. The walls were gray stone and they stretched up into the shadows, where the steeply sloping roof was supported by massive wooden beams. Even though it was the height of summer, it felt cold in here, and a small pile of logs smoldering in the huge fireplace did little to dispel the chill.

The room took James back to the previous year and another gloomy castle, this time in the west of Scotland. Castle Hellebore. It was there that James had first met Dr. Friend. He had been working for Lord Hellebore, a maniac who had been trying to create a drug that would turn ordinary soldiers into superstrong fighting machines. Dr. Perseus Friend had been Hellebore's chief scientist, and James had helped to destroy his laboratory. He vividly recalled the moment when Friend had run back into the burning building to try and save his work, and he had thought that that was the last he would ever see of the man.

How wrong he had been.

For here he was, sitting at the head of a long table built from great planks of dark wood, taking sips from a glass of iced water.

The walls were decorated with murky portraits, faded and

tattered banners, and the odd piece of armor. James guessed the portraits were of members of the von Schlick family. So why exactly was Dr. Friend impersonating the *Graf*? And what did he have to do with Roan's plan to assassinate King George? James had known that the *Graf* fit in somewhere, but he had never connected him directly with Roan herself.

It didn't make sense. Friend had worked for the Russians once, but he had fled to the West. Was he back working for them again? Or was there something more complicated going on? James had the feeling that if he waited long enough he would get answers to all his questions.

He had been sitting here, alone at the table, since his arrival, with two armed guards standing watch over him. Then at last Friend had come in. He had barely looked at James, and had been quietly sipping water at the far end of the table for the last few minutes. His smooth face showed nothing, and so far, he had said nothing.

Now, finally, Dr. Friend turned to look at James. James remembered that he used to wear spectacles. He was wearing none now, but his eyes were pale and steady.

"I used to wonder," he said, "while I was lying for all those long weeks and months in various hospitals around Europe, my whole body gripped by indescribable pain . . ." He paused for another sip, sucking the water noisily between his thin lips. "I used to wonder what I might say to you if I ever saw you again. I practiced lines . . . 'Ah, James Bond, we meet once more, but this time the outcome will be very different.' That sort of thing. But it never sounded right. It was all too—*what is the word*—'corny.' I sounded like a cheap villain from a melodramatic American movie. I was still working on what to say when you stumbled into my room at the clinic, and I was too shocked and surprised to say anything. Not that I *could* say anything, as I did not want to give myself away. So I was silent. Sometimes it is best to say nothing, to keep your mouth shut." The monotonous drone combined with his immobile waxlike features made Friend seem more like an animated dummy than a living, breathing man.

"I expect you want to know what I am doing here, pretending to be the Graf von Schlick," he went on, "and how I got here, and what is going on. While we wait for the ladies, I will tell you. It will amuse me.

"The fire was very strong when I ran into it. I knew at once that it was over, the laboratory would perish, and I would perish, too, if I did not get out of there. Fallen timbers blocked the door I had entered by. But the way out to the lochside was clear; the doors there had burned away. I had just time to recover my medical bag, and I burst out of that hellhole like a human fireball. I plunged into the loch. My flaming clothes were extinguished, but not before most of my body was badly burned. I swam. I had to. For I knew that the eels would come for me. I was leaking blood and pieces of toasted flesh into the water. Luckily the noise and commotion, the heat and falling debris were keeping them away, but some of the bolder ones were already nipping at my skin.

"Somehow I made it to the bank on the far side of the castle and climbed ashore. Then I took a risk. I injected myself with the latest, untried batch of serum. The few vials that I had in my case were the last of it, but I knew that it was my only hope of survival. It gave me the strength and the energy to carry on, and it boosted the healing process.

"I crawled into the woods, then found my way to the house of one of Hellebore's workers, a pilot. He had always been a loyal man, and he had been paid well. I directed him to do the best he could with my injuries and offered him a great deal of money to fly me out of there in Hellebore's aeroplane. Under the cover of darkness we took off and hopped across to Iceland, then to Norway, then down to Switzerland. I kept going by giving myself regular injections. How ironic it was that in that last batch we had managed to perfect the drug. It would have been an enormous boon to medical science. It helped to heal my skin, but the damage was very severe. Very deep. Once in Switzerland I took myself to a hospital and so began the months of painful treatment. As I said, it was not only the serum that kept me going; it was also the thought of revenge. Revenge on you, and revenge on your country."

"So you went to the Russians?" said James.

Friend took another sip of iced water and stared at James.

"It is galling," he said, "that twice now my plans have been upset by somebody as stupid as you." He stopped and looked over to the door behind James.

"Ah," he said. "Here are the ladies."

James twisted in his seat. First into the room was Roan. She was wearing a simple white dress that he had not seen before, and she had removed her blond wig. She had obviously spent some effort on her appearance, and for the first time since he had known her, was wearing makeup, which made her look much older. She kept her gaze fixed straight ahead and didn't even glance at James.

Behind her came another young woman. The man with

baggy eyes was pushing her in a wheelchair. She too was pretty, but her looks were spoiled by tiredness. Tiredness and something else. Her head lolled and she could barely keep her eyes open. Her mouth was slack. Her skin pale and shiny. As she came near to the table her head rolled toward James and their eyes met. For a moment something came alive inside her and there was a brief flare of intelligence; she gave James a pleading look that was gone almost before he registered it. Then her chin flopped down to her chest and her features slackened.

"Good evening to you both," said Dr. Friend as Roan sat down and the other girl was wheeled to her place.

"And you will join us as well, I hope, Vladimir?"

"*Da*," said the baggy-eyed man, and he sat next to Roan.

"You have not been properly introduced, James," said Dr. Friend. "This is my associate Vladimir Wrangel, also known as Agent Amethyst."

Wrangel turned to James with a sour look. Dr. Friend carried on with his introductions.

"The beautiful Roan, Agent Diamond, you know," he said. "And the other beauty is Liesl Haas. She was the real *Graf's* mistress, and I decided to keep her on here for the sake of appearances. I would say that she brightened the place up, but she is so heavily sedated, she may as well be dead."

So that explained it. The girl had been drugged. This promised to be a fun evening.

There was a distant muffled boom followed by a sharper, echoing crack.

"Ah," said Dr. Friend. "Talking of keeping up appearances, that is our cannon. A General Franz von Schlick captured it from the Turks in 1683 after breaking the siege of Vienna. Ever since, as long as a von Schlick has been in residence here, it has been fired every hour, on the hour, from dawn till dusk. It is a charming family tradition. A celebration of victory and freedom. It is where the *Schloss* gets its name. Donnerspitze. *Thunder-peak Castle*."

He clapped his hands and two uniformed servants brought over bowls of cold soup.

"I only eat cold food now," Dr Friend explained. "I cannot bear anything hot near to me. Cold water. Cold food. This cold castle suits me well." He noisily slurped soup off his spoon. "Mm, this is good," he said, and looked at Roan. "I was just telling James about my medical history."

Roan muttered something without raising her head.

"Yes, the doctors were amazed at how quickly my skin healed and how well the new grafts took," said Friend. "Unbeknownst to them I was still secretly injecting myself with the SilverFin serum. Now the serum is all gone, but I am still here. It has not been cheap, but I made sure that I had stashed away some funds in the form of gold coins. I stole them from under the nose of Lord Hellebore himself. I thought it wise to take precautions. He was a ruthless man and not to be trusted."

"Unlike you, I suppose," said James.

"I assume you are being sarcastic," said Friend. "Please don't bother. I have never understood the point of humor. A man should say what he means and be done with it."

"All right," said James. "I'll say it plainly. You're a snake."

"There you go again," said Friend. "I am not a snake. I am a man. A very clever man. Cleverer than Hellebore. He was a great scientist in many ways, but he was also wrong in so many ways. On a military level, the SilverFin experiment was a complete waste of time. We were rushing madly in the wrong direction. We do not need stronger soldiers. Men are cheap and expendable. We can simply breed more of them. The future of warfare is in the technology of weapons and in the advances of intelligence. I like that word, *intelligence*. I have always been an intelligent man. And I used my intelligence to secure my future."

So that's what this is all about, thought James. Dr. Friend was simply showing off, trying to prove to James what a clever piece of work he was. Well, James had had his fill of madmen who thought they were geniuses. They gave him a bellyache.

Or was that the soup?

He swallowed hard. Although hungry, he was struggling to finish the watery liquid in his bowl. It was cold and gray and had lumps of unidentifiable stuff floating in it. In the end he pushed it away half-eaten. After all, he didn't need to be polite in present company. He wondered whether he should pour it onto the floor in disgust.

"It was while I was in Switzerland that I met Wrangel," said Dr. Friend. "Wrangel is a spy. He sought me out because he had learned that here was a man who could speak fluent Russian, German, and English. Here was a man who knew Britain very well. Here was a man who had worked for the Russians. Here was a man who was very clever and ambitious. So I met with his superiors. I went to the very top, and we started to form a plan. When I was well enough, I was made head of a secret unit, and we put Operation Snow-blind into action."

"So you are Obsidian?" said James. Dr. Friend nodded.

The two servants started to serve the next course. Cold ham and raw cabbage chopped with onions and hard-boiled egg, with cold noodles on the side. It didn't look any more appetizing than the soup.

"I sent Wrangel and his team to Lisbon," Dr. Friend droned on, "where they recruited Roan and Dandy. The two of them were perfect for our plans. New blood, freshly arrived on the Continent, desperate to help the Communist cause, young enough and foolish enough not to ask too many questions. Dedicated revolutionaries, blinded by their zeal."

"What do you mean, blinded?" said Roan, a forkful of food halfway to her mouth.

"Did you really think, my dear, that when you killed King George, the ordinary working people of Great Britain would rise up and throw over their bosses? Did you really think that it would be the first step to building your Communist utopia there? The British people are sheep. They are conservative and sentimental and they worship tradition. They love their royal family more than they love themselves."

"Then why did you send us to do it?" said Roan, her voice cracking with emotion.

"I said earlier that I could not understand the point of humor," said Dr. Friend. "But I appreciate now that we are in a rather humorous situation."

"Why?" said Roan.

"The flag I fly does not have the hammer and sickle of the Soviets on it, my dear," said Dr. Friend. "It has a swastika."

Roan threw down her fork with a loud clatter.

"What do you mean?" she said.

"Isn't it obvious?" said James bitterly. "You've been working for the wrong side. He's a Nazi."

"It can't be true," said Roan.

"It is true," said Dr. Friend. "Lisbon is wide open, a chaotic morass of double agents, triple agents, carpetbaggers, and sharks. Even some of the agents themselves have forgotten who they are really working for. Wrangel's team easily identified the Communist cell and destroyed it. The chief Communist spy, Martinho Ferreira, was strangled, and our own man, Cristo Oracabessa, was installed in his place. You believed, Roan, that you were dealing with Communists, but you were not. You were dealing with Nazis. By the time the Russians realized what was going on, it was too late. You and Dandy were in England and your only point of contact was Wrangel, Agent Amethyst."

"But Wrangel is a Russian," Roan protested.

"Not all Russians love Communism, my dear," said Dr. Friend. "Wrangel is a White Russian, not a Red. He lost everything when the Communists took over, and has been working to restore the old order ever since."

"You're joking," said Roan.

"Have you not been listening? I do not joke. Operation Snow-blind was a German operation. Stamped by Hitler himself. A very clever man, by the way. True, it was a bold plan and not without its risks, but we knew that if we pulled it off, it would be a triumph. You have been a great help to the fascist cause, Roan. I thank you. Hitler thanks you."

"No," Roan shouted. "I'm a Communist, not a fascist!"

"What difference does it make?" said James. "One bunch of fanatics are pretty much the same as another, in my book.

A lot of hot air and shouting and the desire to take over the world. The end result: a lot of innocent people lying dead."

"You are wrong," said Dr. Friend. "We are not all the same. I had my experience of the Communists when I was younger, and I did not like what I saw. There was too much suspicion and fear among them. Anyone clever or ambitious was removed and executed. Their leadership is not intelligent. They are peasants. I knew I would never be safe among the Communists. The Nazis, however, appreciate talent, and they appreciate my talents greatly."

Roan was shaking her head and murmuring, "No, no, no . . ."

"Europe is balanced on a knife edge," Dr. Friend continued, ignoring Roan. "Balanced between fascism and Communism. Most countries have a sneaking regard for Hitler and a terrible fear of Communism. There are too many rich men, too many royal families, too many people with too much to lose under Communism, but they fear for their precious freedoms under fascism. Would they really throw democracy aside and embrace Hitler? Perhaps—if it meant stopping the spread of Communism. Your King George doesn't much care for Hitler. He has been a popular king and so the British have no desire to change things. His son, however, Edward, the Prince of Wales, thinks rather highly of what Herr Hitler has achieved. With him on the throne, things might be different. My plan was very simple—to kill the King in a spectacular manner and let everyone believe it was the work of the Communists. In the hysteria following his death, Britain would turn against the Soviet Union, and where would she look to find an ally against the Russian threat? To Germany, of course, the only country in Europe with the guts to stand up against the Communists. With Prince Edward on the throne, England would become Germany's strongest ally. The doctrine of National Socialism, of Nazism, would be very easily rolled out into England. And not just England—other countries would see what a threat the Communists posed. Hitler would become the strongest, most dominant force in Europe, with no other country powerful enough, or brave enough, to stand up to him."

James smiled. At last things that had seemed to make no sense were becoming clear. They had all been made fools of. Merriot, Nevin, Roan, Dandy, James himself. None of them had realized that it was a blind. There never had been a Communist plot. It was the Nazis all along. Ironically, the only person who had known even a little of what was really going on had been Colonel Sedova. She must have uncovered the plot in Lisbon, and had been trying to stop it.

The shadow war, Merriot had called it. Spies and agents working against each other in the darkness. Nobody knowing exactly who the enemy was.

But the war wasn't over. There were more battles to be fought, and James could still end up as a casualty.

"I think you're wrong," he said. "Dead wrong. The English would never welcome Hitler."

"Do you not think so?"

"No."

"Then how do you think we so easily put Dandy and Roan in place at Eton?"

James shrugged. He didn't know what to say.

"With the help of our British friends," said the doctor. "There are many in England who admire Hitler. It was they who assured us that Prince Edward would make a better ally than the King. We needed to be sure, however, that this was true. We had to get close to him. So it was decided that I would replace the real Graf von Schlick, a distant relative. We faked a car accident. Two bodies arrived at the clinic wrapped in bandages. I was one and the *Graf* was the other. Wrangel kept him drugged to keep him quiet until the operation. Unfortunately, the one night that Wrangel could not be there to keep an eye on him, he started to cry out, and you chose to find out what all the fuss was about."

Another piece of the mystery fell into place for James.

"The *Graf* knew some of your plan, didn't he?" he said.

"Yes. He understood more in his drugged state than we had thought. If it wasn't for you, it would not have been a problem. Dr. Kitzmuller, the surgeon at the clinic, was working for us. He is a German, a supporter of Hitler. Under the knife, the real *Graf* was given enough anaesthetic to kill him, and I swapped places with him. At the same time we completed the final stage of my facial reconstruction. I also wear scleral lenses in my eyes, of my own design, colored to match the *Graf*'s own. I can only wear them for short periods of time, but they are sufficient. I do not look exactly like him, but the fire would have altered his face, and the resemblance is enough to convince most people. His wife, though, regrettably had to die, or she might have given us away."

"So before Dandy got anywhere near the King, you'd already killed three people?" said James.

"Eight people," Dr. Friend corrected him. "You are forgetting the Communist cell in Lisbon."

"I'm so sorry," said James. "My mistake, Dr. Friend."

"No," said the doctor. "Perseus Friend is no more. He was not welcome in many places. The Graf von Schlick, on the other hand, a relative of the British royal family . . . well, that opens doors. As the *Graf* I was free to travel to England, where I met the Prince and many of our supporters."

"A lot of good it did you," said James. "The King is still alive. Operation Snow-blind was a failure. All that work, all those deaths, all for nothing."

Dr. Friend sighed.

"Yes," he said. "Once again, you, James Bond, have spoiled my careful planning. Which is why tomorrow, when Dr. Kitzmuller gets here, I am going to skin you alive. . . ."

CHAPTER 28—YOU NEVER GIVE UP, DO YOU?

"I am a practical man, James. I hate waste. You have to die, as I am sure you will understand, but you are young and healthy and strong. Your skin is firm and flexible. My skin, on the other hand, thanks to you, is like the scuffed leather on an old pair of boots. Large areas of my body are still scarred and ugly. I am well enough now for another operation, and I have built a modest operating theater here in the *Schloss*. Some more skin grafts to my back, my neck, and my legs and hands will make me almost normal again. I will peel off your skin, James. It seems only fair after all the trouble you have put me to. An eye for an eye, a tooth for a tooth, a skin for a skin."

"No!"

With a shout, Roan was on her feet, a table knife clutched in her hand. She ran toward Dr. Friend, who sat calmly in his place, watching her, unblinking.

She had not gone four paces, however, when Wrangel slid out of his chair, spun her around by the shoulder, and jabbed her on the chin with his clenched fist. He moved fast and gracefully for such a large man, and the blow was painfully efficient.

Roan dropped to the floor without a sound and lay unmoving on the cold stone slabs.

"It seems that, despite what she has done, the girl feels

something for you, James," said Friend, staring at Roan.

"What are you going to do with her?" James asked, trying to keep his voice as emotionless as the doctor's.

"She failed in her main task, but she did well in everything else. She evaded capture and brought you to me. However, it is of the utmost importance that the British continue to believe that the Communists were behind this plot. We cannot risk her ever talking to anyone about the truth of Operation Snow-blind. Therefore, she will have to die as well."

James grabbed a heavy cut–glass water jug and hurled it as hard as he could at Dr. Friend. The doctor must have been expecting something, for he simply leaned to one side, and the jug smashed harmlessly on the floor behind him.

"A brave show," he said, in the same dreary monotone. "Let's see if you are quite so brave tomorrow when we operate on you without anaesthetic in front of the girl. Sadly, I myself will be asleep, but I think I will get Wrangel to film the process for me. It will please me to study her reactions as she watches you scream in pain and terror. As she watches your handsome body reduced to a piece of meat on the butcher's slab. And when it is over and I am recovered, I think perhaps I shall have the pleasure of executing her myself. Then there will be one less filthy Red in the world."

Roan moaned and started to stir. James went over to her and helped her up. She stood unsteadily, rubbing her jaw. She swayed, and James caught her.

"Thank you," she said quietly.

"Don't mention it." There was bitterness in James's voice.

Roan turned her face to him. Tears were crawling slowly down her cheeks.

"I'm so sorry," she said.

"It's too late for that."

Wrangel gave James a shove.

"Come on," he said. "Move."

"Lock them up in the rooms next to Fräulein Haas," said Dr. Friend. "And be careful not to damage the boy at all. His skin is important to me."

James and Roan walked side by side through the castle, Wrangel and the two armed guards following closely behind. Roan tried to take James's hand but he shook her off.

"You knew they were here, didn't you?" he said. "Near Kitzbühel?"

"Yes," said Roan quietly.

"That's why you so quickly agreed to my plan to escape to here, isn't it?"

Roan nodded. "Amethyst told us that the Lisbon cell had been broken up," she said. "He told us that Obsidian was based in Austria. I didn't know the details; I didn't know anything about the *Graf* or Dr. Friend."

"But you were planning this all along."

Roan said nothing.

"Weren't you?" James snapped angrily.

"Yes." Roan spoke so softly, the word was more of a sigh.

"After everything I'd done for you," said James. "How could you betray me?"

"I've tried to explain," said Roan. "What I'm fighting for is bigger than both of us. You and I, we don't matter. What's important is history. What's important is that we win the struggle by whatever means possible. It broke my heart, darling, really it did. I'll always love you. But sometimes we have to sacrifice the things we love for the greater good."

"I've never heard such rot," said James.

"It's not rot," said Roan, her voice cracking. "I'm fighting for every worker in the world, all the poor people, the masses living under the boot of—"

"Oh, please, spare me another bloody lecture," said James wearily. "I'm fed up to the back teeth of hearing about it. You champion the workers of the world, the faceless masses, but me, a real living breathing person, I mean nothing to you. Why? Because I come from a privileged background? Because I was an Eton schoolboy? Because I was English? Do I not count?"

"I was confused, darling. I didn't know what to do. I was scared of the British and I was scared of the men who'd hired me. I knew how ruthless they were. I'd failed, you see, and I was terrified of what they might do to me. I'd always known that you were important to them. I thought that if I could deliver you to them, they might look more kindly on me."

"Friend was right," said James. "It *is* funny."

Roan sobbed. "If I'd have known what was going to happen," she said, "I'd have done everything differently, but I was desperate to save my skin."

James laughed coldly.

"And in the process you've given them mine."

"I didn't know, darling . . ."

"Well, that's pretty obvious, *darling*," James scoffed. "You didn't know the first damned thing about what was really going on, did you? And now we're both going to die. And as far as I can see it's not going to help the precious workers one jot."

The room they locked James into was small with a low ceiling and a single, square casement window. It had gray walls, a stone floor, a wooden bed, a washstand, and a tatty mud-colored rug.

And it stank.

The smell of decay he had first noticed in the courtyard was even stronger here.

He went immediately to the window and pushed it open, hoping that it might clear the air.

The window swung back only a couple of inches into a sort of sturdy metal cage bolted to the outside wall, but it was enough to let in a waft of foul-smelling vapor from outside. The stench hit James like a blow, and he put his hand to his mouth and staggered back, trying not to gag.

He took out his handkerchief, soaked it in the washstand, and tied it around his face. Then he returned to the window and put his mouth to the opening.

"Roan?" he called out.

After a while there came a reply.

"James? Is that you?"

"Yes. Listen, I'm sorry about the things I said just now. I was scared and angry and disappointed."

"It's all right," said Roan. "You have a right to be. You probably want to kill me, and I wouldn't blame you. Jesus, Mary, and Joseph, but that's an evil smell. We must be right beneath the toilets."

"Maybe," James shouted. "Can you see anything out of your window?"

"Not really, I can't get it open far enough. As far as I

can tell we're on the side of the castle overlooking the valley. There's a long drop out there."

"Even so," James called to her, "if I could get out somehow, I might be able to climb down and go for help."

"You never give up, do you?"

"No."

"I appreciate you trying, darling, but you're just a kid. We've got to accept that nobody's going to come to our rescue. You remember I said once I wanted to stay young and pretty all my life. Well, it looks like my wish is going to come true."

"We'll see about that," said James. "I'm not just going to sit here and wait for the morning. I'd rather smash myself to pieces on the rocks below than have that ghoul dress himself in my skin."

"Would he really do it?"

"He would," said James. "You don't know him like I do."

"I'm awful scared, James. I don't like it here."

"Don't worry," James shouted. "We're not staying."

James carefully searched the room, looking for anything that might be of use. There was a sheet and a thin blanket on the bed; by cutting them into strips and tying them together he might make a rope—but he would have to first get out of the window for that to be any use. He could pull the bed apart and use the legs as weapons—but didn't really relish the idea of taking on the doctor's gun-toting friends armed only with a wooden leg. He could try to batter the door down with the washstand, but the noise would alert the guards long before he would be able to do any damage.

He went back over to the window. With the sash opening

into the metal cage, there was no way he could see properly outside. The first thing he would have to do would be to remove the window from its frame.

That was easily done.

He took off his shoe and removed the knife from its hidden compartment in the heel. He unfolded the blade and used it to scrape some layers of caked-on paint from the first screw in the lower hinge and tried to turn it. It was useless; the screw was rusted into the hinge. The wood itself was soft, however. The window must be at least fifty years old, and it didn't look as if maintenance had been at the top of the doctor's list of things to do when he moved in here.

James dug into the rotten wood with his knife.

Yes. This was going to work.

It took him nearly an hour of gouging, cutting, and chopping, but he worked slowly and steadily, and eventually he was able to pull all six screws out of the frame and lift the window down. Now the opening was clear.

He pulled the bed over so that he could stand on it, adjusted his handkerchief, then climbed up and leaned out to see how the iron cage was fastened to the wall.

There were heavy rusted bolts. The iron bars were half an inch thick, and the walls were solid granite.

Removing the cage was obviously not an option.

While he had been working, his mind focused on his task, James had almost forgotten about the awful stink. He had gotten used to it. But now, as the wind shifted direction, it hit him again. He groaned and retched, then went back to the washstand and wet his handkerchief again. It didn't keep out all of the smell, but it helped a little.

He looked out again. A bright moon was riding high in the sky, but the wind was moving clouds across its face. There were brief periods of illumination followed by long stretches of heavy darkness.

He waited for a clear spot and looked down.

It wasn't encouraging.

Far below he could just make out the tops of pine trees, and between him and them were jagged rocks. Even if he could somehow get the iron cage off the wall, to get down from here, James would need mountaineering equipment.

What about climbing up, then?

He twisted around and looked up, just as the clouds shrouded the moon again.

For the moment he could see nothing except the black shape of the castle walls. His window seemed to be beneath an overhang that looked to be dotted with weeds and small bushes growing out of the cracks in the masonry. He shifted his position and switched his attention to the sides. To the left was Roan's window, to the right was some kind of object projecting from the wall—a rock perhaps, or another bush.

He looked back up just as the clouds thinned and a pale light fleetingly illuminated a patch of wall. He caught a glint of metal. He fixed his eyes on the spot and waited. If there was anything out here he could use, he would grab his chance.

It was frustrating waiting to get a proper look. The clouds slowly lifted, though, until he could make out the shape of some kind of man-made metallic object. It slowly grew out of the darkness until at last it revealed itself to be an ice ax, the long-handled cutting tool used by mountaineers.

What on earth was an ice ax doing hanging on the wall outside his window?

As the moonlight grew brighter it revealed more and more of the scene above him. He saw that the ax was dangling from a rope. He followed the rope up. It was snagged on a dead root sticking out of the wall.

Then it was too dark again to see any more, and James waited patiently for another break in the clouds. Finally the sky cleared and it was as if a searchlight were sweeping over the wall.

With a shock, James realized that the dark mass to his right was a man. He was hanging upside down from a second rope that was tied around his waist and tangled around one ankle. From there the rope went straight up to a piton, a metal climber's hook that had been driven into the stonework about fifteen feet above the dead body.

Now James understood what the awful smell was. God knows how long the man had been hanging there, but it must have been for some time, because he was rotting.

He had been baked in the sun and dried by the wind so that his face looked mummified. It was dark, almost black, the cracked lips were pulled back from the teeth in a grimace. His eyes had long since been pecked out by birds, and the sockets were gaping and empty. The birds had also been busy elsewhere—strips of flesh had been peeled from his face so that here and there the bones showed through.

The back of his head looked flattened, and there was dried blood matted in his hair and hanging down in gluey strips from his scalp.

Hidden from above by the overhang of the castle wall, he

must have been climbing up here and slipped, hitting his head in the process.

It was clear that Dr. Friend knew nothing about him, or he would surely have had him removed.

When you were trying so hard to keep up appearances, it wouldn't do to have a dead body hanging from your castle wall.

James studied the man, trying to hold back his revulsion. There was something about his clothing that seemed familiar. And then he spotted the polished leather of a shoulder holster, still carrying its Enfield Number Two Mark One.

It was the Englishman from the train.

James thought back to all that time ago walking with Merriot under the elm trees on Upper Club. What had Merriot said?

"It was not entirely coincidence that I took you boys to Kitzbühel. I was there on business. . . ."

At the time, neither of them had known that Operation Snow-blind and increased German activities in the Tyrol were connected. Merriot would still not know. The only sense that James could make of all this was that the SIS had been trying to find out what was going on at Schloss Donnerspitze, and the man hanging outside his window was a British agent.

Whatever the case, this poor soul had a gun strapped to his side.

If James could get hold of that gun, it would make him a very happy boy indeed.

CHAPTER 29—FOR KING AND COUNTRY

James slipped a hand between the bars of the iron cage and reached out for the ice ax. Standing on the bed, he had to force his whole body up, folded awkwardly into the cage, his neck against the top, his head looking down. He groped around until at last his fingertips touched the cold metal of the blade. He pressed himself up harder, trying to force his shoulder through the narrow opening. He gave the ax a gentle nudge, and it began to swing away from him; as it swung back, he caught hold of it and gave a tug. It slipped off the root and he took a firm hold of it as the rope snaked down. He had to hold on tight—the rope was surprisingly heavy and the weight of it jarred his shoulder as it fell below the window. He didn't let go, though, and in a moment he had pulled the ax and the rope in through the bars. Now he calculated the distance to the dead body. If he could swing the ax across and hook it onto the corpse, he might be able to pull it close enough to grab the gun.

He grinned.

There was always a way.

He measured a length of rope and knotted it securely to the cage, then he slipped the ax back out and let the cord run through his fingers until it was dangling down below him. He began to swing it back and forth like a pendulum. Once he had built up enough momentum, he gave a heave and hoicked it up toward the man. It thudded uselessly into his chest and fell away.

James swung again. This time the ax smashed into the man's face with a horrible crunch.

James felt awful, as if he were desecrating a corpse.

Don't think about that. The man's dead. He's beyond feeling anything. Besides, if he was a British agent come to investigate Dr. Friend, then he'd be glad to help any way he could.

Even dead.

"For King and country," James said through gritted teeth as he made a minute adjustment to the length of rope.

He swung again. The ax looped up, dropped down, and snagged on the man's belt, where it held firm.

Good.

James shifted his position at the window so that he could get both arms outside the cage, and then he took hold of the rope and pulled, dragging the body across the wall toward him. It came closer, closer; light glinted tantalizingly off the gun nestled in its holster.

Hell!

The ax came loose and raked over the man's belly, popping his shirt buttons before falling off and clattering against the wall.

The body swung away from him.

Never mind. He'd done it once; he could do it again.

"What are you doing out there?" It was Roan's voice, from the other window.

"Don't look."

"I can't, the window's in the way."

"I've found something that might help us. Listen at the door. If you hear anyone coming, try and warn me."

"All right."

James's arms were aching. It was very awkward holding the ax through the bars, and his shoulders were on fire. He never for one moment thought of giving up, though. With a grunt he swung the ax toward the corpse.

It took him five tries before he finally got it hooked into the man's belt again. He sighed with relief and brought his arms back inside so that he could loosen his muscles and knead away some of the pain.

When he was ready, he got back up onto the bed and took a hold of the rope once more. And once more he pulled. The ax was staying put this time, but as the body swung toward him, the pendulum effect caused it to rise higher up the wall. He had to move the rope across to the far side of the cage, hand over hand, and haul it from there. Eventually the angle became too tight and he could move the body no closer. He reckoned that he should just be able to reach the holster now, though, and he secured the rope.

He stuck his left arm out and grabbed hold of the man's shirt. His flesh felt warm and soft. James knew that the warmth wasn't coming from the man's body heat; it was caused by the bacteria that were eating away at his insides and breeding inside him.

He walked his fingers over the heavy material of the shirt, toward the shoulder holster on the other side.

He tried pulling the body closer still, but as he tugged he felt something give way.

The ax must have torn the man's skin, because the next

thing James knew he was showered with foul liquid and the man's guts spilled out from under his shirt and flopped over his chest.

James was glad of the handkerchief covering his nose and mouth, as it stopped him from swallowing or inhaling anything. He fought desperately not to be sick, and told himself that whatever happened he must not let go. If the man's body fell apart, the gun might be lost. But there were coils of intestines over his forearm now, and his hand was buried in it all. The cesspit reek of death and decay was powerful enough to knock him out, and for a few moments he felt dangerously faint.

He held his breath and fought the dizziness, trying not to look. His eyes were drawn to the body, though. There was nothing he could do about it. Slimy, glistening, bluish-gray in the moonlight, the man's guts almost seemed to be alive. James finally managed to tear his eyes away, and his fingers wormed through the tangled mass until he felt the smooth leather of the holster, and there, yes . . . the gun.

He felt for the grip and closed his fingers around it, then eased it out of the holster.

Don't drop it now.

Inch by inch it came out as warm, sticky liquid dripped down James's sleeve. He fought not to think about the rubbery coils his hand was buried in. The bile was rising in his throat, and his heart was hammering hard against his ribs.

But he had it.

The pistol was firmly in his hand. He pulled it free of the stinking mess and flopped back onto the bed.

Gagging and choking, he dropped the gun to the floor

and staggered to the washstand. He tore off his shirt and furiously wiped the filth from his arms and chest and face.

He didn't stop. He couldn't. He had to keep doing something to prevent the horror from taking over his mind.

He wiped the gun clean and then mopped up the mess from around the window before pushing his ruined shirt through the bars and letting it drop down the mountain. He was still wearing his vest, but it was cold in the room and he shivered.

He grabbed the window and jammed it back into the frame, trying to shut out the ghastly thing that was outside.

Finally he sat in the corner with his back to the wall, his chest rising and falling, his eyes screwed tight shut, and slowly, ever so slowly, his body stilled and he became calm.

By concentrating on what he had achieved and what he was going to do next, he forced the terrible images out of his mind.

Finally he lifted the gun and looked at it.

He turned it in his hands and smiled.

Round one to him.

BOOM . . .

James opened his eyes. It was dawn. The von Schlick cannon had fired its first blast of the day.

He glanced at his watch. Five o'clock.

He had cleaned the Mido Multifort with his handkerchief. It was waterproof, and he was happy to say that it was also proof against vile bodily fluids. The mechanism was beautifully accurate. As long as he wound it every night and morning, it kept perfect time.

And he was relying on that to get him out of his cell.

He had made a plan in the night, in between moments of fitful sleep. He had decided that he wasn't going to wait for Dr. Friend and his cohorts to come for him; he was going to take the fight to them. He was getting out, and they weren't going to stop him.

The stench had grown no better in the night, and he could hear birds outside noisily fighting over the fresh food he had served up for them.

His stomach gave a lurch and his mouth filled with saliva.

Best not to think about that.

He sat up, slipped the pistol out from beneath his pillow, and emptied the bullets onto the bed. He tested the firing mechanism, pulling the trigger four times. It all worked smoothly. Carefully, he reloaded it. It was heavy in his hand. He would have to make sure he held it securely when the time came, because he would only have the chance to make one shot.

Satisfied, he hid the gun back beneath his pillow and lay down, gathering his strength but not quite sleeping, for the best part of forty minutes. Then at ten to six he stirred and rolled off the bed. He unstrapped his watch, pulled out the pin, and set the hands to exactly six o'clock.

And then he waited.

Listening hard for the next cannon blast. Counting the seconds in his head so that he would be prepared.

BOOM . . .

As soon as he heard it he pressed the pin, and the second hand started to sweep around the watch face.

He just had to hope that whoever was firing the cannon would have an equally accurate timepiece.

Now James paced the room, warming up his muscles, rolling his shoulders to ease the stiffness. Every now and then he stopped and stretched before dropping to the floor and doing twenty push-ups. He had to be ready and he had to be fit. He needed adrenaline pumping through his body.

Deep inside he felt the familiar tingling of excitement. No more worrying, no more straining to use his poor tired brain to work things out. Now all he could do was act. He had a clear purpose: *to escape from the Schloss.* That was all that mattered.

At five to seven he picked up his watch, fastened it to his left wrist so that the face was on the inside, and got himself ready.

He took the Enfield in his right hand and stood about three feet from the door, aiming squarely at the center of the lock. He steadied his gun hand with his left hand, the watch face at his wrist clearly visible.

The seconds ticked by, the minutes . . .

It was four minutes to seven . . . three.

He eased back the hammer and felt it click into place.

One minute to go. He followed the second hand as it worked its way relentlessly around the dial.

Thirty seconds, twenty . . .

He gently squeezed the trigger, slowly piling on more and more pressure. . . .

Ten seconds, nine, eight, seven . . .

He held his breath.

Five, four, three, two, one . . .

Now!

As the second hand clicked into the twelve o'clock position, he applied the last ounce of pressure.

The pistol exploded in the small room at the exact same moment as the cannon fired on the battlements.

Thank God for German efficiency.

There was a smell of cordite in the air, and smoke drifted toward a crack in the window.

James waited, the gun now aimed at the center of the door. The bang had seemed deafeningly loud. Was it possible that the cannon had completely obscured it?

Well, if anyone opened that door they were going to get a bullet in the chest.

No one came.

Apart from the birds outside, it was quiet.

He relaxed, letting out his breath, and lowered the pistol.

Now he got to work with his knife. He jammed the blade into the shattered remains of the door lock and twisted it until the door snapped open. Then, keeping his gun in front of him, he stepped into the corridor.

Empty.

There must be a guard of some sort nearby, though, who would have the keys to the other cells.

James didn't remember passing anywhere on the way here that had looked like a guardroom, so he went left down the corridor, which sloped downward slightly, and around a corner.

There was a short passageway to the right, with a heavy steel door at the end. There was a small window in the door.

James crept forward and peered through the window.

The two armed guards from last night sat there at a wide desk, with their backs to the door, drinking coffee and smoking. One was reading a book. In front of them was what looked like a telephone switchboard.

They had removed their jackets and were in their shirt-sleeves, their braces crisscrossed over their backs. Without their guns they had lost their menace and looked like a couple of harmless middle-aged men.

James backed away from the window and saw that a cluster of wires ran along the wall. He took out his knife and carefully cut through them.

He took a deep breath.

He raised his gun.

He opened the door.

"*Bewegen Sie sich nicht!*"

His bark alerted the two men, ordering them not to move.

They put their hands up of their own accord, too sleepy and too startled by his appearance to do anything else.

"*Wo sind die Schlüssel?*" said James, his eyes flicking around the room for the keys.

One of the men nodded at a large steel ring that hung on a hook near the door. James sidestepped toward it, his gun never leaving the guards, and he picked it up. As he did so, the man nearest to him made a grab for his rifle, which was leaning against the wall. James's hand whipped out, and the butt of the pistol cracked into the man's jaw. He fell back with a groan.

"*Das nächste Mal erschiesse ich Sie!*" James yelled, and the men got the message. Next time, he'd shoot them.

He ordered them to remove their belts and told the one

he'd hit to tie his friend to a leg of the desk and gag him. He then marched the injured man out of the room at gunpoint.

"*Sperren Sie die Tür auf,*" he ordered him once they were outside, and the man locked the guardroom door.

James prodded him in the back with the barrel of the gun, and they went around the corner to the cells.

Once there, James made the injured guard unlock Roan's door and open it.

Roan was lying on her bed. James told her to get out quickly, and as she did he shoved the guard inside.

He slammed the door shut and locked it.

Roan was grinning like a mad person.

"I don't know how you did it, darling, but you've saved us."

"Not quite," said James. "It's still early and not everyone will be up and about yet, but we've still a castle full of goons to deal with."

Roan kissed him.

"It doesn't bother me one bit. You can do it, darling. I know you can."

CHAPTER 30—SOMEONE HAS LET THE RABBITS OUT OF THEIR HUTCHES

James quickly explained to Roan what had happened, leaving out some of the more unpleasant details, as they unlocked Fräulein Haas's cell. As soon as the door was open, Roan ran to Liesl's bed to wake her while James watched the corridor.

Liesl seemed groggy but generally in a better state than she had been the previous night. Her eyelids fluttered open, and she smiled at Roan and murmured something in German.

"Tell her we're going to try and get her out of here," said Roan, kneeling down and holding Liesl's hand. "But it's not going to be easy with her in that wheelchair."

To Roan's amazement, Liesl hauled herself up and stood, somewhat shakily.

"It is all right," she said. "I speak English."

"You can walk as well," said Roan.

"I am an actress," said Liesl, stepping into her shoes. "So I have been acting for the last few weeks. I have played the part of someone who is very sick and weak. Whenever I got the chance, I have only pretended to swallow their pills, and I have spat them out afterward." As she tried to walk, though, she swayed and gripped Roan's arms.

"I have been hoping desperately that I might find a way

out of this place," she said, "and now you have come."

"There'll be time for thanks afterward," said James. "Do you know of any ways out of here other than the main gates? They're bound to be guarded."

"There is a small gate that leads to a mountain track," said Liesl, "but we will need to go through the *Schloss* to get there."

"Show us," said James.

Away from the large public areas, the *Schloss* was a maze of back rooms and dank passageways. Liesl wasn't sure of the exact route, and twice they got lost and had to backtrack. There was an abandoned and neglected feel to this part of the castle. They passed rooms piled high with forgotten moldering furniture; others were filled with hunting gear or rusting gardening equipment. They went through a utility room where three vast boilers steamed and gurgled, and then another room that looked like a laundry. At last they reached a long spiral staircase and climbed up it to a heavy wooden door at the top.

"I am almost certain that this leads to the old ballroom," said Liesl, gripping the handle. "Otto was going to try and restore it to its former glory. He had dreams of inviting all his friends from Vienna down for smart occasions."

Her face crumpled and she began to cry. "That was before this nightmare began," she sobbed. "Before that monster killed him. Many nights I prayed that he would kill me too."

"It'll soon be over," said James. "We can't bring the *Graf* back, but we can see to it that Dr. Friend gets what's coming to him."

Liesl opened the door and they went through.

James saw immediately that someone had been busy. The ballroom had been restored, but not for dancing. It had been transformed into an operating room. There were heavy drapes at all the windows, and a circle of bright lights in the center illuminated an area of polished steel tables, sinks, and tall stacks of glass-and-metal shelving. A gleaming array of evil-looking surgical equipment was neatly lined up on the shelves: scalpels, saws, wide-bladed knives, clamps, syringes, and other things that looked for all the world like medieval torture implements.

Two canisters of compressed gas with rubber face masks attached stood at the head of an operating table. There were ominous leather straps at the corners of the table to keep a patient still. Two film cameras on tripods waited in the shadows.

"He wasn't joking, was he?" said Roan. "He really was going to skin you alive."

"Me and God knows who else," said James. "He would think nothing of experimenting on humans."

"Indeed I wouldn't," came a voice, and there, walking down the wide sweeping staircase on the far side of the ballroom, was Dr. Friend with Wrangel at his side. Wrangel was carrying a Luger, but the doctor appeared to be unarmed.

"Why are we so sentimental about human life?" said the doctor. "Why is it deemed so precious when there are so many of us? I have done experiments that could benefit millions of people, so what would it matter if a handful of men died in the process?"

"And just how, exactly, does peeling my skin off benefit mankind?" said James.

"It doesn't. It benefits me. We busy men must give ourselves the occasional small treat."

Dr. Friend had changed into white pajamas, and his bald head was uncovered. He was wearing spectacles and looked for the first time a little like his old self. He had tight rubber gloves on his hands.

"I see someone has let the rabbits out of their hutches," he said. If it was meant as humor, the effect was sunk by his flat, dull, monotonous voice. "No matter, I can soon put them back."

"We're not going back," said James, raising his gun and leveling it at the doctor.

"Do you really think for a moment that you can take on me and all my men?" said Friend. He had reached the dance floor and was walking slowly toward the operating table. "There are eighteen of us here. Twenty-five if you include the domestic staff. And what are you? Two girls and a schoolboy."

"I don't doubt you'll win," said James. "But I'll take you to hell with me first. I'm not afraid to shoot."

"The Enfield is notoriously inaccurate at distance," said Friend. "Wrangel would cut you down before you so much as grazed me."

"Is that a risk you're prepared to take?" James shouted.

"Yes," said Friend. "I am a scientist, a rationalist. I have weighed up the dangers, and I consider myself to be relatively safe. You, on the other hand, are in a very precarious position. Wrangel has a superior weapon and is an excellent marksman, and what is more, he has successfully killed several men with his Luger. I wonder, James Bond, how many men you have killed? It is not as easy as you might imagine from watching the movies. Especially as four of my men are even at this moment lining up behind you."

James didn't look. He suspected that Friend was bluffing. He couldn't be sure, though, and he didn't much care. He was not about to let the doctor take the upper hand. Before anyone knew what was happening, he yelled at Roan and Liesl to get down, and threw himself to the floor beneath a metal table.

As soon as he hit the springy wooden boards he emptied his gun at one of the gas canisters, fighting to hold the pistol steady as it bucked and jerked in his hand.

Wrangel got off a shot that thudded into the floor next to him, sending up splinters of beechwood. A moment later there was an almighty bang and the air in the ballroom punched James, taking his breath away. All the lamps blew out, and some of the drapes billowed and tore so that weak daylight spilled in.

James cautiously rolled out from under the table. The burst of pressure on his ears was agonizing and had rendered him temporarily deaf. There was an eerie stillness. The explosion had been considerably more effective than he had imagined. The room was wrecked, the glass shelves shattered. There was equipment and debris strewn everywhere. Whatever else happened, Friend's surgeon, Kitzmuller, would not be operating on James today.

There was no sign of the doctor or Wrangel, but James spotted Roan and Liesl lying stunned near the door. They evidently hadn't ducked in time.

As James had suspected, it looked as if Dr. Friend had been bluffing about the four guards, but the explosion was bound to bring some running now. There was no time to lose.

James hurried over to the girls and tried to rouse them. He shook them, yelled at them, then began slapping their cheeks.

Roan came around first. She smiled sleepily when she saw James, and then her eyes widened with fear. The next thing James knew he was being lifted bodily off the floor.

It was Wrangel. He easily picked James up and flung him across the room. James landed on a metal cart, which spilled over, tipping him into some metal shelving. He landed in a painful heap, broken glass digging into his bare flesh.

He forced himself to get up and face Wrangel.

The Russian had been standing close to the canisters when they exploded. Like James, he was now wearing only his vest. The shirt and jacket had been ripped from his back, and his trousers hung in tatters. He was bleeding heavily all down one side, and his face looked sunburned.

He didn't seem the least bit bothered by his injuries, though, and he advanced on James, arms held wide like a wrestler, walking lightly on the balls of his feet.

James knew that he was no match for Wrangel. The man was bigger and heavier and obviously a trained fighter. James's only hope was to keep out of his way.

Without warning, Wrangel suddenly speeded up and lunged at James, swinging a hard right hook.

James just managed to duck it and aim a blow at the man's belly.

It was like hitting a side of beef. James's hand smacked ineffectually into a solid wall of fat and muscle. Wrangel didn't even register it. Instead, he came powering back with a straight–armed left punch that James took in the side of the head, knocking him into the wall. He collapsed, winded, his head spinning. He did notice, though, with a small sense of triumph, that the blow appeared to have balanced the pressure in his ears and brought his hearing back.

James was on all fours now, panting like a dog and trying to regain his senses. He realized he had landed in a pile of broken furniture and twisted metal. He saw part of a heavy lamp stand, quickly grabbed it, and surged back up at Wrangel, swinging it at his head.

Wrangel put up his arm and swatted the stand away as if it had been a feather duster. He then ripped it out of James's hands and tossed it aside contemptuously.

He didn't need a weapon; he was evidently intending to kill James with his bare hands.

James backed away, picking up anything he could find and hurling it at Wrangel, who came on steadily like a tank. James rammed a cart into him, then hit him with a chair, but all to no avail. Finally he was backed into a corner with nowhere to go. A brief exchange of punches left him on his back, staring up at Wrangel through a swirling fog of dancing lights.

Wrangel picked him up again and then smashed him down onto the operating table on his back. Wrangel's eyes were invisible behind the fleshy pouches of his eyelids, but James could tell that he was enjoying himself. He put his hands around James's throat and began to squeeze.

The fight had been knocked out of James; he could barely move. His hands scrabbled feebly at Wrangel's forearms, but there was no stopping the man.

James's throat was on fire, his head throbbing, his eyes bulging out of their sockets. His lungs were slowly filling with poisonous carbon dioxide, and it felt like they would burst. All the colors in the room were draining away.

Just before he slipped into oblivion, James caught a movement in the corner of his eye, and a moment later Wrangel began screaming with a horrible, high-pitched voice, a long drawn-out "*Eeeeeeeeeeeeeeeeeeeeeee!*"

He let go of James and clutched at the side of his face, tottering backward. When he took his bloody hand away, James saw that there was a scalpel embedded in his neck at the base of his ear.

He kept backing away, on tiptoe like a dancer, his arms windmilling, the weird girlish shriek screaming from between clenched teeth, until at last he collapsed onto his back, accompanied by the sound of shattering glass.

James sat up, coughing and gasping for breath. Roan was standing there with a shocked look on her face.

"I didn't know what else to do," she said.

"Come on," said James hoarsely. "Let's not cry over him. We need to get out of here."

They fetched Liesl, who was just stirring.

"We have to hurry," barked James, yanking her to her feet. "It's only a matter of time before the guards get here."

"Wait," said Roan. "Listen!"

There was the sound of gunfire coming from outside.

"Who are they firing at?" said James.

Roan shook her head.

James ran to a window and ripped down the drapes. Outside was a small empty courtyard.

"We'll go this way," he said, and picked up a film camera. "It looks safe out here."

He heaved the camera through the window, and he and

Roan knocked the remaining pieces of broken glass out of the way.

They climbed out.

The sounds of battle were louder out here. They could hear the crack of small-arms fire and the occasional meatier thump of a rifle.

Liesl was terrified, shaking like a leaf, her eyes darting around but not fixing on anything.

James looked at Roan. She shook her head again. Liesl could put them all in danger.

James spotted a concrete shed and grabbed the girl.

"Get in there," he said, "until this is all over. No sense in taking a bullet."

"Will you stay with me?" said Liesl fearfully.

"I'm going to try and find out what's going on," said James. "But don't worry, we won't leave you here."

"You promise?"

"I promise. Now get in there and keep your head down until it's quiet."

Once Liesl was safely out of the way, James and Roan climbed a flight of steps that ran up from the corner of the courtyard onto the castle wall. From there they crept along the ramparts until they found a vantage point looking down into the main courtyard.

There was a fierce gunfight in progress between Dr. Friend's German agents and another group of men wearing dark mountaineering outfits.

"Who are they?" said Roan.

"God knows," said James. "But they just might have saved our bacon."

The Germans appeared to be losing and were being driven back into the castle.

"What are we going to do?" asked Roan, but before James could reply, a German agent armed with a Luger appeared from farther along the wall. He yelled at them and then started firing.

James and Roan broke away and ran back down the steps in a mad scramble. When they hit the bottom, James glanced back. The man was taking careful aim, but then there came the evil chatter of a machine gun, and bullets raked along the top of the wall. The German gave a cry and tumbled forward, landing in the courtyard with a nasty wet slap.

James and Roan carried on, running away from the firefight, but as they reached the far side of the courtyard, a bizarre sight met them.

Dr. Friend had come out of the building and was limping stiff-legged toward them across the cobblestones, Wrangel's Luger swaying in his hand. He had been standing next to one of the shelves of surgical instruments and had obviously taken the worst of the blast. The whole of the left side of his body was studded with debris. Knives, scalpels, syringes, odd-shaped pieces of broken metal, and shards of glass stuck out of him grotesquely. They were in his face, his shoulder, his arm and ribs, even down his legs.

There was still no expression on his face, and without his glasses his stare was vague and unfocused.

But he recognized James.

"Bond," he hissed, and loosed off a shot.

His aim was wide; the bullet ricocheted harmlessly off the

cobblestones, but it would only be a matter of time before he found his target.

"Come on," James shouted, grabbing Roan by the arm. "We'll just have to take our chances out there."

They dashed back across the courtyard toward the archway that led through to the front of the *Schloss*, two more bullets whining past them like angry wasps. As they careered through the arch, Friend fired again. This time the bullet was closer. It bit into the stonework, inches from James's head, sending up chips of granite and dust.

They emerged into the open space of the main courtyard and passed a long, cream-colored Mercedes-Benz 770 saloon, its doors hanging open, a man crouching in the driver's seat with his arms folded around his head.

Mercifully, the battle seemed to have moved on. There was nobody between them and the big double gates that were standing half open. Beyond the gates was the open road and freedom.

"That way," James yelled, and he pulled hard on Roan's arm. There was almost immediately another shot, and Roan gasped.

James spun around.

"Are you hit?"

"No . . . my ankle. It's twisted."

She couldn't put her weight on one leg, so James put his arm under her shoulder and half dragged, half carried her toward the gates. He looked back at Dr. Friend, who was on the far side of the courtyard, staggering on, dropping bits of glass and surgical tools with each step.

Surely he was too far away to do any damage. . . .

They came to the gate, and James pushed Roan through to safety. He had to delay Friend, though. He leaned his weight against the ancient dark wood of one of the gates and heaved. It swung shut and he moved to the other, but as he did so, a searing pain burned across his temple, and something plowed through his hair. A moment later there came a *boom* that seemed to sound right inside his head, and a distant *crack*.

He lost all control of his limbs.

He was going down.

He heard Roan scream his name, and then he was wading through treacly blackness as a vice tightened around his skull.

He tried to say something, to reassure Roan that he was all right, but nothing came out, and the blackness swallowed him whole.

Roan was lying in the road in an untidy sprawl. She had had no time to do anything but watch helplessly as Dr. Friend had swung his arm across the open expanse of courtyard and fired toward the gates. She had seen the bullet strike James's head, and she had screamed as he fell. When she had started to go to him, however, someone had grabbed her and thrown her to the ground.

It was a woman, dressed all in gray.

For a moment, Roan was too dazed to move. She saw the woman step into the half-open gateway and raise a pistol.

She fired a single shot at Dr. Friend.

Roan watched the bullet punch into the center of his perfect face and emerge from the back of his head in a spray of brains and blood.

The woman now slipped her gun inside her tunic as she turned from the gateway and looked down at Roan.

She stood there with her legs planted widely apart, a solid and immovable object, her clothes too tight for her bulky frame. She had short gray hair and a wide, square peasant's face.

"My name is Colonel Sedova," she said. "But most call me Babushka, the Grandmother. I am with the Soviet secret police. You have caused us a great deal of trouble, Miss Power."

"You know me?" said Roan.

"I have been on your trail for weeks, ever since I uncovered the Nazi plot in Lisbon. At first I only knew you by your code name, Diamond. Then, when the trail led me to Eton, I at last learned your name. But sadly, you and Bond went on the run before I could get to you. We have slowly pieced together the details of Operation Snow-blind, but until now we were never sure of the whereabouts, or the real name of the man behind it—Obsidian. I now know everything."

"Then you'll know that I thought I was working for you," said Roan, struggling to her feet and standing awkwardly, her twisted ankle sending darts of pain up her leg. "I didn't know who Obsidian was either. I knew nothing about Dr. Friend, or the *Graf*, or any of this. I thought I was doing the right thing. I thought I was working for the struggle."

"I understand," said Babushka softly. "You were tricked. You could not have known."

A thickset man with a scar across his face came through the gates carrying a rifle. He glanced back toward the castle. The shooting appeared to have stopped. He said something to the colonel in Russian, and she nodded toward Roan.

The man slung his rifle over his shoulder, drew a pistol from his belt, and casually aimed it at Roan.

"What are you doing?" said Roan. "I'm on your side. You said you understood."

"If only we had got to you first," said Babushka, "how different things might have been. We have a great need of women like you."

"I'll gladly come back to Moscow with you," said Roan. "I'll do anything you ask of me. All I want is to be able to help the Communist cause."

"Yes," said Babushka, "but can we trust you?"

She looked down at the body of James Bond, lying still in the gravel.

Roan looked, too. She wanted desperately to go to him, but she was terrified of the Russians.

"Of course you can trust me," she said. "Did you not just see Dr. Friend try to kill me?"

"This whole thing is a mess," said Babushka. "If we had been successful in Calais, you would have been spared all this. But the boy outwitted us, I am afraid. It was through him, though, that we eventually tracked you down. After Calais, we put all our operatives onto the case to work out where you might have been heading. We looked into Bond's recent history, and one of our guesses was that he might be coming back here, to Kitzbühel. So we put an agent in place, an Englishman called Nicholson. Unfortunately, you decided to deliver Bond into the enemy's hands just before I arrived with my men. Nicholson followed you yesterday and luckily he recognized the cars from here."

"Now here you are," said Roan, forcing a smile, "and, as they say, all's well that ends well."

"Is it ended?" asked Babushka.

"Dr. Friend is dead," said Roan. "This base is finished."

"And what of Bond?"

"What of me?" said James, sitting up.

"Oh, James, thank God you're all right," said Roan, fighting back tears.

"I'm not so sure I am all right," said James. "But I'm awake at least. I've got the devil of a headache, though."

"Doctor Friend's bullet merely creased your temple," said Babushka.

James put a hand to his head; there was a little blood, but nothing worse than a scalded scratch. He got shakily to his feet.

"Colonel Sedova is a Russian," said Roan. "She's come to—"

"I know who Colonel Sedova is," James interrupted. "And I know why she's here. I heard everything."

Babushka muttered something to the OGPU man, and he swiveled his gun toward James.

"This situation is very familiar," said Babushka. "Once before, in London, you held *me* at gunpoint. I asked you, as one soldier to another, to let me walk away."

"And I let you go," said James.

"I suppose I should do the same now," said Babushka.

"Your fight's not with me," said James.

"Isn't it?"

"No. If anything, you should thank me for stopping Dandy. If his bomb had gone off, your lot would really be in the stink."

"My fight is against all enemies of the state," said Babushka.

"I hardly think I pose much of a threat to the mighty Communist empire," said James.

"You would be very valuable to us, James. The British hold several of my agents. I could exchange you for them."

"I'm not coming to Russia with you," said James flatly.

"I can offer you two choices," said Babushka. "I can take you with me, or I can shoot you now and have done with it."

"Then shoot me," said James, wearily rubbing his head, "because I'm not coming with you."

Babushka laughed. "You are a brave young man."

"I am a tired young man. I've had my fill of fighting."

"Let him go," said Roan. "He helped me escape. He has no argument with you."

"Keep out of this," snapped Babushka. "This is none of your business."

"It is *so* my business," said Roan angrily. "James and I are in this together."

"What do you care about him? You tried to deliver him up yourself."

"I was wrong. I know that now. I was trying to save my own neck. It was a dirty thing to do."

James looked Babushka in the eye.

"Did my letting you go that time in London mean nothing?" he asked.

Babushka was still. She was thinking. Weighing up the options in her mind.

"I have made my decision," she said.

But James never learned what that decision was, because at that moment all hell broke loose.

It began when a shot rang out, and the OGPU man at Babushka's side fell with a sigh. At the same time, there was a shout from the trees above the road. An English voice.

"Put your hands up and throw down your weapons!"

Before James could work out what was going on, he saw Babushka drag her pistol from her tunic.

"I am sorry," she said, and pulled the trigger.

James heard Roan shout "NO!" as he threw himself to the side. He knew he wasn't going to be quick enough, though, not at this range. Only a miracle could save him.

He hit the ground and noticed with a surge of relief that he was unhurt.

Maybe a miracle had happened.

But why was Roan lying at his side? And why was there blood on her white dress? Had she put herself between him and Babushka?

He was gripped with panic. He desperately wanted to check that she was all right. The fight wasn't over, though. Three armed men were running down the hillside.

James could see that Babushka was torn between firing at them and shooting at him again.

He didn't hesitate. In one move he rolled over, grabbed the gun that had been dropped by the OGPU man, aimed it at Babushka's chest, and squeezed the trigger four times.

Babushka grunted and was thrown backward into the rocks by the side of the road.

The next moment the three men arrived.

"They weren't going to shoot," said James bitterly as he got to his feet.

"We couldn't take the risk, son."

The men were British, dressed in camouflaged outfits with knitted caps. They moved toward the castle, guns at the ready. A moment later, Nevin appeared, carrying a sniper's rifle with telescopic sights. For once he wasn't wearing his trilby. He pulled James out of the road behind the cover of a rock.

"Can't be too careful," he said. "Are you all right, lad?"

"I'm not shot, if that's what you mean," said James. "But let me go to Roan, she's hurt."

"You stay here—it's too dangerous."

"I've done all right so far without your help!" James shouted. "I can't just leave her lying in the road."

"I've not come all this way to lose you now, lad," said Nevin, holding James by the arm. "When we're given the all-clear, we'll get out from behind this rock. Until then we stay put."

"You're too late, Nevin," said James, tearing himself from the man's grip. "You've missed the party."

He stood up and looked over the rock.

Roan had gone.

Where she had been, there was a small puddle of dark blood. More spots of it trailed away across the stony ground, skirting the *Schloss* before turning away onto a track that led up the mountainside.

"She's not dead," said James, grinning with relief.

A bullet sang through the air, fired from the castle walls. He'd been wrong—the party wasn't over yet.

"There's another girl," said James. "She's called Liesl. She's hiding inside a shed in a rear courtyard. Make sure she's all right, will you? Friend was holding her prisoner."

"Just stay back there," Nevin yelled, putting his sniper's sights to his eye. "I'll make sure she's not hurt."

James wasn't listening. He ran in a low crouch toward the mountain path, keeping his head down, expecting at any moment to be hit by another bullet.

None came, and soon he was on the path and climbing away from the *Schloss*. Gradually, the sounds of the battle dimmed.

It was happening to someone else now. He wasn't a part

of it anymore. The gunshots might as well be firecrackers or jumping jacks.

He looked down at the road. There was no sign of Nevin. Babushka lay where she had fallen.

How many other people would be dead before the end of the day?

He ran as fast as he could now, his lungs burning. Once or twice he lost sight of the trail and had to stop and search for it, but for the most part there were spots of blood every few feet. Roan must be bleeding badly.

He crested a ridge and took one last look back. He could see the rooftops of the *Schloss*, men moving about; a group of them ran into the road.

James squinted.

Babushka had gone.

Maybe someone had taken her body?

She wasn't his concern anymore. Let Nevin deal with it.

All he had to worry about was Roan.

He carried on, climbing ever higher up the mountain. The air grew cooler; the sounds of the battle were quieter still.

Up and up he ran, through a tangle of tall pine trees, their scent filling the air. If it wasn't for the ominous trail of blood on the ground, he might be out for a summer walk. A walk like those he had taken so many times before with Roan in the mountains.

The path emerged from the trees. Green patches of grass covered the rocky ground; here and there wildflowers grew.

And then, up ahead, he saw her. A tiny crumpled shape nestled in the lee of a rock. He sprinted over to her, praying that she was still alive.

When he got to her, he saw that her eyes were open and her lips trembling.

Thank God.

He knelt down next to her and stroked her face. Her arms were folded tight across her chest. Beneath them, her dress was stained a vivid scarlet. She was shaking, her skin so white it looked luminous, her wide eyes black as night.

"Darling," she murmured. "You made it."

James took her in his arms and held her. She felt cold.

"You're going to be all right," he said. "I'll get help. It's over now; nobody's trying to hurt you anymore."

"Oh, that'd be nice," she said, and smiled.

James looked at the blood. "What did you do, you fool?" he said.

"I wouldn't let her, darling. Not after everything. I wouldn't let her kill you."

"It's the bravest thing anyone's ever done," said James.

"I don't think I'm brave," said Roan quietly, and she shivered.

"Why did you come all the way up here?" asked James.

"To find some quiet. No more noise. I love the mountains. I wanted to see some snow. I thought if I came up here I might find some."

"There's no snow," said James. "You've come all the way up here for nothing."

"Oh, the trouble I've put you to, darling. You must think I'm a witch."

"No. I love you," said James. "Nothing you've ever done, or ever will do, can change that. I didn't choose to love you; it just happened."

"And look how I treated you," said Roan. "Remember, I told you . . . you have to open your heart. You have to let it take a few knocks so that it can toughen up. Only thing is, my heart, it took too many knocks, I reckon. It got too hard . . . like stone. I have a stone heart, James, darling."

"No," said James. "Not a stone—a diamond, a beautiful diamond."

"Diamond heart," Roan whispered, and then she gave a small cough.

"Don't talk so much," said James. "You need to save your strength."

"No," said Roan, "there's something I need to tell you."

"What?"

"All that stuff I said, about the great cause. I don't know if I really believe in it anymore, if I ever did. Oh, I know there's wrong in the world, the poor aren't given a chance, but it was Dandy who taught me the politics. He was passionate about it. About Russia. The revolution."

"Please," said James. "It doesn't matter."

"But I didn't want to tell you the truth," said Roan. "I couldn't before. I didn't want to hurt you any more than I had done."

"What do you mean?" said James.

"Dandy," said Roan. "He wasn't just my friend. He wasn't just someone I was working with, a fellow agent . . . he was my husband, James."

"What?"

"We were married. I'd have done anything for him. When I found out he was dead, my world fell in. I hated everyone and everything, I wanted to hurt someone. . . ."

"You wanted to hurt me?" said James.

"I'm sorry."

"So you never felt anything for me at all?"

"Don't be daft. Of course I did. I told you I loved you, didn't I? Well, you should never lie about anything as serious as love. But you can love someone and hate them at the same time."

"Do you hate me still?"

"Oh, look, it's snowing. . . ."

James looked around. He could see nothing.

"I don't think so," he said.

"Can't you see it?" said Roan, with a childlike grin on her face. "White flakes in the air. Oh, they're so beautiful, James. I knew I'd see some snow again before I died."

"You're not going to die."

"Not as long as I've got you to look after me, eh? Of course I don't hate you anymore; you're the most amazing boy I've ever met. . . . Oh, but that pretty snow sure is cold. Look at it, we must be caught in a blizzard."

"There's nothing there," said James, who was shaking with fear. "There's no snow."

Roan took hold of his hand. Her skin felt frozen; her hand seemed very small, like a child's hand. He tried rubbing it.

"It's so beautiful," said Roan. "So beautiful . . ."

"Please don't die," said James. But there was nothing he could do. She was slipping away from him. No matter how hard he held her, no matter how much he loved her, no matter what he said or did, he was helpless in the face of death.

"Please . . ." he whispered. But she could no longer hear him.

CHAPTER 32—FROM ON TOP OF A MOUNTAIN

James sat in the sun on the top of the Hahnenkamm with his back against a rock. The clean air filled his lungs. The buildings of Kitzbühel were hidden from him. He might be the only person in the world, looking at a scene that had remained unchanged for millions of years. The petty squabbles of men meant nothing up here.

From his vantage point he could see the vast range of other mountains spread out around him. To the south, the more distant peaks of the higher Alps were dusted with snow, but here they were a vivid emerald studded with black rocks and the darker green of the pine trees. The sky that stretched over his head in a great endless sweep was deep, deep blue. As James had ridden up alone in the cable car, Kitzbühel had slowly shrunk until he felt he could reach out and take control of it, like a child playing with toy houses and cars. From up in the gondola it had all looked so clean and simple and ordered. That must be how God saw things. From a distance all looked well with the world.

Down there it was different, though. He knew the reality of it. The world was messy and complicated; you could never be sure of anything anyone said or did. Real life was confusing. People made it so. They filled this perfect world with unhappiness, fear, and violence.

He wanted to stay up here forever. Stay up and never come down. Like Peter Pan, he would somehow find a way to stay young forever. How marvelous it would be not to have to grow up and deal with all the messiness in the world. But he knew that you couldn't stop time. You *had* to grow up. And you couldn't keep the world away—sooner or later it would come looking and find you and drag you kicking and screaming back into its chaotic, churning belly.

There were ways of dealing with the world. There were ways of understanding it. James would learn the best way. His body was bruised and battered. He was covered in cuts and scratches, each one reminding him of some part of what had happened since his return to Europe. But his body would heal. He knew that well enough; he had kissed good-bye to plenty of cuts and bruises over the years, even a few broken bones. He knew, though, that it would take much longer for his heart to heal, and for his mind to hide away the bad memories.

He would protect his heart better in the future. He would grow a tough shell around it. Because he was painfully aware, sitting here, all alone, like some eagle in its aerie, that this was his position in the world.

Alone.

He had been alone since his parents had died, and he was alone again now. When it came down to it, there was only one person he could rely on in the world, and he was called James Bond.

Well—he stretched out and looked up at the sky—*there was nothing wrong with being alone.*

He lay there for some time, feeling the massive bulk of the

mountain beneath him, drawing strength from it, letting the tangled thoughts drift away.

Finally James sat up. He was no longer alone. A group of walkers were moving slowly across the mountaintop from the cable car station. They were no bigger than ants. He smiled. It was harder to be alone than you thought. He closed one eye and narrowed the other to a slit, then held his thumb up in front of his face so that it appeared to be hovering over the people. It was a giant's thumb. God's thumb. Poised to obliterate them.

He crushed them.

How easy it would be.

But of course they kept on coming.

After a while he recognized the slight limp of Oberhauser. He seemed to be leading the others. James saw him point toward where he was sitting.

They were looking for him, then. It was *indeed* hard to be alone.

He studied the group more closely now.

There were three of them and Oberhauser, who now stopped, turned, and went back toward the cable car station. One was unmistakably Mr. Merriot—James could see his ever-present unlit pipe. The man next to him in the trilby was surely Dan Nevin. The slightly overweight man lagging behind them and struggling to keep up on the rocky ground James had never seen before.

It was only a matter of time, James supposed. They would have tracked him down sooner or later, wherever he had gone. In some ways it was a relief. He had to get this thing over with.

When Merriot was close enough to be heard, he called out to James. James waved but said nothing in return. A few minutes later the men arrived, red-faced and out of breath.

"Quite a spot," said Merriot, looking around at the view, and James nodded.

"How are you, James?" said Nevin.

"As well as can be expected, I suppose," said James, and he looked at the third man, who was just arriving.

"This is Sir Donald Buchanan," said Merriot, sitting down on a rock and taking his pipe out of his mouth. "Sir Donald is with the government. I suppose you could say he's my boss."

"How do you do, young man?" Buchanan wheezed. He was sweating heavily and looked like a man who enjoyed good food more than exercise. "Pleased to meet you at last."

"Are you?" said James. "I assumed you'd come to arrest me."

"Arrest you? Far from it, far from it," said Merriot, and he gave James a kindly smile. "We understand why you did what you did. We put an intolerable strain on you. It wasn't fair—a young man like you. We were panicked by what had happened, and blinded by a desire to track down the enemy and bag him. It was too heavy a burden to expect you to carry. But, as usual with your adventures, it all seems to have turned out right in the end."

"Has it?" said James. "Roan is dead."

"That is a shame," said Merriot. "She and her man may have been planning a terrible thing, but in many ways she was an innocent. She was caught up in a game that was bigger and more complicated than she could ever have imagined."

"And is the game over?" said James.

"I don't think it ever will be," said Merriot. "The Great Game, they used to call it, this shadow war of spies, double agents, plots, counterplots, secrets, and lies."

"When you put it like that, Michael," said Buchanan, wiping his face with a handkerchief, "it sounds dreadfully grubby."

Nevin laughed and lit up a cigarette.

"It's worse than grubby," he said.

"What happened to Babushka," James asked, "to Colonel Sedova?"

"Disappeared," said Nevin. "Shame. She would have made a good prize. All hell's broken loose in Moscow by all accounts. The OGPU's been wound up and taken over by the People's Commissariat for Internal Affairs."

James was hardly listening. You could change the name of something, but it wouldn't make it smell any sweeter.

"Expect you're wondering how we found you at the castle, eh?" said Merriot.

"You'd sent a man there," said James. "He died."

"Yes," said Nevin. "We found the poor beggar. His name was Walsh. We'd been investigating the *Graf* for something else. Had no idea it was all part of the same plot."

"None of us did," said Merriot.

"We lost contact with Walsh," Nevin went on, "but one of the last messages he sent was about seeing a boy and a girl on the train. It took us a while to put two and two together, and a while longer to realize that it added up to five."

Merriot rested a hand on James's shoulder.

"So, young James," he said, "what is to be done with you?"

James shrugged. For the moment he didn't much care. There was a hollow, empty feeling inside him.

"I have talked to your estimable Aunt Charmian," Merriot went on. "She is here, by the way, in Kitzbühel. I asked if we could talk to you first."

"Oh?" said James. "I suppose you want to rehearse me in what lies I'm going to tell people about what's happened?"

"You always were a clever lad," said Merriot.

"The thing of it is," said Buchanan, "we'd really rather you didn't say anything to anyone."

"Not even to my aunt?"

"Not even to your aunt," said Buchanan. "There are certain parts of the story that would be a great embarrassment to all of us. We could all look rather foolish if any of this ever got out."

"And then there's the matter of the Prince of Wales," said Nevin.

Buchanan coughed and looked away.

"Nobody must ever know the full truth about what happened," said Merriot. "We will ask you to sign various papers and documents—the Official Secrets Act, that kind of thing—and then your lips must remain cemented shut."

"That's it?" said James. "No punishment for running away and helping a wanted woman? You're going to say nothing about my part in it all?"

"No punishment," said Merriot quietly. "We'll cut a deal with you as long as you cut a deal with us. Let's not forget you saved the King's life. He has even offered you a medal. I've declined on your behalf, of course."

"Of course," said James.

"And of course he doesn't know exactly what happened. The four of us here on top of this mountain are the only people in the world who know the whole truth, and that's how we would like it to stay."

"If you speak to anyone—ever—about this," said Buchanan, "then the full force of His Majesty's government will come down very heavily on you. And that would be messy, I can assure you."

James sighed. He was all too happy to forget this episode.

"My lips are sealed," he said.

"Good man," said Merriot. "Now. Specifics. You cannot return to Eton."

"I thought you might say that," said James.

"That part of your life is over," said Merriot. "I will miss you. You never took to the classics, it's true, but you were always a bright and interesting pupil. And what an athlete. You should see the boy run sometime, Sir Donald."

"*Hmph*," said Buchanan, who evidently had no interest in sports.

"We have arranged for you to be transferred to your father's old school in Edinburgh, James, to Fettes. I think you will like it there—the sports are excellent and I know you'll make new friends quickly. We will make up some story to cover your leaving Eton. In fact we will barely have to alter the facts."

"It's a good rule," said Nevin, blowing out a cloud of smoke. "If you're going to tell a lie, keep it as close to the truth as possible—it's much easier."

"I'll remember that," said James.

"We will need to cover your tracks a little, though," said

Merriot. "To keep you safely out of it. Records will show that you left the school a year ago, and could not have had any involvement with the events of the last half. This whole matter is being officially removed from the history books."

"And the Prince of Wales?" said James. "What will become of him? It won't be quite so easy to remove *him* from the history books."

"Leave that to us," said Buchanan darkly.

"I don't think he had any idea of what was being planned," said Nevin. "It's well known that he doesn't like his father, but if he'd known they were going to kill him, he would never have gone along with it."

"Some of his beliefs and enthusiasms are a little worrying, though," said Buchanan. "We'll have to see to it that nothing like this could ever happen again. If necessary we will see to it that he never becomes king."

"Plots, counterplots, dirty secrets, and lies," said James.

"Something like that," said Buchanan. "But what the general public don't know can't hurt them."

"You're good at keeping secrets, James," said Merriot. "In fact, of all of us here, you're the best equipped for this job."

"As a spy?" said James.

"A spy indeed," said Merriot. "It's in your blood."

James ran his fingers through his hair.

"Almost the last thing Uncle Max said to me before he died was, 'Don't ever be a spy.'"

"Wise words I'm sure," said Merriot. "But perhaps our destinies are chosen for us. And we will always need people like you. You're young now, you need a rest, you need to try and live the life of an ordinary boy for a while. But when the time comes, when you're old enough, will you hear the call?"

"There's a war coming, James," said Nevin. "We're trying our damnedest to stop it, but I fear it's going to happen sooner rather than later. My prediction is that within five years, Europe is going to be on fire. We'll need people to put those fires out."

"And people to start them," Buchanan muttered.

"I've had my fill of blood and fire," said James. "I'm not sure I want to fight anymore."

"I'm not sure any of us do," said Merriot. "But if war breaks out I'd sooner have a gun in my hand than a pen."

"Is that the only choice?" said James.

Merriot smiled and looked off into the distance. "Perhaps not," he said. "We schoolmasters sometimes have to give the impression that we know everything, but sometimes I have to admit that we don't." He stood up and held out his hand to James. "Do we have a deal?" he said.

James thought about it.

"I don't suppose I have much of a choice," he said.

"No," said Buchanan. "I'm afraid you don't."

"Can I see my friends again?" said James.

"We can't stop you, I suppose," said Merriot, "but we'd *really* rather you didn't."

"They must know that I left with Roan."

"An affair of the heart, nothing more."

Nothing more?

James shook Merriot's hand.

"Sometimes," said Merriot, "we don't know if what we're

doing is right. But perhaps you have seen enough of what Hitler is up to to know that he's someone who must be stopped."

"Yes," said James.

"Come along," said Buchanan. "I'd like to be back in time for supper. Can we trust the boy?"

"Yes," said Merriot.

"Will you come down with us?" said Nevin.

"I'll stay a little while longer," said James, "and enjoy the last of the sun."

"You can sign the papers in the morning before we leave," said Buchanan.

"As you wish," said James. "But I've shaken on it, and that's really all you need."

Buchanan grunted and set off back toward the cable car station. Nevin gave a tip of the hat and followed. Merriot hung back.

"Good-bye," he said. "I really shall miss you. But I'm sure we shall meet again, somewhere along the way."

"Good-bye," said James. "Thank you for organizing all this. I'm sure it wasn't as straightforward as you've made it seem. I reckon Sir Donald was all for locking me up and throwing away the key."

Merriot winked.

"Clever lad," he said, and turned to go.

"One more thing," said James.

"Yes?"

"Roan? Do you know what her real name was?"

"Her married name was Roan Cullinan," said Merriot. "But she never used it, for reasons of security."

"And her maiden name?"

"Turns out she was who she claimed to be. Roan Power. That was her real name all along."

"Thank you."

James watched as Merriot stuck his pipe back into his mouth and set off after the other two with his long loping stride.

James stayed there until he was sure that the others had gone, and then he stayed a while longer, feeling the heat drain out of the day. At last he stood, stretched his aching muscles, and began the walk down to Kitzbühel. He wouldn't take the cable car. He wanted time to think, and he thought best when he was walking. The winding track down the mountain would take him a couple of hours, but he was in no hurry.

He remembered that other time, coming down the mountain with Miles Langton-Herring. It seemed a lifetime ago.

He was pleased that Charmian was here. She knew how to make him happy and take his mind off his worries. Maybe she would stay for a while—she would like the Oberhausers, and James could show her the mountains.

He felt lighter and happier already. Perhaps it really was as easy as this. He would sign some pieces of paper, and everything would be forgotten, as if it had never happened. He would go to his new school, Fettes, and start again. Nobody would know him, nobody would expect anything of him. Except Perry. James smiled. Yes, he'd forgotten that Perry was at Fettes. The place wouldn't be entirely alien. Oh, some boy would no doubt try to bully him when he got there, to show that he was in charge and James was an insignificant newcomer, but he would deal with that. He hadn't been scared of mere boys for a long time.

At the first turn of the path he found Hannes Oberhauser waiting for him.

"I thought you would come this way," he said, grinning.

"You know me too well," said James.

Oberhauser put his arm across James's shoulders, and they walked together.

"I wanted to make sure that you were all right."

"I'm all right," said James, and he meant it.

"Helga is making *Wiener schnitzel* for dinner," said Hannes. "I know it is one of your favorites."

"It is," said James.

"Your aunt will be joining us. I have met her—she seems a lovely woman."

"She is," said James.

They walked on down the track, and were soon lost among the tall pine trees.

A chamois came out of hiding and looked carefully in the direction they had gone, then, with one bound, he too disappeared.

The mountain was quiet.

ACKNOWLEDGMENTS

As this book brings to a close this chapter of James Bond's life, I wanted to properly thank all the people who have helped me in the writing of the series. Some I have thanked before, but it will do no harm to thank them again. So, in no particular order:

Vicky Fullick
Frank, Jim, and Sidney
Kate Jones
Alexandra Cann
Susan Powell
Bernard Fergusson for his book *Eton Portrait*
Zoë Watkins
Corinne Turner
Fleur Gooch
Kate Grimond
Lucy Fleming
Matthew Fleming
Rebecca McNally
Amanda Punter
Adele Minchin
Kirsten Grant
Francesca Dow
Lucy Chavasse and all at Colman Getty
Michael Meredith
Nick Baker
All the boys and girls who have read the books
John Cox
Ian Fleming